"EVERY BIT AS GOOD AS THE MORE CELEBRATED 87th PRECINCT SERIES!"
St. Louis Globe-Democrat

"EXPERT McBAIN!"
The New York Times Book Review

"CRACKLING DIALOGUE, SNAPPY PACING, AN ABUNDANCE OF CLEVERLY PLACED CLUES, AND A GAGGLE OF QUIRKY CHARACTERS!"
Philadelphia Inquirer

RUMPEL-STILTSKIN

The new Matthew Hope Mystery
by Ed McBain

RUMPEL-STILTSKIN

McBAIN

BALLANTINE BOOKS • NEW YORK

Library of Congress Catalog Card Number: 80-54086

ISBN 0-345-30436-5

This edition published by arrangement with The Viking Press

Manufactured in the United States of America

First Ballantine Books Edition: November 1982

This is for Lars and Cary Lindblad

1

I have it on good authority that a certain type of man, upon getting divorced, will run out to buy himself a motorcycle and will then begin dating nineteen-year-old girls. Me, I had the dent taken out of my Karmann Ghia's fender, had the entire car repainted a muted beige that blends well with the sand on Calusa's beaches, and didn't date anyone at all for the six months following the final decree. My partner Frank insists this was abnormal; he is the "good authority" who offered the Honda-cum-Pubescent-Girl Theory.

But the ritual postures of "dating" are not easily recalled or re-enacted by a thirty-seven-year-old man who was married to the same woman for fourteen years and who himself has a daughter not too far removed in age from all those long-legged, long-haired nineteen-year-old beauties. Joanna—long-legged, long-haired, and beautiful in her own right—has just turned thirteen and has finally begun sprouting the breasts she's been coveting for the past eternity of her life. I love her to death, but I get to see her only every other weekend and for half the duration of her school vacations.

I'm a lawyer by trade, but it was not I who negotiated the terms of my own divorce settlement. In law, as in medicine, there are so-called specialists: the real estate lawyer, the tax lawyer, the corporation lawyer, the copyright lawyer, the

matrimonial or family relations lawyer, who—in the case of
Eliot McLaughlin, at least—might better have been called a
criminal lawyer in that he most certainly committed a crime
of enormous severity when he allowed me to sign such an
onerous separation agreement in a state noted for its liberal
divorce laws. Eliot kept telling me, however, that *I* was the
guilty party. This meant that my former wife Susan, while not
quite discovering me *in flagrante delicto,* had nonetheless
learned that I was having what is euphemistically known as
"an affair" with a married lady named Agatha Hemmings,
who has since divorced *her* spouse as well and who is now
living in Tampa. All water under the bridge, as they say.
There are a great many bridges in Calusa, Florida, and a
whole hell of a lot of water.

My partner Frank says that Calusa is not a bad place in
which to live if a man is recently divorced and suddenly finds
himself footloose and fancy-free. For Frank, who is a transplanted New Yorker, than which there is nothing worse, this
is a tremendously generous admission. He is obliquely referring, of course, to the plenitude of widows, divorcées, and
aforementioned teeny-boppers who clutter Calusa's splendid
beaches seeking solace in the sunshine and who—according
to Frank—are all ripe for the taking. I would be most reluctant to take any of those nubile nineteen-year-olds; in fact, I
would be terrified. What do you talk about *afterward?* The
latest Fleetwood Mac album? As for those blue-haired, tightly
girdled widows in their late sixties and early seventies, I must
confess they do little to stir my middle-aged blood. Middle-
aged, yes. I figure my life expectancy to be somewhere
between seventy and seventy-five (else why all those *widows*
running around?), and thirty-seven is half of seventy-four, so
there you are. The divorcées are quite another matter. In the
past few months I've discovered that they come in all sizes,
shapes, and colors and that an ever-increasing number of
them are between the ages of twenty-six and thirty-five, just
about right for a man my age. Frank, in his partisan New
Yorker way, says it's truly unfortunate that most of them
come from the Midwest. But that's because if you draw a line
due south from Columbus, Ohio, it will go straight through
the center of Calusa. Frank says that Calusa is only Michigan
on the Gulf of Mexico. Maybe he's right.

The eastern rim of Calusa Bay is jaggedly defined by U.S. 41, more familiarly known as the Tamiami Trail. It is Frank's belief that "Tamiami" is redneck for "To Miami." Again, he may be right; if you follow 41 south, it eventually leads to Alligator Alley, which then crosses the Florida peninsula to the east coast of the state. There are five keys off Calusa's mainland, but only three of them—Stone Crab, Sabal, and Whisper—run north-south, paralleling the mainland shore. Flamingo Key and Lucy's Key are situated like massive steppingstones across the water, connecting the mainland first to Sabal and then to Stone Crab—which is where Victoria Miller was singing in the lounge of the newest restaurant on the beach.

It was one of those January nights rare for Calusa, eternally and extravagantly promised to the tourists, but only infrequently materializing. During Calusa's long winter months the mean average temperature is sixty-two degrees, seventeen on the Celsius scale, but this only means that the daytime temperatures hover in the mid-fifties, much too chilly for swimming in ocean or unheated pool, and at night they sometimes plunge into the lower thirties, reason enough for the orange-growers to run scrambling for their smudge pots. But today the weather had been exactly what the snowbirds pray for—a combination of clear blue sky, brilliant sunshine, and temperatures in the high seventies. As I parked the Ghia in the lot behind the restaurant, a soft balmy breeze wafted in off the Gulf and a wisp of cloud brushed past the face of the moon; the blacktop underfoot was suddenly awash in molten silver. There was the sound of piano music in the distance. I began walking toward it.

The Greenery had opened at the start of the season in October. Each year in Calusa a dozen or more new restaurants make their bid for longevity, but if one of the dozen survives by the end of the season it's a miracle of no small proportions. My partner Frank says that a class act hasn't got a chance in Calusa; the migratory midwestern "clods," as he calls them, are looking for places advertising family dinners at $4.95. The Greenery was a class act indeed, and by Frank's reasoning it should have closed a month after it opened. The food and service were excellent, the cuisine Continental (certain death in a town where travelers driving campers are searching for pizzerias or hamburger joints), and the decor was nothing short of stunning, having been designed by a client of ours named Charles Hoggs, who was also responsible for the mall downtown at Riverpoint. The restaurant had, at one time, in *fact* been a nursery, and Charlie had used the existing greenhouse as the entrance, adding the lounge and main dining room behind it as a series of similarly glass-enclosed rooms. The Greenery was never open for lunch, so glaring sunlight wasn't a problem. The owners had hired the services of a woman named Catherine Brenet, with whom I had had an unpleasant professional experience not too long ago, and it was she who kept the various rooms hung with fresh plants delivered on an almost-daily basis from her shop, Le Fleur de Lis, next door to the Royal Palms Hotel downtown on South Bayview. I hoped the Greenery made it—if only for Vicky's sake.

She had sung hard rock back in the mid-sixties, but the music coming from inside the place now, louder as I approached the greenhouse entrance, was the sort of stuff the big bands used to play back in the late thirties and early forties, a little before either *her* time *or* mine. I myself was born in 1943, a year after my father went off to fight World War II. Actually, he did no fighting at all. As an attorney practicing before the Illinois bar, he was assigned immediately to the Judge Advocate General's Office and spent most of the war as a commissioned officer at Fort Bragg. When he was discharged in 1945, it was with the rank of lieutenant colonel. The music I listened to as a teenager in Chicago was a music in transition from pop to rock. My heroes and heroines (in addition to Elvis, of course) were groups with names that by today's standards sound demure if not downright prissy: The Elegants, The Everly Brothers, The Platters, The Champs, Danny and the Juniors, and so on. Victoria Miller did not erupt onto the scene until rock had taken a firmer hold, in 1965, when she had just turned twenty and I was twenty-two and studying law in my father's footsteps at Northwestern. By that time I was presumably too mature, determined, and career-minded to notice any longer what was happening in the world of popular music; at our initial meeting three weeks ago, when Vicky mentioned the title of her first big-hit, million-copy, gold-record best-seller fifteen years back, I was hard put to remember it. The title, incidentally, was "Frenzy." The name of her backup group was Wheat, and the song—later extracted as a hit single—appeared on an album pressed by Regal Records, a firm now defunct but which at the time had its headquarters in New Orleans.

There was a poster-sized photograph of Vicky in the lobby, on one of those wooden tripod affairs that look like artists' easels. The picture had undoubtedly been taken by a professional photographer, which meant that the long black hair framing Vicky's face seemed altogether too sleek, the lips cradling her smile too glossy, her dark eyes sparkling with those phony little pupil-pinpoints of light professional photographers are taught to capture on film in order to make their subjects appear "alive." She seemed, in the photograph, almost an abstraction of herself, all character smoothed and polished out of her face, as bland as bleached flour. She seemed, too, a great deal younger than her almost thirty-five years, and I wondered if the picture hadn't been taken back in the heyday of her career, when she was enjoying the heady success of three gold-record albums in as many years. The script lettering on the photo's white background announced: NOW APPEARING: VICTORIA MILLER, RECORDING ARTIST. She had not been a "recording artist" for almost twelve years now. She had opened here at the Greenery on Friday night, and this was Sunday, but I had spent the weekend with my daughter, Joanna, sailing down to Sanibel and back on my boat *The Windbag*—one of the few material possessions I'd salvaged from my marriage—and had dropped her off at Susan's only half an hour ago. This was my first opportunity to catch Vicky's act, and I was eagerly looking forward to it.

It was ten minutes to nine when a hostess in a long black gown slit to the thigh on the right leg led me to a table near the bandstand. In Calusa many of the "family" restaurants offered early dinners at discount rates to senior citizens. The codgers, as I used to call them whenever I wished to annoy my former wife, also enjoyed these discount rates in Calusa's various movie theaters; catch the five o'clock show, and they let you in for $1.50. The Greenery, however, was a restaurant striving for a clientele somewhat more lofty than all those doddering ladies in their wedgies and their hapless mates in Hawaiian-print sports shirts. The dinner hour started at seven here. Vicky was doing one show each night, at nine o'clock, presumably timed to catch those diners who wanted an after-dinner drink in the lounge, or those customers intent on heavier drinking in the hours before midnight. There was only a handful of people in the room when I took my seat at the table; I did not consider this a very encouraging sign.

Almost every restaurant, bar, or lounge in Calusa offered some sort of "live" entertainment, but usually this consisted of a bearded kid strumming a guitar and singing either folk songs or "a little tune I wrote last summer while hitching through the beautiful mountains of North Carolina." The man playing the piano in the glassed-in lounge, however, was a musician of some note (no pun intended), who had pursued a career as a concert pianist in New York before retiring and building a home on Sabal Key here in Calusa. He often accompanied visiting guest artists at the Helen Gottlieb Memorial Auditorium, and had previously tickled the ivories for the likes of Joan Sutherland, Beverly Sills, and Marian Anderson. Apparently the Greenery was sparing no expense in trying to lure the dinner crowd from its many competitors; January was high season in Calusa, and if they didn't make the big buck now and in the several months to follow, they might very well be out of business the day after Easter.

At nine sharp the lights dimmed. Over the loudspeaker system a voice said, "Ladies and gentlemen . . . Miss Victoria Miller." Vicky appeared rather like an apparition in shimmering white, caught in the circle of a follow spot that led her relentlessly onto the small bandstand. She touched her accompanist briefly on the shoulder in greeting and, head ducked shyly, stepped swiftly into the curve of the grand piano. She lifted her head and tossed her long black hair. She smiled radiantly at the audience. The spot faded, to be replaced by a cool blue beam of light that turned her gown to glare ice. The piano introduction lingered. Vicky seemed to catch her breath. She brought the microphone to her lips and began to sing.

In all truth, she was awful.

"How was I?" she asked.

We were in the Karmann Ghia, driving around Lucy's Circle on the way to the mainland. The dashboard clock read 11:05 p.m. Vicky had changed into street clothes; she was wearing a dark blue skirt, high-heeled navy patent pumps, a white blouse, and a pale blue cardigan sweater. Her long legs were crossed somewhat recklessly, and she kept jiggling one foot. I had known only one other performer in my lifetime, a student at Northwestern who worked weekends as a stand-up comic in a Chicago gin mill on North Wells. After each performance he would be strung as tight as a high-tension wire. Vicky was the same way now, virtually vibrating on the seat beside me. That was good because I planned to take her to bed.

"You were terrific," I said.

"Do you think they liked me?"

"They loved you," I said.

"I thought they did, but you know you never can tell."

"Couldn't you tell?"

"No, I really couldn't."

"All that applause," I said.

"Yes, they did clap a lot," Vicky said.

The traffic around the Circle was maddening. The restaurants were disgorging late diners, and the high school kids were arriving in throngs to join the festivities at the Circle's two disco joints. There was always heavy traffic in the Circle. During the daytime it was impossible to *park* there, and during the night it was impossible to *drive* there, and the whole damn thing was a bad idea except for the merchants who ran the boutiques, souvenir shops, jewelry stores, and the myriad other emporiums offering treasures for sale. But there was only one way to get from Stone Crab Key to the mainland, and that was over the humpback bridge connecting it to Sabal, and then around the Circle on Lucy's Key and over to Cortez Causeway. A horn sounded on my left. I yanked the wheel to the right and swore under my breath as a carload of teenagers raced by; the kid sitting alongside the driver flashed a moon at us.

"Did you think they were talking a lot?" Vicky asked.

"Who do you mean?"

"The people. While I was singing."

"No, no. That's usual."

"Is it?"

"Well . . . I mean . . . don't you *know?*"

"Actually, no," she said.

"What do you mean?"

"I didn't used to perform live."

"You didn't?"

"No."

"You mean when you had those hit records?"

"Yes."

"You didn't perform live?"

"No."

"Why not?"

"Eddie wouldn't let me."

"Eddie?"

"My producer. At Regal."

"Ah."

"Eddie said it was bad for the records, he wanted everybody to go out and buy the *records*, you see."

"Maybe he was right."

"Oh, sure. Three gold records, you know, that's a lot."

"It is," I said.

"But you think they liked me, huh?"

"They loved you."

"I was so nervous. Did it show? That I was nervous?"

"Not a bit."

"I could use a drink," she said. "And some grass. Do you have any grass at your place?"

"No," I said, "I'm sorry."

"Would you mind if we went to my place then?"

"Well . . ."

I was thinking about her daughter. I was thinking that *my* place didn't have a six-year-old daughter sleeping in the room down the hall from Mommy's bedroom. I was thinking that *my* place had a nice big swimming pool in which we could frolic naked before getting down to more serious matters. I was thinking that *my* place had a nice big king-sized bed and that the sheets on it had been changed just that morning, and I was thinking that were we to climb into that king-sized bed to consummate what had been tantalizingly postponed for three weeks now—actually three weeks and two days, since we'd met at a gallery opening on a Friday night, and this was now a Sunday—were we to realize the full potential of our relationship by moving our somewhat tentative courtship off the dime in my king-sized bed tonight, then there would be no six-year-old cherub wandering down the hallway to ask Mommy for a drink of water, not in *my* place. I did not want to go to Vicky's place. My "Well . . ." made that abundantly clear—the slight inflection at the end of the word, the ringingly dubious note conveying reluctance if not downright obstinateness.

"Well," she said right back at me, and both of us fell silent.

We were on the Causeway now. Calusa Bay spread to the right and left of us. Out on the water, I could see the lights of several anchored sailboats. We were silent all the way across the bridge. I stopped for the traffic light on the corner of Cortez and 41. The silence lengthened. My place was northward to the left, Vicky's place was southward to the right. The light on Cortez and 41 is a very long light.

"What we *could* do . . ." I said.

"Yes?"

"Is go to your place for the pot, if that's what you'd . . ."

"Yes?"

"And *then* go back to my place."

"Uh-huh."

"If that's what you'd like to do."

"Because I really *would* like to smoke some dope, you know."

"Okay, if that's what you . . ."

"So if it isn't any trouble . . ."

"No trouble at . . ."

"We could go to *my* place first . . ."

"Yes, that's what we'll . . ."

"And then I could check on Allie and . . ."

"That sounds . . ."

"And tell the sitter I want her to stay a while longer."

"Maybe she could even sleep over," I said.

"No, I don't think she can do that. She's only fifteen."

"Okay, but tell her . . ."

"I'll tell her maybe two, three o'clock—would that be all right?"

"That'd be fine," I said.

"You've got the light," she said.

"What?" I said.

"The green light," she said.

All the way out 41 to the Cross River Mall and then eastward to Vicky's house, visions of sugarplum fairies danced in my head. I had known her for three weeks and two days and had taken her out twice during that time, once to dinner and another time to a late movie. On our second date (I *despise* that word) we were getting very friendly on her living room couch when six-year-old Allison walked in rubbing her eyes and wanting to know who the nice man was and asking whether she could show me the finger paintings she'd made in school that day. I looked at fourteen finger paintings. They were very nice finger paintings. I did not even know the little tyke's last name—Vicky had gone back to using her maiden name after the divorce—but I raved nonetheless over her prodigious talent. She wanted to know why Mommy's blouse was unbuttoned. Vicky wasn't wearing a bra; I had discovered that in the fifteen minutes before Allison's untimely arrival. She buttoned her blouse, and Allison sat on the rug in front of the couch and began drawing with her crayons, her long black hair falling in a curtain over her face as she worked. The clock on the mantel read ten minutes to one. In the *morning*. I asked Allison if she didn't think she might like to go back to sleep so she could wake up nice and early and go to the beach tomorrow. Allison said she hated the beach. "I turn lobster red in the sun," she said. Allison was a born artist. She made seven crayon drawings for me before the little porcelain mantel clock chimed the half-hour. When at last she yawned, hope sprang eternal. But she only got up to go to the kitchen to make herself a peanut butter and jelly sandwich. She offered me a bite. I left the house at two a.m., wondering what the penalty was for biting six-year-old girls in self-defense. I would have to ask Benny Weiss, who was a criminal lawyer.

But tonight . . . ah, tonight.

The omens all seemed ripe for gratification. Vicky had, to begin with, invited me to her opening weekend at the Greenery, which seemed to indicate an interest more than casual. She had chosen *me* with whom to share this big event in her life, singing again in public—well, wait, she'd *never* sung in public before, according to her own testimony—but singing *again*, at any rate, after a hiatus of almost twelve years. And she was now choosing to share with me the afterglow of the event, asking only that she be allowed to pick up some grass at her place, which would help to calm her later in the cloistered privacy of my living room, both of us sitting there and smoking our brains out (I had begun smoking pot only since the divorce) while I removed first the pale blue cardigan sweater, and then the white silk blouse to expose once again those magnificent breasts I had only briefly glimpsed and touched last Friday (before Allison made her entrance and called to Mommy's attention the fact that one rubescent nipple was about to make an entrance of its own) and then the blue skirt and the pantyhose—I *hate* pantyhose; whoever invented them should be shot along with the man who invented those electric hand dryers you find in men's rooms all over America—and then we would wander together into my bedroom where I would draw back the covers and we would slide together between cool clean sheets to discover each other at last. I was feeling extremely horny. I drove much faster than I normally would have; the cops in Calusa, Florida, are not noted for their charity to speeders.

Vicky lived in a small development house on a street called Citrus Lane on the eastern rim of the county. Drive six miles past her house and you found yourself in cattle country. This was one of the things that first astonished me about Florida. If you're born and raised in Illinois, you naturally think of Florida as consisting solely of palm trees and beaches. But there are two million head of cattle in the state, and you don't have to drive very far out of Calusa before coming into miles and miles of fenced-in grazing land—with the cows all facing in the same direction, it seems. A single light was burning in Vicky's house as I pulled the car into the driveway.

"Do you want to come in?" she asked.

"You won't be long, will you?"

"Just to get the grass," she said, "and to look in on Allie."

"I'll wait here then."

"I won't be long," she said, and leaned over, and put one hand widespread on my thigh, and kissed me open-mouthed before she got out of the car. I watched her as she walked to the front door of the house. She was, I guessed, about five feet eight inches tall, her long black hair trailing halfway down her back and swaying gently with each long-legged stride she took. She possessed, I noticed for the hundredth time, a truly glorious ass and splendid legs; once again I envisioned myself taking off all her clothes. Sitting behind the wheel of the Ghia in the darkness, vaguely tumescent, I heard a raccoon making a hell of a racket as he rummaged through someone's garbage. I hoped he would not wake the Dread Allison.

As promised, Vicky was back in no time at all. She did not go around to her side of the car. Instead she put her folded arms on the window frame on my side and said through the open window, "I'm sorry, Matthew."

"What?" I said.

"I can't go with you."

"Why not?"

"Allie's coming down with something."

I don't know why, but I immediately felt she was lying. Perhaps it was only my own disappointment. The red-blooded American male's dream of conquest shattered, rejection rampant in the near-midnight stillness of Citrus Lane.

"She's been coughing all night. The sitter thinks she may have a fever."

"Well, I . . . that's too bad," I said.

"Why don't you come in instead?"

"Well, if your daughter's sick . . ."

"The sitter gave her some Nyquil. She's asleep now."

I hesitated. My previous experience with Allison indicated that she was not a very heavy sleeper. On the other hand, if the sitter had *really* given her something to knock her out . . .

"Well," I said.

I could not shake the feeling that Vicky was lying to me.

"Please come in," she said. "I want you to."

I nodded.

"Will you?"

"Well, all right, I guess so."

"Thank you," she said.

The sitter was waiting in the living room. She was a round-faced, plump little teenager wearing blue jeans, no shoes, and a man's tailored shirt with the tails hanging loose.

"This is Mr. Hope," Vicky said. "How many hours was that, Charlene?"

"Four," Charlene said. "Hi."

"Hi," I said.

Vicky was counting out bills. She handed a wad of them to Charlene, who counted them twice, like a teller at Calusa First Independent, and then stuffed them into the right-hand pocket of her jeans. "Well, g'night," she said.

"Do you want me to walk you home?" Vicky asked.

"What for? It's just across the street."

"I'll watch till you're inside then," Vicky said.

"Sure," Charlene said. She sounded puzzled. "Well, g'night," she said again, and went out the front door. Vicky stood in the doorway, watching as she crossed the street to a house diagonally opposite. There were lights burning there in what I guessed was the living room. Charlene opened a door at the side of the house, waved back at Vicky to signal her safe crossing, and then went inside and closed the door behind her. The light over the door went out, the lights in the living room stayed on. Vicky closed and bolted her own front door.

"So," she said.

"So," I said. I was thinking of six-year-old Allison in her bedroom down the hall. I was thinking of finger paintings and crayon drawings and another early-morning art exhibit. Vicky must have read my mind.

"Don't worry," she said, "she's sound asleep." She caught her breath the way she had before she'd started singing earlier tonight, and then she moved into my arms and pressed herself close to me and lifted her mouth to mine and kissed me.

The grass was very good stuff that had made its way across the Gulf of Mexico on God-knew-which fishing boat to be carried ashore on God-knew-which deserted Florida beach; dope is the second biggest industry in the State of Florida. It should have calmed Vicky after the first few tokes, but it seemed to have no effect at all on her. Neither did the good cognac she poured into two huge snifters. Her tension was almost palpable. She jumped at every sound outside the house—a cat crooning his strident love song to another cat, an automobile passing in the midnight stillness, a locomotive somewhere far in the distance, rushing through the night. We had turned on the television set, and we sat on the couch before it, the black-and-white images of an old movie flickering to provide the only illumination in the room, passing the

second joint between us, alternately sipping at the cognac. I
felt no sense of urgency. I was beginning to believe that
Allison really would sleep through the night, and that there
would be no need for any frantic adolescent fumbling at
buttons, no cause for desperate, hasty kisses designed to
entice and entrap before imminent discovery. But Vicky was
trembling in my arms.

"Come on," I said, "relax. It's all over now."

I was referring to her performance at the Greenery.

She sighed and said, "I only wish it were."

I did not know what she meant.

She caught her breath again; I realized, suddenly that the
mannerism was a nervous tic. And then, all at once, perhaps
because of the strain of her opening weekend, perhaps because of the combined pot and cognac, she began talking
about her fairytale rise to prominence as a rock star back in
the sixties, and as I listened, I felt closer to her than I'd ever
been since I'd known her. There are men—and I shame-
facedly admit that I am among them—who will want to take a
woman to bed because she is what they have been taught to
believe is "sexy," whatever the hell *that* may mean, whatever combination of hip and thigh and lips and hair and breast
may coalesce to create the image of someone quintessentially
desirable. As Vicky told me about her spectacular ascendance
to stardom, I began to like her. And I wanted to go to bed
with her now for that reason alone: because genuinely, after
three weeks and two days, I *liked* her.

She told me that until her "discovery," as it was later
described in all the newspaper and magazine articles written
about her, she'd been doing one-night stands in lounges and
honky-tonk roadhouses in and around Little Rock, Arkansas,
causing very little local stir and seemingly destined for ano-
nymity. Her father Dwayne—who'd been a widower since
Vicky was fourteen, and who'd been nurturing her singing
"career" ever since she got paid ten dollars for her first
gig at a dive called Rocky's Corner in Sweet Home, Arkansas, just outside Little Rock—decided in 1964 that his then
nineteen-year-old daughter was destined for bigger and better
things. He promptly popped her into the family's 1962 Buick
sedan one weekend and drove her across the border into
Memphis and then northward to Nashville, where there were

more record companies than there were fleas on hound dogs. After four days of pounding the pavements and knocking on unreceptive doors, Dwayne and his nubile daughter ran across a young guitar player in the lounge of the Holiday Inn at which they were staying, and he told them there was no way a'tall to make it there in Nashville, the competition was too keen, the town was swarming with too damn many ambitious musicians. Only place to be was N'Orleans, he told them, which was where he was heading soon as he paid his hotel bill and got himself a bus ticket south. The guitar player's name was Geoffrey Hamilton; he would later become the lead guitarist in Wheat, the group that backed Vicky on her first hit album.

Why Hamilton concluded that New Orleans was the "only place to be" remained something of a mystery to Vicky. There were, to be sure, several record companies in that city, but they were mostly cutting jazz, and only a few of them were willing even to *see* aspiring amateurs. One of them was a firm called Regal Records, and its president was a man named Anthony Konig; the "Regal" was a deliberate reference to "Konig," which meant "King" in German. Back then in 1964 Konig was a handsome giant of a man in his early forties, blessed with an inheritance from a father who'd been a wealthy soybean farmer in West Carroll County, and determined to make a mark for himself in the music business. It was not difficult to understand how Victoria Miller, tall, gorgeous, and voluptuously ripe at the age of nineteen going on twenty, had captured Konig's imagination. He immediately arranged for an audition for her and her itinerant guitar-player friend, tossing into the mix a pair of musicians he had previously auditioned—the bass guitarist and the drummer who would later join Geoffrey Hamilton in the group called Wheat.

"That was the real beginning," she said, and caught her breath again. "Oh, Matthew, it seems so very long ago." She turned into my arms, and kissed me suddenly and deeply, and then rose swiftly from the couch, ground out the roach in an ashtray, and said, "I want us to make love now."

"Yes," I said.

"Please," she said, and extended her hand to me.

In the light of later events, it is difficult not to ascribe to

those next three hours in Vicky's bedroom an ulterior purpose
that had nothing to do with the act of love. There was, it
seemed to me even then, an excessive need to please, an
almost compulsive desire to make this a memorable experience, some sort of gala occasion that would enter the annals
of marathon lovemaking as our night of nights, perhaps to
break all existing records in Mr. Guinness's massive tome. I
had since my divorce been with women who trotted out their
bag of sexual tricks like magicians eager to baffle with dexter-
ity and skill. I had been with women who shyly played the
virgin while dispensing energetic head surely superior to any
offered by all the whores of Bombay. I had been with women
eager to learn ("Am I doing this right, Matthew?") and eager
to teach ("I will take you where you've never been"). I had
been with women easily shocked ("Oh, God, this is absolutely *disgusting!*") and easily shocking ("I once did it with
two black guys and a Labrador retriever"), but those three
hours with Vicky Miller, on her bed, in her bedroom, while
her daughter slept the sleep of angels just down the hall, were
more savagely sexual than any I had ever spent with any
woman, or any pair of women, in my life.

By two-thirty in the morning I was spent, satiated, and
silently wishing that little Allison would knock on the bedroom door to ask for some cough medicine or a mustard
plaster. Vicky was just starting, it seemed. I do not know
how she managed to prepare me once again for obedient
service to her unabated lust, but manage she did. When at last
I lay back exhausted against the pillow again, the small
porcelain clock in the living room was chiming 3:00 a.m.,
and her restless hand was already beginning to fidget beseech-
ingly where I ached and throbbed, fearful that all those stories
my mother told me about it falling off if I abused it were
about to come horribly true. Her mouth descended again.

"Vicky," I said wearily. "I have to go."

"No," she said. "You don't."

"Really, it's . . ."

"Stay the night," she said.

"I can't."

"You can."

I was thinking I had to be in the office at nine. I was
thinking that if my own daughter were six years old, I would

not want her waking up at eight to discover a naked stranger shaving in her mother's bathroom. I was thinking I'd had enough. I was thinking I'd had enough to last me till St. Swithin's Day, which isn't even celebrated in the United States of America.

"Stay," she whispered, and lowered her insistent mouth again.

"Vicky, honey, I love you but . . ."

"No, you don't love me," she said.

"Honey, I'm . . ."

"Then stay."

"Exhausted . . ."

"If you love me, stay."

"No . . ."

"Please."

"I can't . . ."

"Matthew, please Matthew, stay Matthew, please darling, stay darling, please Matthew please . . ."

Her voice murmured liquidly and hypnotically against my flaccid cock, plaintively urgent, her body reversed as she hovered above me in a fiercely determined crouch, "Please Matthew, please baby, stay baby, please say yes baby, please Matthew," her mouth swallowing her own murmured words as she enjoined and entreated, devouring and demanding, a rutting feral beast of the field with an appetite too voracious to appease—or so I thought at the time. When at last she recognized defeat, when at last she realized that she could not coax with her supplicating mouth even the tiniest *hint* of desire from me, she reversed her position once again, straddling me, and clasped my face between her hands and leaned forward to kiss me gently and sisterly on the mouth and the cheeks. "Just to sleep with me, Matthew, all right?" she said. "I promise I won't bother you, I want to sleep in your arms is all, will you do that for me, Matthew, just say you'll do that for me, please Matthew," her words interspersed with those gentle flicking kisses and hummingbird caresses of tongue. It was ten minutes past three in the morning. I kissed her lingeringly on the mouth, and then held her away from me and looked into her eyes.

"Vicky," I said, "I really have to go.

"Okay," she said abruptly, "fine," and rolled away from me, and turned her back, and pulled the sheet over her.

"My clothes are at the house . . ."

"Sure."

"The clothes I need for work . . ."

"Sure."

"And my briefcase . . ."

"So why don't you just go?" she said.

"Vicky," I said, "I'd be embarrassed to have your daughter find me here when she . . ."

"You weren't so embarrassed when you came in my mouth," she said.

"Vicky . . ."

"So just *go*, okay?"

I dressed swiftly and silently, and then I went to the bed where she lay with her face turned away from me. Tentatively I kissed her on the cheek.

"Never mind," she said.

"I'll call you tomorrow," I said. "Today, actually. Later today."

"Don't bother," she said.

"Vicky, honey . . ."

"Good night, Matthew," she said.

I debated saying something further, and decided not to. I was starting for the bedroom door when she said behind me, "You'll be sorry." I turned to look at her. She was still lying with her hair spread on the pillow, her face and her eyes averted. Quickly I went out of the room.

That was the last time I saw her alive.

2

My partner Frank calls Summerville and Hope the Old Curiosity Shop of the legal profession, this because we handle a great variety of cases and do not specialize in any one branch of the law. There are three lawyers in our office—Frank, myself, and a young man named Karl Jennings, who'd been admitted to the bar only a bit more than a year ago. Normally, we divide the work among us. If we find ourselves coping with a case requiring skills one or another of us doesn't possess, we will turn the case over to an outside shop. Rarely will we handle litigation of any sort, preferring to defer in such matters to attorneys who regularly handle court work. The firm employs as well a receptionist, a file clerk, and a secretarial pool consisting of two secretaries shared by Frank, Karl, and me. Only once in our history have we been involved in a criminal case, the one we still refer to around here as the "Goldilocks" case. I was about to become personally involved in another one that Monday morning, but I didn't yet know it.

The day started with an unannounced visit from a certifiable nut named Louis Dumont, whom I did not at first recognize as a lunatic. He arrived at ten minutes past nine, while I was still reading the morning mail. Cynthia buzzed from outside and said there was a man named Louis Dumont here to see

me. I asked her to come in for a minute. Cynthia Huellen is a
native Floridian with long blond hair and a glorious tan that
she works at almost fanatically; never a weekend goes by that
does not find Cynthia on a beach or a boat. She is easily the
most beautiful person in the law offices of Summerville &
Hope, twenty-four years old, and employed by us as a receptionist. Frank and I keep telling her to quit the job and go to
law school instead. She already has a B.A. from the University of South Florida, and we would take her into the firm the
minute she passed her bar exams. But each time we raise the
possibility, Cynthia grins and says, "No, I don't want the
hassle of school again." She is one of the nicest young
people I know, and she is blessed besides with a keen mind,
an even-tempered disposition, a fine sense of humor, and the
kind of clean good looks that went out of style in the sixties.
If I were twenty-eight, I would ask her to marry me, even
considering the possibility that this might not sit too well with
a daughter only eleven years younger than she is. The moment the door closed behind her, I asked, "Who's Louis
Dumont?"

"He says it's about the Cummings property. You look
terrible."

"Thank you. Does he have an appointment?"

"No."

"It's nine o'clock in the morning, are you telling me he
just walked in without an appointment?"

"It's nine-fifteen, and yes, that's what he did."

"All right, bring me the Cummings folder, give me a
minute to look at it, and then send him in."

Louis Dumont was a man in his mid-fifties, I guessed, with
a complexion that would have seemed pallid even in Minne-
sota but which made him appear positively moribund here in
Florida. He was almost entirely bald, and he had a pencil-line
mustache under his nose. His deep-set, restless brown eyes
should have provided the first clue to his instability, but it
was only a little past nine in the morning, and I wasn't paying
that much attention after less than four hours of sleep. He
stood silently before my desk, looking over, a short man in a
suit too heavy and too somberly hued for Florida. I guess he
was waiting for me to offer him a seat. I offered him one, and
he took it. He spoke very slowly and very calmly, deceiving

me completely. He told me that ten years ago the property in question was owned by his stepfather, Peter Landon, a widower who died intestate, leaving the building to Louis himself and his stepbrother John.

"Uh-huh," I said. As he spoke, I was rummaging through the Cummings folder again, looking for the probate record on Peter Landon's estate.

"So you see," he said, "the building still belongs to me and my stepbrother."

I now had the probate record in my hands. I read it over silently and looked across the desk. "According to this," I said, not for a moment realizing what violent effect my words would have, "Peter Landon died leaving only one child, a son named . . ."

Dumont leaped to his feet as though I'd touched him with a cattle prod. I saw those eyes then, burning unpredictably bright in his head. "You're just like all the rest!" he shouted, and then put both hands flat on the desk and leaned on his arms, the elbows locked, and yelled in a shower of spittle, "Why won't you recognize my claim? Why are you trying to cheat me out of my inheritance? You fucking sheeny Jew cocksucker shyster, I want what's *coming* to me!"

I'm not a Jew, and I have never sucked even a tiny little cock in all my life, and to the best of my knowledge I'm an honest practitioner of the law. But I was scared to death that if I denied any of Dumont's accusations he would lean farther across the desk and strangle me with his bare hands.

"Mr. Dumont," I said, "I'm basing my response only on what the probate record . . ."

"What the fuck does the *probate* record know?" he shouted. "Does it tell you how Peter took in an orphan and raised him as his own?"

"Well, no, it . . ."

"*I* was that orphan!" he shouted.

"Mr. Dumont, please try to . . ."

"He raised me as his own *son!* And when he died, he left that property to me and that rotten bastard John!"

"Well, I . . . I can find no record of that, Mr. Dumont."

"Records!" he shouted.

"That's all we have to go on," I said. "If the records . . ."

"Records!" he shouted again.

"Mr. Dumont, however close you may have felt to this man who took you in as an orphan . . ."

"He *did!*"

"Nor am I denying it. But however close you may have felt to him and the rest of the family . . ."

"Not that bastard John!"

"Not John, of *course* not John, but Mr. Landon himself perhaps, and perhaps his wife when she was alive."

"I never *met* his wife! What the fuck are you talking about?"

"My point is that in the absence of other evidence . . ."

"Evidence!"

". . . I'm afraid you have no claim as an heir to Peter Landon. In any event, sir, the property has changed hands four times since Mr. Landon died, and the present owner's obligation . . ."

"*Obligation!*" he shouted. "Don't tell *me* about obligation! I know all about those fucking sales and conveyances, I know all about titles and real estate, too, I know all about them, and I know my rights. If I have to bring an ejectment action to get my share of that million dollars . . ."

"Mr. Dumont, we're selling the property for three hundred thous—"

"It's worth a *million,* and I want my share! And I'll tell you something else, you fucking sheeny Jew cocksucker shyster, I'll *kill* any lawyer or judge who tries to keep me from getting what's mine!"

"Mr. Dumont," I said "you're beginning to annoy me. On behalf of my client, I'll offer you five hundred dollars to sign a release and a quitclaim deed. Otherwise, we'll simply disregard your claim. What do you say? Do you want the five hundred?"

"I want my share of the million!"

"Your share of the million is five hundred dollars, take it or leave it."

"I'll take it," Dumont said.

"Fine."

"I'll take it, you cocksucker."

"You go wait outside while I have the papers and the check drawn."

"I want it in cash," Dumont said.

"No, you'll take it by check. I want a record of payment in settle—"

"Records!" he shouted.

"Go sit outside," I told him. "And watch your language in front of that young girl out there."

"You cocksucker," he said, but he left the office.

That was the beginning of my Monday. Ten minutes later I got a call from a man who owed nine hundred dollars to another of my clients, a surgeon who'd performed a gall bladder operation for him. The man's name was Gerald Bannister. He started the conversation by saying, "What's this all about?"

"It's about nine hundred dollars, Mr. Bannister."

"So what's the matter? Ralph thinks I'm not going to pay him?"

"If by Ralph you're referring to Dr. Ungerman, yes, he's afraid that all he's going to get out of this is your gall bladder."

"Ha-ha, that's very funny," Bannister said. "Of *course* I'm going to pay him. Tell him to stop dunning me, okay? My gall bladder, that's very funny. What's he got it in a jar or something?"

"Mr. Bannister, when do you plan to pay Dr. Ungerman?"

"I'll pay him, don't worry."

"I *am* worried. *When* will you pay him?"

"I can't pay him now."

"When *can* you pay him?"

"I can't pay it *all* right now is what I mean."

"How much of it *can* you pay right now?"

"A hundred."

"What about the remaining eight hundred?"

"I'll pay him a hundred a month."

"That's not good enough."

"It's the best I can do."

"You'll have to do better."

"I *can't* do better than two hundred a month."

"You didn't *say* two hundred, you said a *hundred.*"

"I meant two hundred."

"A hundred now, and two hundred a month for the next four months, is that it?"

"That's it."

"All right, I'll need you here to sign the notes. And remember, Mr. Bannister, *you're* the one who's setting this schedule . . ."

"I know I am."

"I'm simply warning you that any future delinquency won't be tolerated."

"Thanks for the warning."

"I'll prepare the notes. When can you come here to sign them?"

"Next week sometime."

"Make it tomorrow."

"I can't make it tomorrow."

"When *can* you make it?"

"Thursday."

"All right, nine o'clock Thursday."

"One o'clock Thursday."

"One o'clock, fine."

"I never been dunned like this in my life," Bannister said, and hung up.

It was almost ten when Cynthia buzzed to say that Frank wanted to see me in his office. There are people who say that Frank Summerville and I look alike. I cannot see any resemblance. I'm six feet two inches tall and weigh a hundred and ninety pounds. Frank's a half-inch under six feet, and he weighs a hundred and sixty, which he watches like a hawk. We both have dark hair and brown eyes, but Frank's face is rounder than mine. Frank says there are only two types of faces in the world—pig faces and fox faces. He classifies himself as a pig face and me as a fox face. There is nothing derogatory about either label: they are only intended to be descriptive. Frank first told me about his designation system more than a year ago. Ever since, I've been unable to look at anyone without automatically categorizing him as either pig or fox.

He took one look at me now and said, "Look what the cat dragged in." I did not believe I looked all that awful. It was true that I'd had very little sleep last night, but I had felt vaguely refreshed after showering and shaving this morning, and moreover I was wearing one of my best suits, an English tropical I'd had hand-tailored for me at Chipp in New York.

That was before the divorce. Since the divorce I have not been able to afford any hand-tailored suits.

"The Downings are coming in about those wills," Frank said. "I don't know what to advise them, Matt. I hate to be put in the middle of this."

"What's the problem?"

"They're taking a six-month cruise around the world, and they want to sign new wills before they take off. But Sally's reluctant to make her brother-in-law the alternate executor of the will . . ."

"You mean if Howard predeceases her?"

"Right. She doesn't *like* her brother-in-law, plain and simple. She feels that if Howard dies first and then *she* goes, her no-good brother-in-law will make a mess of the estate."

"Has she any reason to believe that?"

"The man pissed away his half of the fortune Howard's father left them. Sally's afraid he'll do the same with *their* estate once both of them are dead."

"So? Who does she want as alternate executor?"

"*Her* brother."

"Then what's the problem?"

"He's no better than *Howard's* brother. A two-bit gambler from what I understand, running up to Miami every weekend to play the dogs or the frontons."

"So where's King Solomon?" I said.

"They'll be here in twenty minutes. What do I tell them?"

"Would she accept one of us as executor?"

"She might."

"Or a bank? What's their bank?"

"First Union."

"They've got a good trust department, why don't you suggest them?"

"She's dead set on her brother."

"How does Howard feel about it?"

"He's holding out for *his* brother."

"Then tell them to cancel the goddamn trip," I said.

"I'll suggest First Union."

The buzzer on his desk sounded. Frank clicked on.

"Yes?" he said.

"There's a policeman here to see Mr. Hope," Cynthia said.

"You expecting the fuzz?" Frank asked.

"No," I said.

He was waiting in the reception area, a beefy young man with china-blue eyes and sandy-colored hair. He introduced himself as Sergeant Halloway and politely asked if I would mind coming along with him.

"What for?" I said.

"You're Matthew Hope, aren't you?" he said.

"I'm Matthew Hope," I said.

"Mr. Hope," he said, "a woman named Victoria Miller was found dead earlier this morning by the colored lady come to clean her house. People live across the street said a tan Karmann Ghia bearing the Florida license plate HOPE-1 was still parked in deceased's driveway there at three in the morning. Highway Safety and Motor Vehicles says that's your car, Mr. Hope. Also, it seems a baby-sitter named Charlene Whitlaw was introduced to a man named Mr. Hope in deceased's house at around midnight last night, which puts you at the scene of the crime for at least three hours. So what they want to do is ask you some questions is all. You think you'd like to come with me?"

In Calusa the police station is officially called the Public Safety Building, and these words are lettered in white on the low wall outside. Less conspicuously lettered to the right of the brown metal entrance doors, and partially obscured by pittosporum bushes, are the words "Police Department." The building is constructed of varying shades of tan brick, and its architecturally severe face is broken only by narrow windows resembling rifle slits in an armory wall. This is not unusual for Calusa, where the summer months are torrid and large windows produce only heat and glare. I had spent a lot of time in this building last March with a client named James Purchase, whose wife and two daughters had been brutally stabbed to death in his house on Jacaranda Drive. The detective I'd worked with then was a man named George Ehrenberg. When I asked Sergeant Halloway, in his car on the way downtown, whether Ehrenberg was on duty today, he told me curtly that Detective Ehrenberg didn't work in Calusa anymore, he was working for the Lauderdale police now. I asked

Halloway if Ehrenberg's partner was around, a man named Detective Di Luca.

"Vinnie's on vacation," he said. "He won't be back till the twenty-first."

"Oh," I said. The twenty-first was a week away.

An orange-colored letter-elevator rose like an over-sized periscope from the floor, diagonally opposite the entrance doors to the third-floor reception area. There was a desk against the paneled wall facing us, and a girl sat behind it, typing furiously. The clock on the wall above her head read ten minutes to eleven. All of it looked very familiar—except that Vincent Di Luca was on vacation, and George Ehrenberg had transferred to the Fort Lauderdale P.D. The man who was waiting to talk to me introduced himself as Detective Morris Bloom. He was a heavyset man in his mid-forties, taller than I by at least an inch, and wearing a rumpled blue suit and a wrinkled white shirt with the tie pulled down and the top button open. He had the oversized knuckles of a street fighter, a fox face with a nose that appeared to have been broken more than once, shaggy black eyebrows, and dark brown eyes that seemed on the imminent edge of tears. I recalled that George Ehrenberg had also possessed an ineffable air of sadness, and I wondered now if everyone on the Calusa police force was pained by the job he had to do. Bloom told me at once that he was investigating a homicide here, and said he would like to inform me of my rights before he asked any questions. The word "homicide" had been spoken at last. Sergeant Halloway had told me only that Vicky had been found dead. In this state suicides and homicides were investigated in exactly the same fashion, and so it had been reasonable for me to believe that if I'd been the last person to see Vicky alive, a visit from the police was almost certainly in order. But now it was official. Homicide. Either way I felt rotten. If I had *stayed* with her last night—

"I'm an attorney," I told him. "I'm familiar with my rights."

"Well, Mr. Hope, the way I look at it, you're technically in custody here, and I'm *obliged* to advise you of your rights. I've been a police officer for close to twenty-five years now, and nothing gives me a bigger pain in the ass than interpreting Miranda-Escobedo. But if I've learned one thing about interrogations, it's that it's better to be safe than sorry. So, if you don't mind, I'll just reel off your rights to you, and then we'll be over and done with it.''

"If it makes you feel better,'' I said.

"Nothing about murder makes me feel very good, Mr. Hope,'' he said, "but at least this way we'll be starting off even, everything according to how the Supreme Court wants it, okay?''

"Fine,'' I said.

"Okay,'' he said. "In keeping with the 1966 Supreme Court decision in *Miranda* v. *Arizona*, we are not permitted to ask you any questions until you are warned of your right to counsel and your privilege against self-incrimination. First, you have the right to remain silent. Do you understand that?''

"I do.''

"You are not obliged to answer any police questions, do you understand that?''

"I do.''

"And if you *do* answer any questions, the answers may be used as evidence against you.''

"I understand.''

"Next you have the right to consult with an attorney before or during police questioning.''

"I *am* an attorney. We can skip the rest, can't we?''

"I guess so,'' Bloom said dubiously. "Do you understand all of your rights?''

"I do.''

"Are you willing to answer my questions?''

"I am.''

"Okay, I'll start with the big one: *were* you with Victoria Miller last night from midnight to sometime after three a.m.?''

"If you mean at her house, it was more like eleven-thirty. Mr. Bloom, can you tell me what happened?''

"Well, you see, Mr. Hope, and no offense, but you're here because I want to learn from *you* what happened. Because, Mr. Hope, and I'm sure you realize this, being a lawyer, since you were with her for three, four hours last night, I guess you must understand that the possibility exists you maybe killed her.''

"She was alive when I left her,'' I said.

"What time was that?'' he asked at once.

"Sometime between three and three-thirty."

"Would you remember the time exactly?"

"Three-fifteen, three-twenty, somewhere in there."

"Anyone see you leaving the house?"

"Not to my knowledge."

"Lady across the street was up watching a movie on TV, she says she saw your car parked over there when she turned off the lights at three a.m."

"Yes, I was still there at three."

"How come you're so sure of that?"

"A clock chimed the hour."

"A clock where?"

"In the living room. A little porcelain clock."

"Were you in the living room when the clock went off?"

"No. We were in the bedroom."

"Uh-huh. In bed?"

"Yes."

"Mr. Hope, excuse me, but did you have sexual relations with Victoria Miller last night?"

"Yes, I did."

"How long had you known her, Mr. Hope?"

"A little more than three weeks."

"Had you been intimate with her all that time?"

"No. Not until last night."

"Are you married, Mr. Hope?"

"Divorced."

"From what I understand, Miss Miller was a singer . . ."

"Yes."

". . . who was performing out there at the Greenery, out there on Stone Crab."

"I was with her there last night, yes."

"While she was singing?"

"Yes."

"From what time to what time?"

"I got there at a little before nine. The show ended at ten, and we sat talking to some friends of hers until . . . it must've been about a quarter to eleven. We got back to her house at eleven-thirty."

"Anyone there when you got there?"

"Yes. Vicky's sitter. Vicky paid her, and after she was gone we sat down to . . ."

I hesitated.

"You can tell me about the dope," Bloom said. "I'm not looking for a drug bust. We found a couple of roaches in the living room ashtray and two unwashed brandy snifters. So what you did was sit down to smoke some grass and have a few drinks, am I right? Then what?"

"We went into the bedroom."

"To make love?"

"Yes."

"Until three, three-thirty in the morning?"

"Yes."

"Did you see the little girl at any time last night?"

"No. She was asleep."

"*Ever* see the little girl?"

"Yes, once."

"When was that?"

"A week ago Friday."

"But you didn't see her last night, huh?"

"No."

"Not when you came in, and not before you left either."

"No. The sitter had given her some Nyquil to put her to sleep."

"The sitter told you this?"

"She told Vicky. Vicky reported it to me."

"How'd you get along with her?"

"Vicky? Fine."

"No spats, no lovers' quarrels, no . . ."

"We weren't lovers."

"Until last night. What were you *before* last night?"

"Friends."

"Good friends?"

"Casual friends."

"But last night it wasn't casual."

"No, it wasn't casual."

"So how about *last* night? Any spats *last* night?"

"No. Well, wait . . . yes. I suppose so. I guess we had a small argument. What might be considered an argument."

"Oh? What about?"

"She wanted me to stay, I wanted to go home. We discussed it briefly, and I left."

"How'd she feel about that?"

"She was angry, I guess."

"But you left anyway."

"I left."

"And you say she was alive when you left, huh?"

"She was very much alive."

"I think maybe she was," Bloom said, and nodded. "Mr. Hope, this line of work, you develop what Ernest Hemingway used to call a built-in shit detector. You familiar with Ernest Hemingway? The writer?"

"I'm familiar with him."

"You learn to sense whether somebody's telling the truth or somebody's lying, I'm sure it's the same in your line of work. I think you're telling the truth. If I'm wrong, sue me," he said, and shrugged. "I don't have to remind you not to leave town, this isn't a movie. The autopsy's being done right this minute at Calusa General, and I might want to get back to you after I have the results. From what you've told me, they'll be finding sperm in the vaginal vault, which won't help us any when it comes to determining whether the killer raped her beforehand or not. But unless they come up with something besides the *obvious* cause of death . . ."

"What was that, Mr. Bloom?"

"She was beaten to death."

"Beat—"

"Yeah, nice, huh? We figure it had to be a man because of the sheer power involved, broke her jaw and her nose and a dozen ribs, cracked her skull wide open, probably by pounding it on the tile floor in the bathroom. That's where the maid found her at nine o'clock this morning, in the bathroom, blood all over the fucking floor. But you never know, it could've been a woman, too. Some women, when they get mad, they're strong as an ox, you know? I had a case when I was with the Nassau County cops, this woman no bigger than my thumb strangled her two-hundred-pound husband. You think he could've brushed her off like a fly, am I right? But she had this unnatural strength in her hands. This *rage* in her fingers, you know?" He demonstrated by clasping his huge hands together, the fingers interlocked, and squeezing an imaginary throat between them. "Guy didn't have a chance against such fury. I'll tell you something, Mr. Hope, never start up with a guy who's really angry. He'll kill you before you can bat an eyelash." He relaxed his hands, nodded soberly, and said, "I moved down here 'cause I figured you don't get such shit in a nice place like Calusa, am I right? Only high-class cat burglars down here, prowling the condos. Instead, some bastard beats a girl to death in the middle of the night." Bloom shook his head. The sad brown eyes looked even sadder. He sighed and then said, "You know anybody who might've wanted that little girl badly enough?"

"What?" I said.

"The little girl."

"I don't understand."

"Badly enough to have killed the mother for it."

"I still . . ."

"The little girl's gone, Mr. Hope. Whoever killed Victoria Miller took the little girl with him."

3

I could not shake the feeling that I was at least partially responsible for Vicky's death and her daughter's abduction. I did not even know little Allison's last name, and this oversight caused in me a remorse almost as deep as the lingering guilt. My partner Frank maintains that the three guiltiest minority groups on the face of the earth are Jews, Italians, and Divorced Men. I cannot speak for either of the two ethnic groups, but I can certainly affirm that guilt played a large part in my signing the settlement agreement proposed by Susan's attorney and later offered to me by my own attorney, Eliot McLaughlin. Susan has never allowed me to forget the fact that I was "whoring around" as she puts it, with a woman crazy enough to have attempted suicide over me, and that if it had not been for my "adolescent behavior" my daughter would not now be shuttling back and forth between two homes but instead would be enjoying a bona fide family relationship "like all the other little girls in Calusa." Susan forgets that the divorce rate in Calusa is roughly what it is in the rest of these United States: forty percent of all married couples get divorced here annually. Most of my daughter's close friends, in fact, are the victims of—well, there I go. *Victims*. It is difficult to resist Susan's propaganda, especially when each time I arrive to pick up Joanna she will say, "It's your *father*," in a tone of voice that makes it clear she is *really* saying, "It's your son-of-a-bitch, no-good, philandering father." Frank says this feeling of guilt will never pass. He tells me he knows men who have been divorced for ten or more years who still dream nightly about their former wives. I have dreamt about Susan only once since the divorce last June. That Monday morning, as I left the Public Safety Building and began walking the ten blocks to our offices on Heron and Vaughan, I had the feeling I would be dreaming about Vicky and about what had happened last night for a long, long time to come.

It was going to be another beautiful day. The digital clock on top of the Southern Florida Bank and Trust Company building flashed the hour—11:20 a.m.—and then the temperature: it was seventy-two degrees already, and the sun was still forty minutes from its zenith. The sky behind the building was cloudless and blue; the early morning mist that had been there when I'd made the drive downtown in Sergeant Halloway's radio motor patrol car had burned off completely. In Calusa the cops patrol one man to a car, and they hang their hats on a hook over the visor on the passenger side. From the rear the hanging circle of the hat looks like a person's head and creates the illusion of a second officer in the car. The illusion works only with the tourists; any resident of Calusa, *including* the thieves, knows there is only one cop in that car. As I waited for the light to change in front of the Harris Brothers Department Store on U.S. 301, a patrol car went by. The driver's hat was hanging as usual over the passenger seat. The driver turned to look at me, and so strongly did my sense of guilt return that for a moment I believed there actually *were* two patrolmen in that car, and that both of them were closely scrutinizing me. The light changed to green. I crossed the street in the hot morning sun.

There was yet another feeling, almost as difficult to dispel as the one of guilt. I could not forget that when Vicky came out of her house last night to tell me her daughter was coming down with something, I'd immediately thought she was lying. I tried to rationalize this now as I had last night. I'd been disappointed, I'd been rejected (or so it seemed at the time), and so I'd chosen to believe that Vicky was inventing an excuse to spare my feelings: she hadn't *wanted* to be alone with me at my place, and a concocted cough and attendant fever seemed the easiest way out of it. But that was *before* she'd invited me in, that was *before* we'd shared the joints and the cognac and the tumultuous acrobatics in her bed. So if she hadn't been lying as a way out of prolonging our evening together, why *had* she been lying?

She had entered that house promising she'd be gone only as long as it took "to get the grass and to look in on Allie." Three or four minutes later she had returned with what I felt certain was a false story. It seemed reasonable to assume that in those three or four minutes she had learned something that had caused her to change her mind about leaving her young daughter alone in there with a sitter. It seemed further reasonable to assume that fifteen-year-old Charlene Whitlaw might know just *what* that something was.

Unless a kid is lucky enough to get into Calusa's exclusive public high school "for the gifted," officially called Bedloe by the School Board but snidely referred to as "Bedlam" by the parents of children who have not passed the stringent entrance exams; or unless a kid is rich enough to afford one of the area's two private preparatory schools—St. Mark's in Calusa itself, and the Redding Academy in nearby Manakawa— then the secondary school educational choices are limited to three schools, and the selection is further limited by that part of the city in which the student happens to live. It would be nice to report that white parents in Calusa dance joyously in the streets when faced with the possibility of their children attending Arthur Cozlitt High, which has an unusually high percentage of black students. This, alas, is not the case. I have had at least a dozen irate parents trotting into my office in the past several years, asking if there was not some sort of legal action they might take to effect a transfer from Cozlitt to either Jefferson or Tate, each with a more normally balanced ratio of black to white students.

Calusa is a city of a hundred and fifty thousand people, a third of them black, a tiny smattering of them Cubans who have drifted over to the West Coast from Miami. There used to be a restaurant called Cuban Mike's on Main Street, and it made the best sandwiches in town, but it closed last August when someone fire-bombed the place. The whites blamed the blacks; the blacks blamed the rednecks; and the handful of Cubans in town kept their mouths shut lest fiery crosses appear on their lawns one dark night. One of these days Calusa is going to have a racial conflagration that will blow the town sky-high; it is long overdue. In the meantime everyone here pretends that this is still the year 1844; I think Frank and I may be the only people in all Calusa who notice that at any performance given at the Helen Gottlieb, only half a dozen people in the audience will be black—in an auditorium that seats two thousand.

Charlene Whitlaw lived on Citrus Lane in the southeastern part of the city, which meant that she normally would have attended Cozlitt High. But a call to the School Board—on the brief stop I made at my office—garnered the information that she was a student in her sophomore year at the highly prized Bedloe on Tantamount and Crane. I told Cynthia I would be going there before lunch and would be back in the office at three, in time for my only afternoon appointment.

Cynthia asked me what had happened at the police station. I told her, and she promised to fill Frank in when he returned from Globe Title and Guaranty. The Ghia had been baking in the sun all morning; the black vinyl seats were hot to the touch. I drove southward on Oleander, an avenue paralleling 41, but not as well known by the tourists, and then turned east on Tarpon and began a series of jigs and jogs in an attempt to avoid traffic lights; full-stop signs were easier to cope with in Calusa, and left turns onto busy highways were to be avoided at all costs.

It was a little past twelve-thirty when I pulled into Bedloe's parking lot on Tantamount. The kids were all outside eating lunch in the sunshine. I asked a bosomy seventeen-year-old in cutoffs and a tight pink sweater where the main office was, and she directed me to a low, white-stucco building in a cluster of similar buildings that sprawled leisurely across the campus. On the playing field a dozen or more boys and girls were yelling too loud as they played a game of pick-up volley ball. A fussy secretary with a pencil in her hair told me that Charlene Whitlaw was at present on her lunch hour—as was every *other* Bedloe student—but that she was scheduled for an English class in Building Number Four, the one with the

purple door, at one o'clock. Belatedly, she asked me who I
was. I told her I was Charlene's uncle.

The kids began ambling back to their classes at ten minutes
before the hour. Charlene was wearing the same blue jeans
and man's tailored shirt she'd had on last night; I wondered if
she'd slept in her clothes. She recognized me the moment she
came around the side of the building, and a frightened look
darted into her eyes. She had, after all, been interviewed by
the police sometime early this morning, and it was she who'd
told them a man named Mr. Hope had come into Vicky's
house last night at eleven-thirty. She must have thought for a
moment that I was there to do to her what I had done to
Vicky, or at least what she *assumed* I'd done to Vicky.

"Charlene," I said at once, "it's all right, I just want to
ask you some questions."

"I didn't tell them anything," she said, and began backing
away from me.

"I've already been to see the police . . ."

"Just your name," she said.

"Yes, that's okay, I'm a lawyer," I said, "there's no
problem."

Telling people you're a lawyer seems to have a soothing
effect on them, in direct contradiction to the inescapable fact
that the nation's prisons are full of *hundreds* of lawyers who
have committed unspeakably heinous crimes. My words seemed
to calm Charlene. She took a tentative step closer.

"I didn't think you did it," she whispered.

"You're right, I didn't."

"Was it Mr. Bloom you talked to?"

"Yes."

"He scared me," Charlene said.

"He shouldn't have, he's a very nice man."

"It was terrible what happened, wasn't it?"

"Awful."

"Who do you think did it?"

"I don't know."

"The man who called?"

"What man?" I said at once.

"The one who called last night."

"Did he give you his name, Charlene?"

"No. He just said to tell Vicky he'd be stopping by to collect."

"Collect what?"

"He didn't say."

"Did he say money, or . . ."

"No."

"Or . . . anything at *all?* What the something might be that he was coming to collect?"

"No, he just said, 'I'll be stopping by to collect,' that's all."

"When was this, Charlene?"

"Well, actually he called three times."

"Last night?"

"Yes. The first time was just after the taxi picked up Vicky to take her to the Greenery. That was about . . ."

"Yes, what time was . . . ?"

"About ten to eight, just after I got there."

"But she'd already left when he called, is that right?"

"Oh, sure, she had to sing at nine, you know."

"Yes, I know that. What did he say that first time?"

"He just said he wanted to talk to Vicky, please, and I told him she wasn't there just then. I never tell people who call when people I'm sitting for'll be back. That's a bad mistake. I saw this movie once where a person who's planning to rob a house makes a call and the sitter answers and he finds out from her when everybody'll be home and all, and that way he knows there's just the sitter in the house, you see. So he can come rob it."

"Uh-huh. When did he call the next time?"

"About ten-thirty."

"And what'd you tell him then?"

"I told him she was out walking the dog just then, and couldn't come to the phone. She doesn't even *have* a dog, but I didn't want him to know she'd be back late 'cause then he'd know I was all alone in the house. With just Allison, you know. Who's only six, you know."

"And the last time?"

"When he called again, you mean?"

"Yes."

"About a quarter past eleven, just before you guys got

back. That was when he said to tell her he'd be stopping by to collect.''

"But he didn't say what that might have been? Money, or trash, or laundry, or . . .''

"No.''

"And he didn't leave his name? Or a number where he could be reached?''

"No. I asked him who should I say called, but he said to just give her the message.''

"What did he sound like, Charlene?''

"Gee, I don't know.''

"Well, what kind of voice did he have? Did he sound young or old or . . . ?''

"Gee, I really couldn't say. I mean, he didn't sound *really* old, you know. I mean, not like you or my father.''

"Uh-huh.''

"But he didn't sound like a teenager, either, if that's what you mean.''

A loud bell sounded somewhere on campus. The kids lounging around outside began filing in through the purple door. The doors on the other buildings, I now noticed, were all painted in different colors. This was a school for the gifted, but it was apparently necessary to color-code the doors so that the students could find their classrooms. My partner Frank, in his inimitable fashion, once said that a school for the gifted in the State of Florida was the equivalent of a 600 school in New York City. A 600 school, I think, is a school for slow learners.

"I have to go to class now," Charlene said.

"Just a few more questions," I said.

"Okay, but really I *do* have to . . .''

"Was Allison coughing a lot last night?''

"Allison? No. Who said she was coughing?''

"Did you give her some Nyquil to put her to sleep?''

"No. I gave her a glass of milk and some graham crackers at ten o'clock. Vicky said she could stay up late to watch her favorite show on television, but that she had to go to bed right after it. So I gave her the milk and graham crackers and put her to bed.''

"But no Nyquil.''

"No."

"And no coughing."

"None at all."

"Did you tell Vicky you thought Allison might have a fever?"

"No, why would I have told her that?"

"Did you tell her about those various phone calls?"

"Oh, sure, of course."

"Charlene," I said, "thank you. You'd better hurry up, you don't want to get a late slip."

"Did they have late slips when *you* went to school, too?" she asked, as if amazed that such a practice had been in effect during the days of the Holy Roman Empire.

"Yes," I said. "Charlene, thanks a lot."

"I hope they get him, " she said.

She seemed not to know that little Allison had been abducted. I did not tell her otherwise. I watched as she opened the purple door and went into the air-conditioned classroom, and then I walked back to where I'd parked the Ghia, wondering if I should tell Morris Bloom what I'd learned about the mysterious phone calls last night. As Bloom had informed me, though, this was not a movie. I decided to share with him everything I knew.

He was not too terribly appreciative.

He told me, first of all, that this was a homicide he was investigating here, not to mention a kidnapping, and that whereas he could maybe understand my wanting to follow up on something I thought might be pertinent to the investigation, he nonetheless would hate to think that an amateur (the word rankled) by conducting his own investigation might somehow give the killer an edge he certainly didn't need. He reminded me that in accordance with Section 1201, Subsection (b) of the Federal Kidnapping Statute, the failure to release a victim within twenty-four hours after he'd been unlawfully seized, confined, inveigled, decoyed, kidnapped, abducted, or carried away would create a rebuttable presumption that such person had been transported in interstate or foreign commerce, which meant that the FBI could be called in on this at nine o'clock tomorrow morning, which would be twenty-four hours from when the maid had found Victoria Miller dead and her daughter missing. Until that time the case was the sole province and responsibility of the Calusa Police Department, which would get all kinds of heat if something should happen to that little girl, something maybe as bad as what had happened to her mother.

"Now, Counselor," he said (and the word "Counselor" rankled, too, because it was more often than not used sarcastically, even among contesting attorneys in a courtroom), "we do not know why this man—if it *was* a man—took that child. In most kidnappings there is a ransom motive involved, but you don't kill a woman and then hope to get ransom money from her. We've learned from the murder victim's father—and I'm telling you all this so you can understand my position, Counselor—a man named Dwayne Miller here in Manakawa, that his daughter's former husband is a man named Anthony Konig who lives in New Orleans, and we've been trying to reach him all day to determine whether the killer has contacted *him* with a ransom demand. He would seem the only likely person to contact, unless the killer thinks this Dwayne Miller is also a candidate, in which case . . ."

"Did you *ask* Miller whether he'd been contacted?"

"Yes, and we've also set up equipment at his house to handle a trace, should anybody call there. He understands this is a matter of life and death, Counselor, and he loves his little granddaughter and wouldn't want any harm to come to her, so he knows better than to talk about this to anyone, even though the tendency in a tragedy is to share it with neighbors and friends. The present tragedy up here is to cool the kidnapping, wait for the man who took that kid to make the first move. We've informed the papers and the television stations in Tampa and Manakawa about the *murder,* but we haven't said word one about the kid being missing. We want the killer to make the first move, you understand? Maybe he thinks we don't even *know* yet that a child was involved here, maybe he thinks *we* think she was off visiting a friend or something, and we don't yet know she's gone. We want him to make the call, either to the little girl's father, this Anthony Konig who I now got the New Orleans cops trying to locate so we can get the telephone company in there, in his *house* there, to install their stuff, or else to the kid's grandfather, who's ready and waiting to keep the guy talking forever, or else to us, or the newspapers—which God forbid I hope he *doesn't* call because they would like nothing better than to get involved here and maybe screw up the whole thing even if it means endangering the kid's life. We're going to be ready and waiting when he calls, *if* he calls, and we've got the edge if he thinks none of us know anything and he has to explain it all at great length while the phone company is trying to trace the call.

"So, Counselor," he said, "it would be nice to have your word that from this minute on you won't be running all over the city of Calusa questioning anybody you think might have some connection with this case, as I would hate to have the blood of a six-year-old girl on my hands if I were you, Counselor."

"I thought this wasn't a movie," I said.

"It isn't."

"Then stop talking to me as if I'm a fucking Los Angeles private eye."

There was a long silence on the line.

"Okay," Bloom said at last, "I'm sorry." He was silent again. "I don't like kidnappings," he said. "I've got a daughter of my own."

"So have I."

"Okay, I *said* I was sorry, I'm *sorry*, okay? But please do me the favor, okay? Stay out of it. We already knew about those phone calls last night, the sitter told us all about them when we talked to her this morning. Okay, Mr. Hope? Please?"

"Okay," I promised, "I'll stay out of it."

But that was before Anthony Konig came to visit me at four o'clock that afternoon.

My three o'clock appointment was with a client whose next-door neighbor's driveway was encroaching on his property by a full two feet. He didn't want to force the man, whom he genuinely liked, to rip up the driveway, but at the same time he wanted to know if there was any danger in permitting the encroachment to continue. I told him there was indeed danger of the neighbor's later asserting rights to the land by virtue of the location and continued use of the driveway. I told him we would have to prepare an agreement that would permit the encroachment but wherein the neighbor would agree not to assert any rights in the future. He seemed doubtful. I assured him everything would be fine and there was nothing to worry about. He still looked doubtful when he left at three-fifteen.

In the next forty-five minutes I placed or answered a dozen phone calls to or from: 1) a man in the Mortgage Department at Florida National who informed me that a former client of ours named Jonas Carlton had just sold a house subject to their mortgage and that the mortgage called for the entire note to be paid upon sale or conveyance of the property; the bank now wanted to call the note due; 2) Jonas Carlton, first at his office and then at 3) his home on Sabal Key. I got no answer at either place. It occurred to me that he might have moved in the time we'd handled the original purchase of the house for him, so I called 4) Florida National to ask if they had a number for him that might be different from the one in my files. Indeed, they had. I then called 5) Jonas Carlton again, in Manakawa this time, seventeen miles to the south of Calusa. I got no answer there, either, so I made a note to try him again in the morning. That was when the phone rang with 6) a man from the Internal Revenue Service who told me that a client of mine was claiming a two-thousand-dollar tax reduction on the purchase of a new home in 1978, and could I provide them with a certificate from the builder, stating that the transaction complied with the requirements for the reduction. I told him I could, and then buzzed Cynthia to ask for the file. She informed me that I had a call waiting from 7) a man whose name she couldn't pronounce. That was because the man's name was Kajchrzak. He spelled it for me, and then said that he had been born Frederick Wilson, but that he had been adopted by the Kajchrazk family when he was just an infant and had been known as Frederick Kajchrzak for the past thirty-four years. He now wanted to change his name back to Frederick Wilson, but his adoptive parents resented his lack of loyalty to the family name and had told him they would oppose any application for change. I asked him to come see me, and we made an appointment for the following week. Cynthia buzzed again to say she had the file I wanted. I asked her to come in. She put the file on my desk, and told me that another call was waiting on three. This one was from 8) a client named Arthur Lorring who told me his son had been charged with doing ninety miles an hour in a clearly posted thirty-mile-an-hour zone on a motorcycle with a young lady on the back seat. I told him I suspected this might be considered something more than a simple speeding violation, and gave him the name of a colleague who might handle such a matter better than Summerville and Hope. I then called 9) Benny Weiss, who is a criminal lawyer. I told him to expect a call from Lorring and filled him in on what the kid had done. He confirmed that this would be considered a violation of Chapter 316.192, Reckless Driving, and that Lorring's son would undoubtedly go to jail for ninety days and would be lucky if he got off without paying a fine as well; in Benny's opinion, the kid *deserved* ninety days. I then returned a call from 10) a client of ours who was buying a liquor store, and who had called while I was out to say that the seller's attorney wanted the value of the liquor inventory to be determined by the shelf price less twenty percent. I told him I wanted the *book* value to be the basis for determining the value of the inventory, since this was the customary method, and suggested that I call the seller's attorney. He said I should go ahead, so I called 11) Abraham Pollock, known in the profession as Honest Abe, and told him the retail price was unacceptable to us. He moaned and groaned and said, "Have a heart, Matthew," more times than I could count, but he finally agreed on the wholesale price plus twenty percent. The call I made just before Cynthia buzzed to announce Mr. Konig was to 12) my dear daughter Joanna.

Susan answered the phone.

"Hello, Susan," I said. "May I speak to her, please?"

"She's not home from school yet," Susan said.

"Oh. Well, okay, I'll . . ."

"She had Choir today."

"Right, I forgot."

"But I'm glad you called."

This surprised me. Susan was rarely, if ever, glad I had called.

"Oh?" I said.

"Yes. Are you busy this weekend?"

I did not say anything. Was Susan about to extend an invitation to a party? A brunch? A walk on the beach? A beheading?

"Because if you're not," she said, "do you think you could

take Joanna again? I know you just had her, but this is important."

This, too, surprised me. Normally, Susan didn't even like the idea of my seeing our daughter once every other weekend.

"I'd be happy to," I said.

"What it is," she said, "I've been invited to the Bahamas for the weekend."

"For the *weekend?*" I said. The Bahamas seemed a long way away for just a weekend.

"Yes. Georgie Poole is flying down in his plane on Friday afternoon, and we'll be spending all day Saturday and Sunday on his boat, and then flying back to Calusa again on Sunday night. So can you pick up Joanna at school on Friday? And then take her back again on Monday morning, on your way to work?"

"Sure," I said.

"Thanks," she said. "I'll tell her you called."

She hung up. I stared at the phone receiver. Georgie Poole was one of the richest men in all Calusa, a bachelor in his mid-forties who, it was reputed, had a penchant for television cuties in situation comedies, hence his frequent trips to Los Angeles where, it was further reputed, he had vast real estate holdings on the Pacific Coast Highway. Apparently, his eye had now fallen upon my former wife, a cutie in her own right, and I felt so sorry for the poor bastard that I thought I might send him a dozen roses in consolation. Well, that wasn't quite true. Susan might have begun behaving like a bitch the moment she'd learned about Aggie and me (God, that seemed like a century ago!), but she hadn't always been that way, and it was impossible now to forget the many good times we'd enjoyed together. The problem between us—aside from my philandering, which was a secondary problem created by the major problem—was not that one of us had grown up while the other stayed immature; when people give that as a reason for divorce, I always assume they're lying. Instead, it was that we'd *both* grown up—but in opposite directions. Somehow the people we'd been when we first got married had evolved into people neither of us knew fourteen years later, and that was unfortunate, that was genuinely sad. I did not like exchanging harsh words with Susan. I did not like the edge to her voice whenever I called the house I used to share

with her. I did not like the unkind things she said about me to
Joanna, which Joanna repeated as a dutiful and loving daughter. But neither did I like suppressing the frequent sympathy
(guilt, Frank would call it) I felt for her. I had once loved her
more than life itself. As I replaced the receiver on the cradle,
I silently wished her well. A woman could do worse than
Georgie Poole.

The intercom buzzed again. It was four o'clock on the
longest Monday I'd ever lived through. I flicked the toggle
and Cynthia told me there was a man named Anthony Konig
waiting to see me.

"*Who?*" I said.

"Anthony Konig. He doesn't have an appointment. Nobody today seems to have an . . ."

"Send him right in," I said.

The first impression Konig made was of size. He was a
man of about fifty-eight or -nine, I guessed, with a massive
head that matched his enormous girth; I estimated his height
at about six four and his weight at close to two hundred and
fifty. His hair was thick and white and worn rather long,
spilling recklessly onto his forehead and over his collar. His
suit was as white as his hair, and his pastel pink shirt was
fronted with a narrow black tie fastened with a simple gold tie
tack. Pig-faced, with pale blue eyes magnified behind thick-
lensed glasses, he possessed as well a veined, rather bulbous
nose and a surprisingly delicate mouth with a Cupid's-bow
upper and somewhat pouting lower lip. He extended one
fleshy hand and said without preamble, "I'm Victoria Miller's husband, I have a letter from her I think you should
see."

"Her husband?" I said.

"Her *former* husband."

"What sort of letter?"

"About wanting me to have Allison in case anything happened to her. Said I should contact you."

"Contact *me?*"

"Yes. If anything happened. You're her attorney, aren't
you?"

"No, sir, I'm not."

"Then what the hell *are* you?" he asked.

"A friend."

"A *friend?*"

"We saw each other socially a few times. That was the extent of our . . ."

"Then why the hell did she say I should contact *you?*"

His voice, until now, had been the well-modulated, evenly inflected vocal instrument of an educated Southerner. A bit whiskey-seared and therefore somewhat rumbling, it nonetheless had revealed not the slightest trace of an accent. Now, as he became more agitated, his face reddening, his white eyebrows pulling into a frown, the regional roots became more apparent.

"Mr. Konig," I said, "perhaps she'd only *planned* to talk to me about . . ."

"No," he said, "she told me she'd already taken *care* of it. I have her letter right here in my pocket, where's that damn letter?" he said, and began fumbling at the inside pocket of the white suit, pulling out first a black pocket-sized checkbook, and then an empty eyeglass case, and finally a letter which he first wagged in the air and then plunked on my desktop. "Well, go ahead," he said, "*read* the damn thing."

The envelope was addressed to Mr. Anthony Konig on St. Charles Avenue, in New Orleans' Garden District. I pulled the letter free and unfolded it. It was dated January 7; that would have been last Monday. I read it silently.

Dear Tony,

As you know, I will be opening on Friday night (that's the eleventh, better mark it down, ha-ha) at this restaurant the Greenery that has been open here on Stone Crab Key for several months now. I am a little nervous about this because I have never really sung in public since I made it big and not counting when I used to do little gigs in Arkansas, and this will be my first time anyway since I quit the business. But it is mostly about Allison that I am writing to you now.

I know you will be happy to know that if anything should happen to me I want you to have custody of our daughter. I am sure you will bring her up the way she was accustomed to before the divorce and that you will continue being the good father to her that you have always been. I sometimes think it might have been better for all of us, Tony, if we hadn't split up the way we did, but that's neither here nor there.

I'm just saying I want you to have her now if, God forbid, anything should happen to her mother. I've been seeing this man named Matthew Hope, he's an attorney here in Calusa and a very nice person, and he is the one you should contact if the need should arise.

So that's it for now, Tony, wish me luck Friday because I sure think I'm going to need it. Allison sends her love and says she is looking forward to her visit with you next month.

Take care of yourself now, hear?

Regards,

Vicky

I looked up at him.

"Well?" he said.

"I'm sorry, Mr. Konig," I said, "but I see nothing here that would indicate . . ."

"Let me see that damn letter," he said, and lurched out of the chair and virtually snatched it from my hands. "Here," he said, skimming it, "what does *this* mean if not what I've been telling you? *I've been seeing this man named Matthew Hope . . .*"

"Yes, that's certainly . . ."

"*. . . and he is the one you should contact.*"

"Yes, but she doesn't say I'm her attorney."

"She *says* you're an attorney, she says so right here."

"I *am* an attorney. That doesn't make me *her* attorney."

"Damn it, the meaning is *clear*. She talks first about wanting me to have Allison, and then she says I should contact you if the need should arise, those are her exact words, *if the need should arise*. Now what the hell does that mean if it doesn't mean you've got a paper from Vicky saying I'm to have custody?"

"I have no such paper, Mr. Konig. Perhaps, as I said earlier, she *planned* to discuss the matter with me, and then in the press of rehearsals for her opening, or . . ."

"Then why'd she write me if it wasn't something she'd already taken care of?"

"I don't know. Did you correspond regularly?"

"Well, yes, but it was always just chit-chat and never anything serious. This letter . . ."

"Yes, this letter sounds serious."

"Worrying about something happening to her and all, and then something *does* happen, she gets herself murdered . . ."

"Yes."

"So I've got to believe she was *afraid* of it happening and left instructions for my daughter to come live with me and not somebody else."

"She left no such instructions with me, Mr. Konig."

"You keep saying that, but the letter tells me otherwise."

"I know nothing about her wishes concerning custody."

"Your name's right *here* in this goddamn *letter!*"

"I know it is. She said we were seeing each other, and that's true. But as for any specific instructions, either written or verbal, regarding custody of Allison in the event . . ."

"Well, sir, I don't understand it," Konig said.

"Neither do I."

"I simply do *not* understand it."

"In any event," I said, "I'm certain instructions in a letter wouldn't be binding on a court."

There was a long silence. We stared at each other across my desk.

"I want my little girl," Konig said. "I don't have a lawyer here in Florida, he's up in N'Orleans where I live. If you'll represent me on this, find out exactly what the law says about custody, I'd be grateful."

"I'd be happy to, Mr. Konig. Would you mind if I held on to this letter?"

"Not at all."

"Where can I reach you here in Calusa?"

"I'm at the Breakwater Inn, got down here late Saturday, caught Vicky's second night there at that restaurant on Stone Crab."

"You've been here since Saturday?" I said.

"Yes, sir. Drove down from N'Orleans early Friday morning."

"Mr. Konig, there's something I think you should know . . ."

"What's that?"

". . . but I'm not sure I'm the one who should tell it to you. Maybe you ought to go see the police."

"What for? I've never yet met a policeman worth the tin in the badge on his chest. Are the police going to make sure nobody else gets custody of my daughter? I've wanted her all these years, Mr. Hope, I'll be damned if I'll let anyone *else* have her now that Vicky's gone. What is it you have to tell me?"

I took a deep breath.

"Your daughter's been kidnapped," I said.

"What?" he said.

"I'm sorry."

"Oh my God," he said. "Oh my God. What . . . who do I . . . what . . . oh my God!"

On one of my cards I wrote down Morris Bloom's name and the address of the Public Safety Building. Then I buzzed Cynthia and asked her if she was free to drive Mr. Konig downtown. He was still shaking when he left my office, and he looked ten years older than when he'd come in.

I did not get home until a little before six. I snapped on the television set and then went to the wall bar to mix myself a double martini—it had been too long a day. I was stirring the Beefeater and vermouth when the *Six O'Clock News* came on. My partner Frank says that in New York (and I gather he considers this a sign of sophistication) there are so many murders committed every day that the newspapers and television will cover only the goriest of them; to make headlines in

New York, you've either got to kill a cop or else use a meat ax on your entire family and the upstairs neighbor as well. Calusa has its share of homicides, but we're not quite that jaded about our response to them; our newspapers and television stations will rarely ignore even an inconsequential .22-caliber killing. "It doesn't take much to attract a crowd in Calusa," Frank says dryly. Frank sometimes gets on my nerves, but he is a very good lawyer, and I guess the closest friend I have in the world.

The news commentator now, despite Bloom's earlier warning to me, reported both the murder *and* the kidnapping. Either the killer had already made contact or else the police strategy had changed since last I'd spoken to Bloom. I wondered if Konig's visit to him had had anything to do with the decision to release the news. I also wondered what Konig's reaction had been when he'd learned about his daughter. He had seemed a volatile man, and men like that can sometimes—

The thoughts that came to me next were sudden and chilling.

Vicky had written a letter that seemed to state she'd made specific plans for her former husband to have custody of their child in the event anything happened to her. If indeed she'd been afraid that someone was about to harm her, the *someone* couldn't have been Konig; she'd have been crazy to have written him. But if Konig had wanted custody of his daughter "all these years" as he'd told me in my office just a little while ago, and if he'd already learned from Vicky that she planned to *give* him custody in the event of her death . . .

The telephone rang.

I poured the martini glass almost to the rim, and began walking with it toward the bedroom. The phone kept ringing. Outside on the bayou behind the house, a heron—startled by the sound—took sudden wing. I sat on the edge of the bed, the martini glass in one hand, and lifted the receiver.

"Mr. Hope?" Tony Konig."

"Yes, Mr. Konig, how are you?" I said.

"Fine," he said. "Well, considering. They don't seem to have much to go on yet. They want to put some equipment in my house back home, trace a call should he make one. Do you think he'll call, Mr. Hope? They usually call in cases like this, don't they?"

"Yes, usually."

"In any event, have you looked up the law for me? I've got to keep thinking they'll find her, you see. I've got to keep thinking this'll all be over one day soon, Allison'll be back one day soon."

"I had someone in the office do some checking for me, and I also called Hopkins and Cole—they're a big shop here in town, they do a lot of custody work."

"What'd you find out? Does that letter from Vicky mean anything?"

"Not as regards custody. As I suspected, it might serve as evidence of intent, but it wouldn't be binding on a court."

"A *court?* Why does this thing have to go to court?"

"I'm not saying it does. But if someone challenged your right to custody . . . well, let me take this in order, Mr. Konig, if that's all right with you."

"Go right ahead."

"The letter's virtually meaningless. Would you know whether Vicky left a will?"

"I don't know, I'm sorry. Why? Would a will be binding on a court?"

"It would be highly persuasive, yes, and would most likely control unless you were found an unsuitable parent. But even if Vicky died intestate—without leaving a will, that is— you'd undoubtedly get custody of your daughter. In the large majority of instances, the courts have awarded custody to the natural father rather than the maternal grandparents, say, or an aunt, or an older sister, or what have you. Tell me, is there anyone who might *challenge* your custody?"

"Sure. Vicky's father. Dwayne Miller."

"Why?"

"Because he's a crazy old bastard who thinks he runs the world."

"Would he have grounds for such a challenge?"

"Like what?"

"Could he claim you're an unfit father?"

"Ridiculous."

"Could he say your home's an unsuitable place in which to bring up a little girl?"

"Utter nonsense."

"Were you making support payments for Allison?"

"Each and every month."

"Ever miss any of them?"

"Never."

"Ever been in trouble with the law?"

"Few parking tickets . . . and once for speeding, three, four years ago."

"Do you see Allison regularly?"

"At least once a month, and usually over the entire summer."

"Has Allison ever lived with her grandfather?"

"No."

"Well, let me give you some actual rulings, Mr. Konig. *Torres* v. *Van Eepoel*, 1957, right here in Florida: *A natural parent has a right to the custody*—by the way, she *is* your natural child, isn't she?"

"What do you mean?"

"She wasn't adopted? She wasn't the child of any former marriage Vicky may have . . ."

"No, no, this was a first marriage for both of us. Allison's mine, that's for sure."

"Okay, *Torres* v. *Van Eepoel:* 'A natural parent has a right to the custody of his or her children absent conduct or conditions that justify a deprivation of the right in the interest of the welfare of the children. This legal right is one that should not be regarded lightly.' "

"Damn right," Konig said.

"*Modacsi* v. *Taylor:* 'The love and affection of another person, no matter how great, is not sufficient to deprive a fit and proper parent of his child.' "

"Keep on reading, Mr. Hope."

"*Behn* v. *Timmons*—this was a recent one, 1977, also here in Florida: 'The parent has a natural God-given right to enjoy the custody, fellowship, and companionship of his offspring; except in cases of clear, convincing, and compelling reasons to the contrary, a child's welfare is presumed to be best served by care and custody by the natural parent.' "

"Mr. Hope, you've *already* earned your fee," Konig said. "I can't tell you how relieved I am. What do I have to do next?"

"Nothing."

"Nothing? What do you mean, nothing?"

"Once Allison is found . . ."

"I'm praying that'll be soon, Mr. Hope."

"You can simply pack her up and take her home with you."

"Just like that?"

"Just like that."

"Well, fine then, everything seems to be in order. Mr. Hope, I can't thank you enough . . ."

"Few other things, Mr. Konig. Are you sure Vicky never mentioned a will to you?"

"Never. Anyway, what difference would it make? You just told me . . ."

"Yes, I feel you're safe as regards guardianship of Allison's *person*. I'm talking now about guardianship of her *property*. Even if Vicky died intestate, her lineal descendant—your daughter, in this case—would normally inherit. I'd like to know whether or not anyone's been designated guardian of her property. If not, a court would have to appoint one."

"Well, I don't know if there's any will. Is there some way you can find out for me?"

"I'll check around. The legal community in Calusa is a relatively small one. If Vicky had a will drawn . . ."

"Yes, please check for me," Konig said.

"I'll be happy to." I hesitated. "Mr. Konig," I said, "before we end this conversation, and in fact before I do any further work for you, there're a few things I'd like to know. I hope you won't take offense, but the questions have got to be asked."

"What are they?"

"First . . . did you kill Vicky?"

"What?"

"I said . . ."

"You can't be serious."

"I'd like an answer, if you will."

"I did not, sir. I loved that woman with all my heart."

His voice sounded on the edge of tears. I hesitated before asking the next question, but it was another essential one, and it could not be postponed, not if I was to continue representing him.

"Mr. Konig," I said, "if what you've just told me is true . . ."

"It is the God's honest truth."

"Then I'm going to assume, and you correct me if I'm wrong, that you don't *already* have physical custody of your daughter."

"Already have . . . ?"

"Yes, that you didn't just come up to my office as a smoke-screen, asking me about custody when you'd *already* taken Allison away from that house . . ."

"I just told you . . ."

". . . taken her away from there *after* Vicky was killed—if what you say is true, that you're not the one who killed her."

"I didn't kill her. And I didn't kidnap my own daughter, either."

"Did you try to reach Vicky last night by telephone?"

"No, sir, I did not."

"You didn't call the house there three times last night?"

"I did not, sir."

"You didn't tell the baby-sitter there that you'd be stopping by to collect?"

"No, sir. Did someone do that?"

"Yes, Mr. Konig," I said. "Someone did that."

"It wasn't me."

"All right," I said. "All right, I'll start asking around tomorrow morning. About the will. Are you still at the Breakwater Inn?"

"Yes, I'll be here till after the funeral Wednesday."

"And after that?"

He started to give me his home phone number in New Orleans, and then thought better of it; the police would be monitoring that phone, hoping to hear from the kidnapper. He gave me his office number instead and said I could leave word there with his secretary. He'd be checking with her from time to time and would get back to me as soon afterward as he could. He thanked me again and then said good night. There was still that edge of sorrow to his voice.

But I couldn't stop thinking of his massive size and of what Bloom had said to me this morning: *We figure it had to be a man because of the sheer power involved.*

4

I called Jim Sherman at ten o'clock on Tuesday morning.

Jim was one of the two owners of the Greenery, a tall, rather muscular man in his late thirties, whose hair had gone prematurely white when he was only twenty-two. Blue-eyed and tanned to a rich burnished bronze, he worked very hard at creating the image of a dissipated beach boy, even though he owned a million-dollar restaurant and three spacious condominium apartments out on Whisper Key—renting, I'd been told, for a cool two thousand each for every month in season. His partner, Brad Atherton, was somewhat older than he, forty-five or -six, I guessed, with dark hair getting a bit thin on top, and eyes as startlingly blue as Jim's. He was shorter than Jim, though, less flamboyant in style and dress, and somewhat soft-spoken, a combination of characteristics that perhaps accounted for the rumor that he and Jim were sharing a homosexual relationship, with Brad the passive or "female" partner. I had no evidence that either of them were what popular opinion held them to be, and frankly I didn't care *what* their sexual persuasions were. When Anita Bryant began quoting the Bible as source material for her vicious crusade against homosexuals, I stopped drinking the orange juice she was advertising on television. I knew Jim wouldn't be at the restaurant that early in the morning, so I called him at his home on exclusive Flamingo Key.

"Hullo?" he mumbled, and I knew at once that I'd awakened him.

"Jim," I said, "this is Matthew Hope. I'm sorry to be calling so early in the morning."

"No, no, not at all," he said, but I visualized him peering bleary-eyed at a bedside clock.

"I'm sure you heard about Vicky Miller . . ."

"Awful," he said. "Terrible shock. Police were at the restaurant last night, asking questions. God, such a lovely girl."

"Yes," I said. "Jim, the reason I'm calling, I know you must have made some sort of contract with Vicky . . ."

"For the singing engagement, do you mean?"

"Yes. There *was* a contract, wasn't there?"

"Do you need it for some reason?"

"No, no. I was simply wondering who might have represented her. Was there an attorney who handled it for her?"

"Yes, there was."

"Who, can you tell me?"

"Some firm downtown with a dozen names. Let me think a minute. Jackson, Harris, does that sound right? Jackson, Harris, Something, Something, and . . ."

"Would it be Blackstone, Harris?"

"*Blackstone,* Harris, right."

"Blackstone, Harris, Gerstein, Garfield and Pollock?"

"That's the whole crowd," Jim said.

"Would you know who Vicky's attorney there might have been?"

"I'm sorry, no. This was a simple thing, Matthew. I handed Vicky the contracts, asked her to have her people look them over, and she brought them back to me signed two days later." He paused. He was wide awake now. "Who do you think did this, Matthew?"

"I don't know."

"Beat her to death, huh?"

"Yes."

"The son of a bitch," Jim said.

"Yes. Jim," I said, "thanks for the information, I want to get moving on it."

"Glad to be of help," he said, and hung up.

I called Honest Abe Pollock, with whom I'd had a conversation only yesterday concerning my client who was trying to buy a liquor store. The first thing Abe said was, "Have a heart, Matthew. It takes a little while to figure what a whole inventory cost."

"I'm calling about something else," I said.

"Thank God," he said. "Make it an easy one, it's still too early in the morning."

"Victoria Miller," I said. "The woman who was killed Sunday night."

"What about her?"

"I understand your firm looked over the contract she made with the Greenery. For her singing engagement there."

"That's news to me," Abe said.

"Can you find out who did it for her?"

"You know how many lawyers we have here, Matthew?"

"How many?"

"I don't even know *myself*," Abe said. "A *lot*, believe me. *More* than a lot. When do you have to know?"

"Now."

"When you say *now*, do you mean *now* now, or do you mean ten *minutes* from now, or do you mean tomorrow *morning* now? Define your terms, Matthew."

"I'd like to talk to whoever was her attorney, Abe. If you can help me locate him . . ."

"What's so important about a singing contract?"

"That's not the important thing."

"Then what is?"

"Whether or not she left a will."

"You want me to look for a *will*, too? Have a heart, Matthew."

"Just find out who represented her up there, and I'll go bother him, okay?"

"Just a second," Abe said. "I'm putting you on hold, I'm not hanging up."

"Thanks," I said.

I waited.

Cynthia came in with a cup of coffee for me. She was wearing dark blue tight-fitting slacks, high-heeled blue pumps, and a pastel blue blouse. I looked at her in surprise; she rarely wore slacks to the office, preferring instead skirts that showed to good advantage her long, eternally tanned legs. She caught my look.

"What?" she said.

"I'm surprised is all."

"No good?"

"Very nice," I said.

"Then what?"

"You usually wear skirts."

"For a change," she said, and shrugged. "Is there a rule?"

"Of course not."

"Good. Frank says I look terrific."

"Ah, but Frank is not a leg man."

"*Chacun son goût,*" she said. "Do you know you're holding a telephone in your hand?"

"I'm waiting for Abe Pollock."

"He always takes forever," she said. "We're out of real cream, I put Dari-Rich in it."

"Fine, thank you, Cyn."

"*De nada,*" she said, and breezed out of the office.

I kept waiting. When Abe finally came back onto the line, he said, "Matthew, this is going to take a while. There's a big meeting going on up here, another one of our usual multimillion-dollar deals . . ."

"Yeah, yeah."

". . . and I can't get hold of anybody. Are you going to be in the neighborhood any time later?"

"I have a closing at Tricity in about twenty minutes."

"Good, that's right next door. Can you stop in here after you're done? I'll know who was handling this by then, and you can talk to him directly."

"It may not be till twelve, twelve-thirty, Abe."

"I'll be gone, I have an early lunch. But I'll leave word for you, and I'll ask him to wait till you get here, okay?"

"I'd appreciate it."

"No problem. On this other thing, give us till the end of the week sometime. Just between you, me, and the lamppost, my client can't add two and two, it's going to take him *forever* to go through those books and dig out the wholesale prices on all that booze. Will Friday be okay?"

"Fine, Abe."

"I would say 'Have a nice day,' " Abe said, "but I think it's going to rain."

In Calusa, during the rainy season, you can usually expect a thunderstorm along about three or four every afternoon, at which time the humidity and the heat have combined to leave the suffering citizenry virtually limp. The rain, when it comes, mercilessly assaults the sidewalks and the streets, but only for an hour or so. During that short while, the torrential downpour brings at least a semblance of relief. But once the rain stops, you'd never know it had been there at all. Oh, yes, the gutters are running with swift-flowing muddy water, and there are huge brown puddles everywhere, and here and there a truly flooded street—but the heat and the humidity follow as closely behind the brief storm as does a rapist his victim. Within minutes you are sweating again. That is during the rainy season. January was not supposed to be the rainy season. We were not supposed to get rain in January. As Abe had predicted, though, it began raining very hard along about noon, just as I was leaving the closing at Tricity, and I was soaking wet after the short run from the bank to the front door of Blackstone, Harris, Gerstein, Garfield and Pollock.

Most law offices with tongue-twisting firm names will allow their switchboard people to answer with a curt "Law offices," or an ever briefer "Legal," but not the firm of Blackstone, Harris, Gerstein, Garfield and Pollock. As I stepped liquidly into the huge carpeted reception area beyond the massive oaken entrance doors, the blonde behind the desk across the room was chirpily reciting into her telephone mouthpiece, "Blackstone, Harris, Gerstein, Garfield and Pollock, good morning." Making my way soddenly across the room, shaking water from my hair and the sleeves of an expensive jacket I was certain was about to shrink to my daughter's size, I heard the receptionist saying apologetically, "No, it *isn't* a very good morning, is it, sir?" She listened again. "Well, that's right, sir," she said, "it isn't even *morning* anymore, is it, it's already afternoon." I was standing at her desk now. She looked at me, rolled her eyes heavenward, and then said into the mouthpiece, "And not a very good one at that, no, sir, whom did you wish to speak to, sir?" She nodded, said, "One moment, please," and then plugged in one of her rubber snakes. "May I help you, sir?" she asked me.

"Abe Pollock said he would leave a message for me. I'm Attorney Hope."

I don't know why lawyers announce themselves that way to other lawyers or to people who work for law firms, but we do. I guess it is a sort of secret password that tells the other guy it isn't a truck driver or a bill collector or a garbage man calling on the phone or in person—this is a *lawyer,* an exalted "attorney" like himself. Anyway, it's what we do. At my local bank I'm Mr. Hope. In the law offices of Blackstone, Harris, Gerstein, Garfield and Pollock, I was *Attorney* Hope.

"Yes, sir," the receptionist said. "I have it right here."

She handed me a memo slip with Abe Pollock's name printed on the top of it. In his scrawling hand, he had written:

Miller's lawyer was Dale O'Brien, expecting you here around noon, will wait for you.

"Would you let Attorney O'Brien know I'm here, please?" I said to the receptionist. "I'm expected."

"Yes, sir," she said, and plugged into her switchboard. She waited a moment, and then said, "Attorney Hope to see you." She nodded, said, "Right away," and then said to me, "You can go right in, sir, it's through that door and the third office on your left."

"Thank you," I said.

As I went through the door leading to the inner offices, her switchboard lit up again, and I heard her saying, once again, "Blackstone, Harris, Gerstein, Garfield and Pollock, good afternoon " I was beginning to feel like a member of the firm: at least I had passed the first test, memorizing the name. I found the third office on the left and peeked in. A woman in her late twenties, I guessed, was sitting behind a secretary's desk in a little anteroom beyond which was a closed, walnut-paneled door. She was searching for something in the top drawer of the desk, her head bent, but she heard me the moment I approached, and looked up at once.

"Oh, hi," she said.

Her hair was the color of fall leaves, a reddish-brown that evoked for me suddenly and inexplicably the seasonal changes I missed so much here in Calusa. Her eyes were predictably green, the only imaginable color to complement that russet hair, the green of a lush tropical glade, summer in her eyes and autumn in her hair, springtime in the clean fresh look of her generous mouth, no lipstick on it—where was winter to make her complete? A spate of freckles spilled from her high cheekbones onto her fox-faced nose. A pair of oversized eyeglasses were perched on top of her head like skylights on a rusting roof. She squinted at me for a moment and then pulled the glasses down over her magnificent eyes and smiled radiantly—and my heart stopped. I knew at once that I would ask her to go to Brazil with me as soon as my business with O'Brien was finished, or perhaps the Galápagos, or Alaska or Hawaii or Russia or the moon, perhaps even *before* my business with O'Brien was concluded, perhaps right this minute, right here and now before I even *saw* O'Brien."

"You're Mr. Hope," she said.

"Yes," I said. I was staring at her shamelessly. "Mr. O'Brien's expecting me."

She stared back at me. Behind her glasses, those hypnotic green eyes blinked. She said nothing. Neither did she reach for an intercom switch or a telephone receiver. She just sat there behind her desk, staring at me. I thought perhaps she hadn't heard me. I thought, Just my luck, I meet the most beautiful woman in the world and she has a hearing problem, I will have to shout, "I love you," in her good ear, whichever one that happens to be.

"Mr. O'Brien's expecting me," I said again, a little louder this time.

"I'm Dale O'Brien," she said.

I looked at her. She *could* have been a Dale O'Brien, I supposed. Her hair and her eyes were the hair and the eyes of a Dale O'Brien, or certainly *some* kind of an O'Brien. Not to mention the freckles. There had once been a Dale *Carnegie*, of course, and he'd been a man, and there was at present a Dale *Robertson*, who was also a man albeit an actor, but there was also a Dale *Evans*, who was a woman married to Roy

Rogers, whose horse's name was Trigger. At the moment I felt like Trigger's backside.

"I'm sorry," I said. "Abe didn't tell me."

"Don't apologize," she said, "it fools almost everyone. I'm a male chauvinist trap. So's my friend Dana. She's a surgeon at Ben Taub General in Houston. Dr. Dana Canfield, right? So everyone automatically thinks of Dana *Andrews,* who's a man, but does anyone think of Dana *Wynter,* who's a woman? Being any kind of professional only compounds the felony. How can I help you, Mr. Hope? Come on inside, I was out here looking for some paper clips."

She rose from behind the desk in one swift motion, gracefully unfolding what had to be at least five feet nine inches of big-boned, well-padded femininity, long russet hair cascading to her shoulders, green eyes bright and amused and intelligent behind the oversized glasses, good breasts swelling the lapels of her brown suit jacket. She stepped around the desk. The matching skirt to the suit, slit on the left side to just above her knee, revealed a beautifully proportioned leg that tapered gently to a narrow ankle in a tan high-heeled pump.

I could not take my eyes off her. I felt like a schoolboy.

"Well *do* come in, Mr. Hope," she said, and laughed a small embarrassed laugh. Her cheeks, I noticed, were beginning to flush beneath their faint dusting of freckles.

Her office was simply furnished. A large cluttered desk with a leather swivel chair behind it, two similarly upholstered chairs angled in front of it, bookcases lining three of the walls. The framed diplomas on the wall told me she'd got her B.A. from the University of California and her law degree from Harvard. There were two certificates of admission to the bar: one for the State of California, the other for Florida. She went behind her desk, sat in the swivel chair, tented her hands like a proper attorney, and said, "You want to know about Vicky's contract."

"Is that what Abe told you?"

"He caught me on the fly. *Isn't* that it?"

"I *really* want to know if she'd drawn a will before her death. Is it Miss or Mrs?"

"Pardon?" she said.

"Your marital status."

"It's *Ms.*," she said pointedly and with a smile, "but I'm not married, no."

"Will you have dinner with me tonight?" I asked.

"Pardon?" she said again.

"Dinner," I said. "Tonight. With me. Attorney Hope."

"Well, yes," she said, sounding very surprised.

"Phew," I said.

There are very few so-called intimate restaurants in Calusa; in fact, many of the eateries here serve their dishes on bare Formica-topped tables, and the napkins are more often than not of the paper variety. Billy Banjo's was a notable exception to the rule. Situated on Calusa Bay, behind the luxurious Trident Tower Hotel on Route 41, the plant itself was a long, low, elegantly modern, wood-and-glass structure that hugged the shoreline and afforded a splendid view of Flamingo, Lucy's, and Stone Crab keys across the water. Not quite on the same cuisinary level as the Greenery, it compensated instead with damask tablecloths and napkins, highly polished silver, and stemware that glistened in the warm glow of tapered candles.

Dale had told me in her office that afternoon that *she,* at least, had not drawn a will for Vicky, and that if one existed she was unaware of it. We both suspected that if any Calusa attorney had prepared such an instrument for her, the Probate Court would be hearing about it soon enough. There was really no further business to discuss; we both understood we were together now for a purely social evening. Dale, in fact, was dressed somewhat resplendently for the occasion, wearing a green, sarong-wrapped skirt with a matching top piped in red at the sleeves and tied at the waist with a rolled red scarf. Her russet hair was swept up tidily on top of her head, and her green eyes behind their oversized glasses echoed the deeper green of her outfit. She was wearing small diamond earrings as well and a diamond ring on the third finger of her left hand.

The ring caused me several moments of panic until she explained it had been her mother's engagement ring, and she saw no reason why she shouldn't wear it. I suggested she might wear it to better advantage on her *right* hand, although even this might—in our primitive symbolistic culture—signal either a broken engagement or a temporary hiatus in a long-standing relationship. She confessed then that wearing it on the telltale finger of her left hand was a gesture not entirely without malice aforethought. Had she possessed the necessary courage, in fact, she'd have worn her mother's inherited *wedding* band as well—both rings combined might have served even more formidably to keep the wolves away from her pantry door. She explained, in more detail than I might have hoped for, how waitresses wearing wedding bands had discovered that their tips were lower than those whose fingers were not so adorned. Similarly, she herself had learned in the six years since she'd begun practicing law, first in California and next in Florida, that the engagement ring—albeit her mother's—immediately announced to any male client that she was "spoken for," and put matters on a simple businesslike basis from the word go.

"What about males who *aren't* clients?" I asked.

"I take off the ring," she said simply.

"But you're wearing it tonight," I said.

"Only because it matches the earrings," she said, and smiled in what I thought was an encouraging manner.

Since my divorce I had discovered that many women—in an attempt to impress or to inspire trust or even simply to keep a conversation going—would inundate me with intimate trivia about their various tastes and prejudices. I had listened to women telling me what their favorite colors were, which movies they had adored or despised, which television shows they watched on a regular basis, which perfume they wore, whether they preferred to paint their toenails or leave them *au naturel*, and on and on *ad infinitum*. Not so with Dale O'Brien.

She was, I began to suspect, a more reticent sort of person, perfectly content to tell me where she'd gone to college (University of California in Santa Cruz, which I'd already learned from one of the framed diplomas in her office), and then law school (Harvard, again already learned from the *other* framed diploma), and where and when she'd begun practicing law (back in San Francisco in 1974, at a starting salary of $22,000), and how long she'd been practicing here in Florida (it would be four years in June), but unwilling to reveal very much about her personal self as opposed to her professional self. In the beginning I might have been a client seeking advice on a legal matter, eliciting credentials in passing. Well, wait a moment. She *did* tell me she was thirty-one years old; I had guessed wrong in assuming she was still in her late twenties. She also told me that she owned the house I'd picked her up at earlier, a pristine Mediterranean gem on Whisper Key, which had—coincidentally—been designed by our client Charlie Hoggs. But more and more I suspected that Dale O'Brien was the sort of woman who would reserve any exchange of confidences for when she was securely tucked into a man's bed, and then only *after* they had made love (a consummation devoutly to be wished), at which time the flood of intimacies would pour forth as from a burst dam.

I kept waiting for an opportunity to probe a bit more deeply. It did not come until she mentioned, casually, that she shared her house with a cat named Sassafras, who—

"I used to have a cat who loved listening to music," I said at once.

"Oh? What kind of music?"

"Jazz mostly. Miles Davis. Oscar Peterson. He used to stretch out on the living room floor, exactly midway between the two speakers. His ears used to twitch in time with the beat. The Modern Jazz Quartet, he loved the Modern Jazz Quartet."

"What happened to him?"

"He died just about when my marriage did. I sometimes think of him as a metaphor for the divorce."

She hesitated, as though debating whether or not she was willing to move the conversation on to this more intimate level. Her eyes met mine. "Was it very painful for you?" she asked.

"Someone once told me that divorce is a kind of killing. I think it may very well be." I shook my head. "I sometimes feel I've done my daughter a great disservice. It might've been easier to have stayed married, kept the family together at any cost."

"No," Dale said.

"People *do* make arrangements," I said.

"Was there someone else involved?"

"Yes."

"On whose part? Your wife's or yours?"

"Mine."

"What happened?"

"She's divorced now, too."

"Do you ever see her?"

"No. She lives in Tampa."

"Tampa's not that far away."

"I don't think it would matter if she lived right around the corner."

We were silent for several moments. Again she seemed weighing whether she should switch the conversation back to safer ground. At last she said, "Was your marriage failing otherwise?"

"If you're seeing someone outside your marriage, then I would say it's failing, yes."

"Okay," she said, and smiled. "End of direct examination."

She spooned sugar into her cup. She seemed preoccupied with stirring it into her coffee. Her head bent, she said, "I was almost as good as married myself, once upon a time."

"When was that?"

"When I first began practicing. In San Francisco. I lived with an artist out there." She lifted her head; her eyes met mine again. "He used to paint these cutesy-poo pictures of animals with big eyes and lolling little tongues. I thought they were marvelous. I left him the minute I realized they were crap."

"When was that?"

"Four years ago, on the fifteenth of May. That's when I moved out. I came to Florida the following month."

"And you still remember the date, huh?"

"Oh, sure. Biggest decision I ever had to make in my life. I mean, I'd been living with him for two years, that's a long time. And I loved him, you know. I suppose I loved him. Until . . ."

She shrugged.

"Until you found out you didn't like his paintings."

"No, that came after I found out I didn't love him. I can remember the exact moment, isn't that strange? We were in Los Angeles one day, walking in MacArthur Park, it was a Sunday, and I mentioned how much I loved the lyric in that song, the one about MacArthur Park, the lyric about someone having left a cake out in the rain, you know the lyric. And he said he'd never understood what the hell that song was all

about. I looked at him. He was walking along with his hands
in his pockets, he was a great big shambling bear of a man,
with a beard, and he wore these little Benjamin Franklin
eyeglasses, and he was looking down at his feet as we walked
through the park—it was one of those miserably smoggy Los
Angeles days—and he had just told me he had never understood a song that for me had only summed up a whole
generation! I didn't say anything. We just kept walking through
the park, and when we got back to the apartment we sat
around smoking dope, and then he wanted to make love, and
for the first time in my life I told somebody I had a headache,
I told this man I'd been living with for two years, this man I
thought I adored, that I had a headache and could we wait
until later, please? I moved out two weeks after that.''

"You didn't just . . .''

"No, no, I didn't leave a note tacked to the bathroom door
or Scotch-taped to the refrigerator, nothing like that. We
talked about it, a week after our walk in the park, talked
about it like mature, sensible adults, while inside my heart
was breaking because I didn't love him anymore. I think I
was more hurt than he was. We talked about it all night long
that night, and then we *did* make love, we finally made love
for the first time since that day in MacArthur Park when all
the cool green icing melted down, and even the lovemaking
wasn't any good anymore. He gave me one of his paintings
when I moved out. I still have it someplace. I never look at
it.''

"So,'' I said, "here we are.''

"Alone at last,'' she said, and smiled.

We lingered over coffee and a sinfully rich concoction
called Chocolate Coconut Supreme; it was a little after ten
when I paid the check and walked Dale out toward where I'd
parked the Ghia. The rain had stopped, but the sky was still
overcast with threatening clouds, and the temperature had
dropped drastically. In Calusa, whenever you mentioned how
cold it was, or how rainy it was, or how suffocatingly hot it
was; whenever, in short, you mentioned how absolutely *shitty*
the weather could be here at times, the natives (and this
included all those transplanted migrants from the north) would
invariably say, "Ah, yes, but think how bad it is anyplace
else.'' Anyplace else apparently included such idyllic spots as

Barbados or the Virgin Islands or Antigua or Acapulco. Why the snowbirds bothered coming to Calusa at *all* was something I would never be able to fathom. When it gets cold in a warm climate (and please remember that Calusa is only on the northernmost fringes of the subtropics) it can seem colder than four below in Utica, New York. It felt that cold right this minute.

Dale took my arm and moved in close to me. We both ducked our heads against the wind and braved our way across the parking lot. Inside the car I turned on the heater—the first time I'd done so since last February. I also turned on the radio, twisting the dial till I found the station I was looking for, a program originating in Manakawa and promising "Music for Us."

The music was completely wasted on at least *one* of us.

At Dale's front door, she thanked me for a lovely evening, and then offered her hand in farewell. I told her I'd call her again soon, if that was all right with her ("Yes, please do, Matthew") and then I walked through the raging wind to my car. As I crossed the Timucuan Bridge and headed for the mainland, Artie Shaw's "Stardust" flooded the automobile.

I found it small solace.

5

Wednesday morning dawned cold and gray and bleak. The temperature on the thermometer outside my kitchen window hovered at the thirty-one-degree mark, which meant it was one degree below freezing—point five below zero on the Celsius scale. The cable-television forecast from the National Weather Service in Ruskin, Florida, reported winds from the southwest at twenty-seven knots, seas to twelve feet, and a zero possibility of precipitation. Temperatures in the Tricity Area (which included Tampa, Sarasota, and Calusa) were expected to rise no higher than the mid to upper forties. It was altogether a rotten day for a funeral.

There were seventy churches of varying denominations in Calusa, ranging from Catholic to Baptist to Jewish (Orthodox and Reform) to Presbyterian to Lutheran to Seventh Day Adventist and including two for the Mennonite sect, its followers identified by the black clothing and beards worn by the men, and the plain dresses and simple white caps worn by the women. The services for Victoria Miller, born and raised in the South's Bible Belt, were held at the Bay Ridge Baptist Chapel on Bay Ridge Road and Williamdale Avenue. There were perhaps three dozen people listening to the memorial service that day, among them reporters from Calusa's morning and afternoon newspapers, and a man sent up from *Time*'s regional office in Miami. It was perhaps a comment on the impermanency of fame that the *Time* reporter was not accompanied by a photographer; neither were the pair from the Calusa *Herald-Tribune* and the Calusa *Journal.*

The service was brief. The mourners filed out of the low white building afterward, following the coffin, wearing an odd assortment of outer garments. When the temperatures dropped in this part of Florida, no one seemed prepared for the sudden cold, even though it had in recent years become the rule rather than the exception. Winter overcoats stored in mothballs were pulled out of dusty trunks, mackinaws made reluctant appearances, but for the most part the citizens were underdressed, wearing raincoats that served them well during the months of July, August, and September but did little to protect them in the frequently harsh winter months. The mourners walked briskly to their automobiles, coat collars raised, hands thrust into their pockets, faces raw and red from the wind. Overhead, a gray canopy of clouds moved restlessly across the sky. There was only one limousine—for Anthony Konig and a man I assumed to be Vicky's father, Dwayne Miller. Although Konig had earlier described him as a "crazy old bastard," he seemed to be no older than fifty-five or -six—a bit younger than Konig, in fact—a tall, powerfully built man who hurled his enormous bulk into the waiting car as if it were a side of beef. The hearse moved out. We began following it to the cemetery.

I was surprised to see a police car parked just outside the cemetery gates. As the cortege approached, the door on the passenger side—distinctively marked with the City of Calusa's gold seal and the word POLICE in blue against the white background—opened, and Detective Morris Bloom stepped out. He was wearing a heavy black overcoat, a gray fedora, a maroon muffler, and black leather gloves, as though he were still dressed for the wilds of Nassau County up there in New York State. It occurred to me as I pulled the Ghia in alongside the wrought-iron fence that he was the only one here today who was properly dressed for the bitter cold and the biting wind. He spotted me as I got out of my car, and immediately walked over.

"I owe you an apology," he said.

"What for?"

"The private eye shit."

"You already said you were sorry. On the phone."

"It's always better in person," he said, and smiled unexpectedly. "I apologize."

"I accept," I said, and returned the smile.

"I've got the FBI crawling all over my office," he said, "giving me orders like I'm a Meter Maid. If there's anything I hate worse'n the narcs, it's the feds."

"Any word from him yet?"

"Not a peep. It doesn't make sense, does it? This is Wednesday, he took that little girl on Sunday night, but no ransom demand yet. No sense at all."

"Nobody says a murderer has to make sense."

"Ah, but they do," Bloom said morosely. "They do, Mr. Hope. You get the craziest fucking bedbugs—" He glanced around quickly, fearful his obscenity might have been overheard, especially here in so sacrosanct a place as a cemetery. But we were walking several yards behind the rest of the mourners, trailing them on a gravel path that ran staight as an arrow through rows and rows of grave markers. He lowered his voice nonetheless. "You get these lunatics, they're raving about God knows what, but at the same time they know *exactly* why they committed bloody murder. They've got the grievances all ready to spill out, chapter and verse, in detail you could set your watch by. Why*ever* this guy did it—if he *is* a guy—he can tell us all about it, all his grievances, didn't like the kind of songs she sang, didn't like the way she did her hair, who the hell *knows* with these fucking lunatics?" he said, and this time he did not check to see if he'd been overheard.

"I'll tell you what bothers me," he said. "She divorces her husband, but he comes all the way from New Orleans to see her perform here. That bothers the hell out of me, I've got to tell you. When he came to see me Monday, he told me he'd been in town since late Saturday. That puts him here a day before the murder. I don't like that."

"Well, he had a legitimate reason for being here," I said.

"Yeah, *what?* To see his wife do her act? They've been divorced for, what is it, five years? Why such loyalty?"

"She wrote to him last week . . ."

"Oh?"

"Said she wanted him to have custody of the child in case anything happened to her. He may've wanted to discuss that in person."

"Where's the letter?"

"I have it at the office. I'll send it over by messenger if you like."

"Yeah, do that. Custody of the little girl, huh? That's interesting. I'll tell you, Mr. Hope . . ."

"Make it Matthew," I said. "Or Matt if you prefer."

"I prefer Matthew," Bloom said. "He was one of the good guys."

"Good guys?"

"In the Bible."

"So was Matt."

"In the Bible?"

"On *Gunsmoke*."

"I still prefer Matthew. You call me Morrie, okay? Except when we're downtown and there's brass around. Then it might be better to go with the Detective Bloom shit, okay?"

"Okay," I said.

When we reached the end of the path, the coffin had already been lifted over the open grave, and the hydraulic equipment was ready to lower it into the earth. The minister stood with a Bible in his hands, squinting into the wind, facing the assembled mourners who had taken seats on folding chairs set up before a white lattice bower. The bower covered the poised coffin and the open waiting grave. Baskets of flowers carried from the funeral home had been placed on either side of the grave. Some of them had been blown over by the wind, strewing blossoms onto the ground. There were no folding chairs left when Bloom and I approached the bower. We stood off to one side as the minister opened his Bible.

"O sing unto the Lord a new song," he said, "for he hath done marvellous things: his right hand, and his holy arm, hath gotten him the victory. The Lord hath made known his salvation . . ."

His words carried on the wind, blowing over the heads of the mourners and northward toward the Trail. Konig and Miller were sitting on chairs in the first row; whatever their differences, they seemed united now in grief. Sitting to Konig's right, also in the first row, were Jim Sherman and his partner at the Greenery, Brad Atherton.

"Make a joyful noise unto the Lord, all the earth: make a loud noise, and rejoice, and sing praise. Sing unto the Lord with the harp; with the harp, and the voice of a psalm. With trumpets and sound of cornet make a joyful noise before the Lord . . ."

The girl sitting at the end of the first row, just alongside Brad, looked familiar. She was perhaps twenty-two or -three, a slight girl with enormous brown eyes and dark hair blowing in the wind now, wearing a wrinkled black overcoat that looked as though it had been rescued from the bottom of a cardboard valise carried south in the year nineteen aught two when Calusa—by approval of its fifty-seven voters—first incorporated as a town. She sensed my eyes upon her, jerked her attention sharply from the minister, turned to the left where I was standing alongside Bloom, and suddenly nodded. I must have expressed surprise. She nodded again, her dark eyes beseeching response. Puzzled, I nodded back. Apparently satisfied, she turned again to where the minister was concluding his recitation.

"Let the floods clap their hands: let the hills be joyful together before the Lord; for he cometh to judge the earth: with righteousness shall he judge the world, and the people with equity. Amen."

"Amen," the mourners repeated in ragged unison.

"Oh, God, Jesus, *no!*" someone shouted. "Not *yet!*"

The words hung on the air like an exhalation of vapor, drifting up and beyond the man who had spoken them. He alone was standing now in the midst of the seated mourners, a man of about thirty-eight or -nine, I guessed, some six feet tall and weighing at least a hundred and eighty pounds, his face twisted in torment, blue eyes streaming tears, long black hair worn the way hippies used to wear theirs in the sixties and early seventies. His clothes, too, seemed the attire of someone from a bygone time, threadbare blue jeans and a faded denim jacket, beads hanging on his blue T-shirted chest, a beaded Indian band across his forehead—Woodstock reincarnate here and now in Calusa, Florida. Almost before the gathering had located him, almost before they had pinpointed the source of the vocal explosion, he was in motion, moving past the others in the second row of folded chairs and walking swiftly to the coffin where it was poised for imminent descent now that the minister had finished.''

"Don't *do* this yet,'' he said to no one. "Please don't put her in the ground yet,'' and he moved toward the suspended coffin as though wanting to throw himself across it protectively, a maneuver that might have sent both him *and* it tumbling together to the ground. Anthony Konig was on his feet at once, moving surprisingly fast for such a big man, stepping between the outmoded hippie and the shining black coffin, seizing his left arm, swinging him around and saying in a hoarse sharp voice that knifed through the keening of the wind, "Eddie, get hold of yourself!'' Vicky's father followed not a beat behind, coming around on the other side of the man and grabbing his right arm as he was preparing to swing it at Konig. "Calm down,'' he said. "Now *jess* calm down, boy!''

"Who the hell is *that?*'' Bloom whispered beside me. Together, Vicky's father and her former husband began walking the man away from the grave and up the path toward the parked automobiles. "Better see what that was all about,'' Bloom said, and lifted the collar of his coat, and began walking after them.

The other mourners were rising. There was the clatter of wooden chair legs scraping against the gravel. The wind persisted. Beneath the wind I heard the murmuring hum of the hydraulic mechanism as it began lowering the coffin into the grave. The dark-haired girl in the wrinkled black overcoat suddenly materialized at my side.

"I have to talk to you,'' she said.

The wind tossed her hair across her forehead and across her wet brown eyes. Behind her, Jim Sherman was shaking the minister's hand, and his partner Brad was telling him what a fine service it had been earlier in church and how appropriate had been the psalm here at graveside. I kept searching the girl's face, trying to place her.

"I'm Melanie Simms,'' she said, "I work at the Greenery. I waited on you the night you came to hear her sing. Do you remember?''

I remembered only vaguely, but I nodded, anyway.

"I saw you with her later, I know you were a friend of hers, Mr. Hope. There's something you've got to know."

She was talking in a whisper, I could barely hear her under the louder sound of the wind. I leaned closer to her. In the distance, up near the black limo, I could see Bloom in conversation with the man who'd almost jumped on the coffin.

"Just before she was killed . . ." Melanie said, and suddenly cut herself off, and turned sharply to look over her shoulder. Jim and his partner were approaching. Jim's white hair blowing in the wind, Brad wearing a green felt hat that hid his balding pate, their footfalls crunching on the gravel path. "I'll call you," she said, and turned away, and began walking swiftly toward the parked cars.

"It was a nice service, don't you think?" Jim asked.

"Yes," I said. I was still watching, Melanie. She turned once to look at me, nodded again as she'd done while the minister was speaking, and then opened the door of a yellow Mustang and climbed in behind the wheel. The engine caught. She looked at me again through the closed window and then backed the car out of its space and nosed it toward the cemetery gates. Together, the three of us began walking up the gravel path.

"Did you locate that attorney?" Jim asked.

"Yes, I did, thank you, Jim."

"What attorney?" Brad asked.

"Vicky's attorney. The one who looked over the contract we made with her."

"Why?" Brad said, looking suddenly worried. "Was there something wrong with that contract?"

"No, no, everything in order," I said.

At the end of the path we shook hands, and Jim and Brad went to the car they'd come in together. The black limo was gone now, and so were Konig and Miller. But Bloom was still standing alongside the wrought-iron fence, talking to the man who'd tried to jump on the coffin. I walked over to them and caught him mid-sentence.

". . . should have been notified is all I'm saying."

He stopped talking, looked at me, and then looked at Bloom questioningly.

"It's all right," Bloom said, "this is Vicky's attorney, Matthew Hope." Bloom knew this was a lie, and I knew it was a lie, but I recognized why he felt it was necessary. "This is Eddie Marshall, used to be Vicky's producer when she was with Regal."

Marshall looked at me again, appraisingly this time. "Oh, right," he said, "they mentioned your name in the paper. You were the last one to see her alive."

"Yes," I said.

He studied me more closely, nodded, apparently decided it was okay to include me in the conversation, and then said to Bloom, "They may not even know she was *killed* is what I mean. They were the *group*, they should've been notified."

"He's talking about the band," Bloom said to me.

"Wheat," Marshall said, nodding again, "the group that backed her. Did anybody even *think* of contacting them? I mean, they were the ones who were closest to her. So where are they *today* when we're putting her in the ground? Vicky was saying good-bye to this fuckin apple, and Wheat wasn't here to send her off. That wasn't right. I just couldn't help myself, I had to *say* something."

"Well, I'm sure the band must've heard about it," Bloom said gently. "It was on network television Monday night."

"Sure, if they were watching."

"It's in all the newspapers, too, Mr. Marshall. If they'd *wanted* to be here, they'd have *been* here." He paused, and then said, "How'd *you* hear about it?"

"The newspapers."

"When?"

"Late last night. I'm on vacation, I work in Georgia, I'm a d.j. at a radio station up there. Left last Friday to go fishing on the Keys, didn't learn about Vicky till I read the story last night, big follow-up story on her career. Are you familiar with the Keys?"

He was referring, of course, not to Calusa's less celebrated keys, but to *the* Keys, the ones that meandered westward from Florida's southernmost tip, leisurely sprawling into the Gulf of Mexico from Key Largo to Key West, where Ernest Hemingway once made his home, and where Tennessee Williams still does.

"Yes," Bloom said, "it's nice down there."

"Borrowed a boat from a friend of mine in Islamorada Sunday, when I got there. Stopped off at Disneyworld first—

have you ever been to Disneyworld in Orlando?—drove right
on down afterward and went out on the water.''

"What's your friend's name?"

"Jerry Cooper."

"Is that a man or a woman?"

"A man."

"So you left Georgia last weekend, is that it?"

"Yes, on the eleventh, last Friday."

"And got to Islamorada when?"

"Sunday afternoon."

"And went right out on the boat."

"Yes. Didn't come back in till last night. Didn't even
know Vicky was planning a comeback, learned all about it in
the paper. I'd have been down here in a flash if I'd known,
fuck Disneyworld, fuck the Keys, I'd have come straight to
Calusa to catch her opening.''

"When *did* you get here?"

"Early this morning. Hopped right in the station wagon
last night and started driving.''

"These other guys in the band . . ."

"The group."

"Yeah, Wheat," Bloom said. "Can you tell me their
names?"

"The way I can tell you my own. Geoff Hamilton on lead
guitar, Georgie Krantz on bass, and Neil Sadowsky on drums.''

"Got any idea where I can find them?"

"Geoff runs a music school in El Dorado, Arkansas. Teaches
guitar mostly, but I think he gives mandolin and uke lessons,
too.''

"How about the others, whatever their names are?"

"George's a piano tuner up in Falmouth, on the Cape. Cape
Cod. Got a wife and three kids. Plays a gig every now and
then, locally or in Boston, but what he really makes his living
at is the tuning.''

"And the last one, what's his name?"

"Neil Sadowsky, drummer with the group. I don't know
where he is now. He was living in New York last time we
talked, oh, six months ago.''

"Spell those names for me, will you?" Bloom said, and
took out his notebook. Marshall spelled all the names for
him, and Bloom wrote them down in a neat, precise hand.

"Where are you staying here in Calusa?" he asked.

"No place yet, I just got here this morning."

"Here's my card," Bloom said. "If you remember anything about where this Sadowsky guy might be, give me a call."

"If I'm still here," Marshall said. "I'm not due back till Monday morning, but after what happened . . ." He shook his head.

"Cutting the vacation short, huh?"

"Maybe."

"Yeah," Bloom said, and nodded. "Terrible thing. Well, I got to go," he said. "Keep in touch, Matthew."

"I will," I said.

He spread his hand in a farewell fan, smiled over it, and then walked quickly to where the police car was parked.

"Have you got a minute, Mr. Hope?" Marshall asked. "Or are you in a hurry?"

"No hurry," I said.

"I'll walk you to your car."

We began walking. The wind howled around us.

"I wanted to ask you . . ." Marshall said, and hesitated. "The newspaper suggested you'd been seeing Vicky regularly . . ."

"Well, not really."

"Well, whatever," Marshall said, "that's none of my business. I'm saying—in light of what happened afterward— it's good to know she might have had someone she could trust. Were you there at the opening?"

"No, I didn't get to see her till Sunday night."

"At Greensleeves, is that the name of the place?"

"The Greenery."

"How'd she sound?"

"Not very good."

The Ghia was where I'd parked it against the wrought-iron fence, its nose facing us. In the State of Florida you get only one license plate when you register your automobile and you affix this to the rear holder. This saves the state a lot of money each year, but it leaves the motorists with an empty holder at the front of the car. I had filled the emptiness on the Ghia with a metal plate that read: I'D RATHER BE SAILING. Marshall stopped at the car, glanced at the front plate, and said, "You're a sailor, huh?"

"Yes," I said.

"Me, too. Loved those couple of days I spent out on the water." He shook his head. "So she was bad that night, huh?"

"Yes, I'm afraid so."

"Yeah, well, that was Vicky, all right. I loved her to death, but she had a voice like a nasal drip, monotonous, persistent, annoying as hell. It took every ounce of musical knowledge I possessed to make those albums sound like money, you know what I mean? Her looks didn't hurt, either, she was really gorgeous back then. The picture I used on the "Frenzy" sleeve—that was the first album—I poured her into this red sequined gown slit down to her navel and halfway up the leg. She had magnificent breasts and we showed everything but the nipples, believe me, great legs too, it was a stunning picture, we had it taken by a guy in New Orleans who used to work for *Life* magazine back in the forties and early fifties. What we were trying to sell, Mr. Hope, was *youth* and *sex* and a feeling of *wildness*, do you know, *frenzy*, Vicky in that red gown with her head thrown back and a wide smile on her face, one hand on her hip, lots of breast and leg and thigh showing. We were trying to make her a symbol for the sound I'd manufactured in the studio, beefed up her voice, used every trick I knew, made Wheat sound like the Beatles and the Stones all rolled together and blowing at the same time! They ate it up, wanted to eat *her* up as well, believe me, we had more damn calls—television shows, nightclubs, Vegas, New York, concert tours, everybody wanting her to make personal appearances, fat chance. That would've been the end of Victoria Miller, dead on the spot, the end of Wheat, too, the end of the whole big dazzling ball of wax." He shook his head. He had delivered all this with such speed and intensity that, paradoxically, it left *me* feeling somewhat breathless.

"Poor darlin," he said. "What'd she sing that night?"

"All the golden oldies."

"Wrong choice. What was she wearing?"

"A white gown."

"Slinky?"

"Slinky."

"Low cut?"

"Not very."

"But I'll bet she looked terrific, didn't she?"

"Yes, she looked beautiful."

"What'd the critics have to say? Were there any reviews?"

"One, but I haven't seen it yet."

Marshall shook his head again. "She never should have tried it," he said. "Not that way. If she'd wanted to make a comeback, all she had to do was pick up the phone, let me know what she wanted, I'd have dropped everything and come running. But the way she . . ."

"Did she know where to find you?"

"Oh, sure."

"Then you've been in touch over the years?"

"Christmas cards. With little notes scribbled on them, how are you, what're you doing, like that."

"Did she send you one this past Christmas?"

"Never missed a Christmas."

"But she didn't mention the opening."

"No, I only learned about that last night. God, if I'd *known*, I'd have been here in a *minute!* Me miss her opening? After all we'd been through together? No way. Did she seem worried that night? When you went to see her, I mean?"

"I didn't think so at the time, but later, yes, it seemed to me she *was* troubled about something."

"Did she say what?"

"Not really. We talked mostly about how it had gone that night, the show. She wanted to know if there'd been an unusual amount of chatter in the audience, thought she'd detected . . ."

"Yeah, that can be death, people talking during a performance, poor darlin'."

"I told her I hadn't noticed anything out of the ordinary."

"Well, good for you, I thank you for that."

"By the way, she mentioned that you were the one who hadn't allowed her to make any public appearances. In the past, I mean. When you were working together."

"Ah, then she *did* mention me, huh?"

"Yes. She said—well, I really can't remember her exact words, but it was something about Eddie not letting her perform live, and when I asked her who Eddie was, she said you'd been her producer at Regal."

"That's what I was, all right," he said. "And a lot more, I guess."

"Like what?"

"Mentor, adviser . . ." he said, and let the words trail.

"This must be hitting you pretty hard."

"Yes."

"I'm sorry."

He nodded bleakly, and then took from his pocket one of those leather cigarette cases with a lift-off top. I thought he was lighting a cigarette at first—until I caught a whiff of the smoke drifting on the air.

"Is that dope?" I asked.

"Little bit of grass," he said. "Want a stick?"

"No, thanks."

"Don't you smoke?"

"I smoke."

"What is it then? Are they tough on pot down here?"

"Let's say they frown upon smoking it in public."

"Who cares?" he said, and shrugged. "You sure you don't want one? I've got a dozen more in the wagon, you won't be depriving me."

"No, thanks," I said, "that's okay."

He sucked on the joint, let out a slow stream of smoke, and said, "You were telling me she seemed worried about something."

"Yes."

"Did she say *what?*"

"No."

"Had someone threatened her, do you think?"

"I don't know."

"Well, did she *mention* any threats?"

"No."

"A threatening letter maybe?"

"Nothing. Although . . ."

"Yes?"

"Someone *did* call Vicky on the night she was murdered."

"Who?"

"I don't know, the sitter took the calls. The man wouldn't leave his name."

"It was a *man* then?"

"Yes."

"What'd he say?"

"Well, *nothing* the first two times."

"How many times did he *call?*"

"Three. And all he said the last time was 'Tell Vicky I'll be stopping by to collect.' "

"Collect what?"

"I don't know."

"Well . . . did Vicky *owe* him something? Money or . . . I don't know . . . what does a person come by to *collect?*"

The name leaped into my mind without warning, "Allison," and came from my mouth before I even realized I'd thought it, "Allison," and hung on the air to bring her to vivid recall for only a moment, a six-year-old darling in a granny nightgown, showing me her finger paintings and later sitting at my feet while she scribbled with her crayons—Allison.

"No, I don't think so," Marshall said, shaking his head. "People don't say they'll be coming by to *collect* a child. They'll pick *up* a child, or . . ."

"I've heard the expression," I said. "To collect someone. *Especially* when it's a child."

"Well . . . who would have been coming by to collect *Allison?* Was Tony Konig in town?"

"Yes, but . . ."

"He wouldn't have been coming by for a six-year-old child at *that* hour of the night, would he?"

"No, that doesn't sound likely."

"Maybe Vicky arranged to have . . . I don't know . . . *something* picked up. A rug to be cleaned, a vacuum to be repaired, a toaster, a lamp, who knows? And this was the serviceman calling to say he'd be stopping by to collect it."

"At *night?*"

"No, the next day, whenever. Got the message on his answering service, called her back to let her know he'd be stopping by for whatever it was."

"Maybe," I said, and looked at my watch. "Mr. Marshall . . . I really have to get back to the office."

"I'm sure that's what it must have been," Marshall said.

"Most likely," I said. We shook hands. "It was nice meeting you," I said. "Good-bye, Mr. Marshall."

"Good-bye, Mr. Hope," he said, and smiled forlornly.

* * *

All the way back to the office, I kept marveling at Bloom's interrogatory technique. He had listened sympathetically while Marshall had rattled on about the injustice of no one having notified Vicky's backup group that the funeral would be taking place today, and then, quietly and unobtrusively, had gone about the very important business of establishing just where some of the people who'd figured most importantly in her life might have been on the night she was killed. Marshall himself had been out on a boat down near the Keys, borrowed from a friend in Islamorada. I had no doubt that Bloom would be calling the friend to verify this. Geoff Hamilton, the group's lead guitarist, was living in El Dorado, and George Krantz, the bass player, was up on the Cape, in Falmouth. If I knew Bloom, he would call Information to get telephone numbers for both these men, and then would follow up with full-scale, long-distance interviews. As for Neil Sadowsky, the group's drummer, I had no idea how Bloom might go about tracking him down in New York, but I was certain he would figure out *some* way; the next time I saw him, I fully expected him to tell me he'd found out not only where Sadowsky was living, but also his shoe size.

It was almost ten-thirty when I entered the parking lot outside our offices, and pulled into the space marked MATTHEW HOPE, just alongside the one marked FRANK SUMMERVILLE. A yellow Mustang was parked in one of the RESERVED FOR CLIENTS spaces, and Melanie Simms was sitting behind the wheel. She was reading a magazine, but she looked up the moment I pulled in, and she had already opened the door of her car by the time I cut the engine. She brushed the hair away from her face with the back of one hand and waited for me to get out of the Ghia.

"Hello," I said.

"I got your address from the phone book," she said, and looked over her shoulder as though afraid we were being observed. "I was hoping you'd come straight here."

"Come on in," I said.

There was something essentially birdlike about Melanie Simms, a combination of nervous mannerisms that, I realized now, added up to what could have been mistaken for fear. Lacking the calm, unruffled grace of the bigger wading birds on Calusa's shores, she moved instead with the quick, erratic energy of a tiny creature poised for flight, her head bobbing, her eyes darting, her arms held close to her body like folded wings. She was, I noticed, nibbling at her lower lip. Suddenly she glanced over her shoulder again, and I knew this was not part of the avian syndrome—she *was* genuinely afraid of something or someone.

"Cold enough for you?" Cynthia asked the moment we stepped into the reception area.

"Thought I'd go to the beach this afternoon," I said.

"Ha! Anthony Konig called, wants you to call him back right away. Ditto Mr. Carlisle at Tricity, and Mr. Loeb at Pierson, Smith."

"Get me Konig, the others can wait. Miss Simms, would you mind taking a seat, please? I won't be a moment."

"Thank you," she said. She looked around, discovered with a start the bank of leather chairs facing Cynthia's desk, and sat awkwardly, first crossing her legs, and then uncrossing them, and then making certain her skirt and black overcoat were firmly tucked under her. I went into my office just as Cynthia was dialing. She buzzed me an instant later.

"I've got Mr. Konig for you, on three."

"Thank you," I said, and stabbed at the lighted button in the base of my phone. "Mr. Konig," I said, "it's Matthew Hope."

"Yes, how are you, thanks for calling back so soon. What'd you find out?"

"Her attorney knew nothing about a will."

"Who's that?"

"A woman named Dale O'Brien. That doesn't preclude the *existence* of one, you understand. It simply means . . ."

"Yes, that her attorney didn't draw it. Have the police found one? At the house, I mean."

"Not that I know of."

"Would you ask Bloom? I'd ask him myself, but that man really irritates me."

"Yes, next time we talk."

"What's the next step? How do we find out for *sure* if there was one?"

"Well, if an attorney drew one and has the original in his possession, he'll be filing it in Probate. Our own firm, for example, checks the obituary notices every day, and then cross-checks those against our list of clients. If Vicky drew the will herself, that's another matter. But she'd have needed witnesses, and usually a person will call in friends or neighbors to do the witnessing. So if anyone has knowledge of the will, maybe he'll come forward.''

''And maybe not. What do we do *then?*''

''You wouldn't happen to know where she banked, would you?''

''No. Why?''

''Because people usually keep their wills in safe-deposit boxes. That could be a problem. We'd have to petition the court to appoint a temporary personal representative who'd then have the power to open the box.''

''Can you find out whether or not she had one?''

''I'll have someone start checking the local banks, yes.''

''What if she didn't?''

''We'll worry about that when we come to it. There's no great rush. If anyone has custody of a will, he's required to deposit it with the clerk of the court within ten days after receiving information of a death. I'll keep checking Probate. If nothing turns up, we'll figure out our next move then.''

''Well, it would set my mind at ease,'' Konig said. ''If I knew whether or not there was a will.''

''I understand.''

''Don't go away yet. Main reason I called is to tell you what Dwayne Miller said to me in the limo this morning.'' He hesitated and then said, ''I think he killed Vicky. I think he killed his own daughter and then stole my little girl afterward.''

''Mr. Konig,'' I said, ''this really is something you should be telling Detective Bloom.''

''No, I don't want to be telling this to him, he's got his thumb up his ass, he'll never find who done this.''

''I really think . . .''

''You're my lawyer, Mr. Hope, it's *you* I want to talk to. This was on the way back from the cemetery,'' he said, lowering his voice. ''We were dropping me off first, I'm staying at the Breakwater Inn, I'm sure I told you that. Up to then the old bastard was sweet as mother's milk, all condolences and grief. But all at once he started ranting and raving about the mistake Vicky'd made. Said he'd *told* her she was making a mistake, said there was nothing to gain by her making her comeback at a little restaurant out on Stone Crab. Told her . . ."

"Mr. Konig, how does any of this indicate that Mr. Miller . . ."

"Just hold on a minute," Konig said. "He was getting more and more riled as we got closer to the hotel. He told me he'd seen Vicky Thursday night, night before she opened out there at the restaurant there. Told me they had a big argument about her trying to make her comeback this way, said he told her she shoulda tried to contact Eddie Marshall instead, wher-*ever* he was, get him to supervise her career the way he did last time around. Told her that singing at that shitty little restaurant wasn't the way to do it. Wouldn't get her any notice, would immediately class her with all the *other* piss-poor performers down here 'stead of the star she was and the star she could be *again* if only she got Eddie to *work* for her again."

"I still don't understand why you feel this would cast suspicion . . ."

"Told her if she went ahead with it, he'd disown her."

"He said that?"

"God's truth."

"That if she opened at the Greenery, he'd disown her?"

"Her and Allison both."

"Well . . . did the threat have any substance?"

"What do you mean, Mr. Hope?"

"Has he *got* anything that would have made a disinheritance meaningful?"

"Only four hundred acres of orange groves in Manakawa County is all. Plus half a dozen motels on the Tamiami Trail, between here and Fort Myers, and God knows *how* much in securities. Let me tell you something, Mr. Hope. Until I married Vicky, it wasn't *her* making any money out of her records, it was her *father*. *He* was the one socking it into his bank account, *he* was the one came out of the whole thing with millions to spare."

"So—from what you're telling me, if I've got it straight— he warned that he would disinherit Vicky . . ."

"That's right."

". . . if she opened at the Greenery as scheduled."

"That's absolutely right."

"So why do you feel a threat of disinher—"

"Because of what he said next."

"And what was that?"

"This is still Thursday night, mind you, this is him telling me what he was feeling the night before Vicky opened. And these are his exact words, Mr. Hope, may I drop dead on the spot here if this isn't what he said to me just as the car was pulling up to my hotel."

"What were those words, Mr. Konig?"

"The words were, 'She refused flat out, the ungrateful little bitch. I shoulda killed her then and there.' That's what he said, Mr. Hope, may I be struck by lightning if those weren't his precise words."

"And you feel . . . ?"

"Well, how *else* can you take something like that? A man says he shoulda killed her then and there, that can only mean instead of *later*, am I right? He shoulda killed her *then* and *there*, when she refused to listen to him, instead of waiting till *after* she opened there at the restaurant against his will."

"I don't think his words necessarily meant . . ."

"I'm telling you that's what they meant, Mr. Hope."

I was silent for a moment.

"Well?" Konig said.

"Maybe," I said. "Thanks for telling me, I'll pass it on to Bloom."

"Don't pass anything on to that asshole, he doesn't know how to do his damn job. Just go straight to the FBI with it, that's what you should do, Mr. Hope."

"Well, I'll think about it," I said.

"Let me know what you decide, will you? I'll be here at the hotel till two, two-thirty."

"I'll call you," I promised, and we both hung up. I sat looking at the phone for several moments, and then I buzzed Cynthia and asked her to send in Melanie Simms. She came into the office in her birdlike manner, stopping just inside the door to look around, and then turning to make certain she had closed the door behind her, and then taking a tentative step forward, and stopping, and then moving forward again to the chair before my desk.

"I'm sorry I kept you waiting," I said.

"No, no," she said, "that's perfectly all right." She had begun nibbling at her lower lip again. She sat, and then blinked owlishly at me, and said, "Mr. Hope, I think I know who killed Vicky."

She blinked again, and I blinked back at her. It was not usual for anyone in these offices to be discussing homicide; it was even less usual to have two different people in the space of ten minutes tell me they knew the identity of a murderer.

"Have you gone to the police with this?" I asked.

"I don't want to get involved," she said.

"I think the police . . ."

"Mr. Hope," she said, "I know you were a friend of hers, I *think* you were, anyway, and I'm just wishing with all my heart that you'll take this information I'm about to give you and do with it what needs to be done. My brother said I should stay out of it, just forget what I heard and let things take their natural course. But I liked Vicky a lot, Mr. Hope, she always had a kind word for everybody at the Greenery, even when she was busy rehearsing and trying to get the songs right. So I feel I *owe* this to her, I feel I've got to tell this to somebody who can maybe *do* something with it."

"That would be the police," I said. "If any of this is evidence important to the investigation—or indeed to a trial later on—the police would have to hear it from you directly, anyway. Sooner or later you'd have to . . ."

"I'll worry about that when the time comes. Meanwhile, I want your word that you won't say where you *got* this information."

"I can't make that promise."

"Why not?"

"Because if it *is* information regarding a crime, I would feel obliged to give it to the police."

"I thought this was like a confession box," Melanie said.

"If you're talking about lawyer-client privilege . . ."

"Yes, whatever you call it."

"You're not my client, Miss Simms. I have no reason to keep confidential anything you say here."

"Oh."

"I'm sorry," I said. "I really *do* believe that if you have information about Miss Miller's death, you should go to the police."

"No, I can't go to the police," she said, "my brother would kill me."

The word "kill" sent a shiver up her spine, causing her shoulders to pull up into an involuntary shrug. She sucked in a hissing stream of breath, and then clenched her hands tightly in her lap, as though trying to squeeze the last remnants of the tremor from her body. She turned swiftly to look at the closed door. She turned back to me again. She crossed her legs. She uncrossed them. She crossed them again, and then tucked her skirt and her coat around her. In a whisper she said, "It was Mr. Sherman."

"Jim Sherman?" I said.

"Yes, sir."

"You think Mr. *Sherman* killed Vicky?"

"Yes, sir."

"What makes you think so?"

"What makes me think so is what I heard last Friday night."

"And what was that, Miss Simms?"

She turned to look at the closed door again.

"Is that locked?" she asked.

"No, it's not."

"Could you lock it, please?"

"Miss Simms, there's a receptionist sitting just down the hall, she won't allow anyone in here without first . . ."

"Please lock it, Mr. Hope."

Sighing, I rose from behind my desk, went to the door, and locked it. The notion of Jim Sherman killing Vicky, or *anyone*, for that matter, was entirely absurd, and I was beginning to think Melanie Simms was a bit unhinged. But I came back to the desk and sat in the swivel chair behind it once again and patiently said, "All right, the door is locked."

"This was Friday night," she said. "I was working the lounge. That was where I waited on you Sunday, do you remember?"

"Yes," I said.

"It was quiet around then, this must've been about eight, eight-fifteen, the people hadn't yet started coming in for the show. The *dining* room was busy, but not the lounge."

I tried to visualize the lounge as it must have looked on Vicky's opening night, the room lush with fresh plants supplied by Fleur de Lis, Boston ferns and Swedish ivy, vining philodendron and dieffenbachia, votive candles in ruby-red holders on white tablecloths, the pleasant hum of conversation, the clink of ice in cocktails—but no, that would have been closer to nine, when the room was crowded with people waiting for the show to start. Melanie was talking about an earlier time, the Happy Hour already gone, the lounge dim and relatively empty, the bartender listening to the piano player as he stroked all the old tunes from the old Broadway—

"The phone behind the bar rang, and Danny picked it up. It was Vicky calling from her dressing room. She said she was dying of thirst and could someone bring her a Perrier with a little lime in it. Danny mixed the drink, and I carried it back to her. The dressing room at the Greenery, what it is, it used to be part of the ladies' room, like a little sort of lounge area off to the side, you know? That's when the restaurant first opened and Mr. Sherman and Mr. Atherton had no plans for bringing in entertainment. But then they hired Vicky and she needed a place to change, so they put up these fancy screens, you know, and a red velour curtain on these brass rings, and they fixed it up with a dressing table with lights around it, and a nice chair and a couch, you know, everything a person would need. I'm explaining it in detail like this because you have to understand how I could hear what they were *saying* in there. I mean, there's no *door*, you see. Just the screens, and the velour curtain behind them, which you push back on this big brass rod. That's how I happened to hear what they were saying. What Vicky and Mr. Sherman were saying.

"I didn't know if I should go in at first. You can't knock on a *curtain*, you know, and I was standing outside there with the Perrier and lime on a tray, and listening to them, and I had the feeling I *shouldn't* be listening to this, it was none of my business what they were saying, but at the same time Vicky'd asked for the drink, she'd called the bar to say she was dying of thirst, so what should I do? I figured she'd made her call *before* Mr. Sherman got there, before this argument between the two of them started, and I felt pretty sure she wouldn't want me breaking in on them with the Perrier. But there I was with it, and listening to everything they said, and I didn't know whether I should just pull the curtain back, you know, and say 'Hi,' as if I hadn't heard anything, or maybe just go back to the bar and tell Danny she'd changed her mind, I just didn't know. So I just stood there.

"What they were arguing about, I began to figure out, was the material she'd picked to sing there at the Greenery for her opening night, the same stuff she was singing on Sunday night when you were there. But on *Friday* there was still time to change it. I mean, on *Friday* that girl from the *Herald-Tribune* was going to be there listening to Vicky so she could write a review on her—what's her name, the girl on the *Tribune*, Joan something . . ."

"Jean Riverton," I said. Jean was hardly a "girl." She was fifty-four years old and what might have been best described as a virulent boil on the backside of Calusa's creative community; her reviews, all too often scathing, could shut down a performance overnight. I had missed the one she'd written on Vicky's opening because I'd been out on the water with my daughter until late Sunday afternoon.

"Yes, Jean Riverton, that's her name," Melanie said, "you know the girl I mean. She was supposed to be there Friday night—well, actually she *was* there, but not just then, this was still maybe eight-fifteen, eight-thirty—and Mr. Sherman was telling Vicky it still wasn't too late to put at least a *few* rock-and-roll songs in the repertory . . . is that the word, repertory?"

"Yes, repertory."

"Instead of giving them a program of all that—excuse me, but this is exactly what he said—all that old-fart stuff from the forties and fifties. He told Vicky she was known as a rock-and-*roll* singer, that was how she'd made her reputation, she wasn't Dinah Shore, she wasn't Rosemary Clooney, she wasn't Ella Fitzgerald, she wasn't Teresa Brewer, she wasn't Sarah Vaughan, she was Victoria *Miller* and that stood for hard rock and what she was planning to sing tonight was soft *shlock*. That was the word he used, shlock, what does shlock mean?"

"Well, just go on," I said.

"Mr. Sherman told her he'd been telling her this for the past two weeks now, ever since rehearsals started with that mummified relic—those were his words, too—who played for all those opera singers at the Helen Gottlieb, but Vicky wouldn't listen, she just wouldn't listen, and now she'd be going on in a half-hour, *less* than a half-hour, and couldn't she for Christ's sake *please* ask the piano player to play at least *one* of the songs she'd made famous, didn't the piano player at least know 'Frenzy,' everybody in the whole *world* knew 'Frenzy.' Vicky very calmly said yes, they *had* gone over this a hundred times in the past two weeks, and she thought it'd been decided that the crowd in Calusa was an *older* crowd and that the songs she used to sing back in the sixties wouldn't be the proper songs to sing for them, especially not in an intimate lounge like the one there at the Greenery, and *especially* not with just a piano accompaniment, even if the piano player *was* only a mummified *relic*—she was imitating Mr. Sherman there, you know, mimicking him—and that she certainly didn't want to discuss it now, twenty-five minutes before she went on, so would he mind getting—this is what she said, Mr. Hope, so you'll have to excuse me—would he mind getting the fuck out?

"Well, the discussion till then had been more or less on a civilized level, you know, nobody *really* raising his or her voice, just the two of them having at it like a husband and wife who are arguing over money or the kids or whatever, but all of a sudden Mr. Sherman went through the roof. He asked her who the hell she thought she was, ordering him out of a dressing room that had cost him close to two thousand dollars to set up for her, lights around the goddamn dressing table—excuse me—and full-length mirrors all over the place, and the couch she asked for so she could *rest* before a performance and the heavy velour curtains and the ornate screens, who the hell did she think she *was,* some kind of *star* still? Some kind of star selling million-copy gold records instead of a has-been selling real estate in a grubby office on Sabal Key? Don't you tell *me* to get out of here, you . . .' "

Melanie stopped abruptly. She clasped her hands in her lap again, and then looked down at her shoes and—her face beginning to flush—said, "This is what he said, I'm only repeating it, Mr. Hope. He said, 'Don't you tell *me* to get out of here, you cheap little cunt,' and that was when one or the other of them, I don't know which one because I couldn't see what was going on, I could only *hear* from where I was standing outside the curtain, one of them slapped the other

one, I don't know if it was Vicky slapping Mr. Sherman or
the other way around. But there was the sound of this *slap,*
you know, and then just silence. I stood there thinking I'd
better not go in after all, I'd better just go back to the bar and
say she'd changed her mind, or maybe just pour the drink out
and take back the empty glass. When Mr. Sherman started
talking again, his voice was very, very low, I could hardly
hear him, so maybe *she* was the one slapped *him* after all, and
he was steaming as a result, you know, and talking very low
the way people do when they're boiling mad. He said, 'Fine,
very good, so long as we understand each other. If that *other*
cunt, the one on the *Tribune* gives you a bad review tonight,
and if people stay away from this restaurant because of you
and that forties shit you plan to sing, then lady, you are dead.
Believe me, lady, you are dead.' I knew he'd be coming out
then, and I knew he'd realize I'd been listening if he caught
me standing there, so I ducked outside the screens and went
back to the bar with the drink and told Danny she'd changed
her mind. But you know, Mr. Hope, Joan Riverton's review
. . . *Jean* Riverton's . . . was very bad the next day, in the
paper, I mean. It was really awful. And I don't know whether
Mr. Sherman was saying Vicky'd be dead, you know, meaning she'd be *fired* or something, or whether he meant she'd
really be dead, which is what happened to her, didn't it?
Somebody killed her on Sunday night, and it was Mr. Sherman who said, 'Believe me, lady, you are dead.' ''

    She took a deep breath. She nodded, and then looked down
at her hands—still clasped in her lap—and then looked up
again, directly into my eyes, and said like a challenge, ''That's
what I heard last Friday night.''

6

Although I'd promised to call Anthony Konig as soon as I decided what to do with the information he'd given me about Vicky's father, I didn't talk to him again till Thursday afternoon, after I'd concluded my one o'clock meeting with Gerald Bannister, the delinquent gall-bladder patient. I was, in fact, just about to dial the 504 New Orleans area code when Cynthia buzzed to say Konig was waiting on three. I punched the lighted button in the base of the phone.

"Hello, Mr. Konig," I said.

"You promised you'd call."

"I'm sorry, things got a bit hectic around here yesterday. Where are you now?"

"Still at the Breakwater, looks like I'll be here through the weekend at least. I've got to see about ordering a stone for Vicky, and I want to make some sort of arrangement with a florist, get fresh flowers put on the grave every now and then. Have you checked those banks yet?"

"Yes, sir, someone in the office did. Vicky had a checking account and a small savings account at Calusa First, but no safe-deposit box."

"How about the other banks in town?"

"Nothing at any of them."

"So we still don't know, am I right? About a will, I mean."

"That's right. But I'll keep checking with Probate, you needn't . . ."

"I think you ought to go see Vicky's father."

"What for?"

"If anyone'd know about a will she left, it'd be Dwayne."

"What's the rush, Mr. Konig?"

I was thinking the man's daughter had been kidnapped, most probably by the same person who'd killed his former wife, and all he was worried about was a will which—*if* it existed—might name him as guardian of whatever his daughter would inherit. It seemed to me that Anthony Konig should have been less concerned about his daughter's goddamn *property* and more concerned about her *safety.*

"I like to get all my ducks in a row," he said.

"Why don't we first get Allison back," I said. "*Then* we can start worrying about . . ."

"Well, that's just the point. When we *do* get her back, I want to know where I stand. If I'm her designated guardian . . ."

"Mr. Konig, forgive me, but I'm sorry I even *mentioned* that possibility. If there *is* a will, and if you *are* the named guardian, there'll be plenty of time to do what needs to be done later. In the meantime . . ."

"I'd like you to go see Dwayne," he said.

I said nothing.

"Mr. Hope?"

"I hear you, Mr. Konig."

"*Will* you go see him?"

"If you feel it's that important."

"It'd set my mind at ease. And while you're there, you might fish around a little, see if it isn't true what I told you."

"I'd rather not do that."

"Well, then just find out whether there's a will or not. I've got nothing personal to gain by this, Mr. Hope, I hope you realize that. I don't imagine I'd have free hand as guardian to do whatever I *wanted* to do with Allison's property . . ."

"As a matter of fact, you wouldn't. The court would require a very strict accounting."

"Which is what I thought. But I'd sure as hell hate to think Vicky may've named her *father* as guardian. So if you could find out for me whether he knows about any will, I'd appreciate it.''

"I'll do what I can."

"Thank you," he said, and hung up.

He had not told me where I could find Dwayne Miller. I buzzed Cynthia, asked her to get me Detective Bloom at the Public Safety Building, and then slipped the signed Bannister notes into a manila envelope, marked it Bannister-Ungerman Notes, and tossed it into the basket with the rest of the material awaiting filing. Cynthia got back to me almost at once.

"Detective Bloom on four," she said.

I picked up the receiver.

"Hello," I said, "how are you?"

"Hungry," he said.

"Hungry?"

"I went to see my doctor last Saturday, the yearly check-up, you know? He told me I'm fifteen pounds overweight, my blood pressure is one-twenty over ninety-four, and my cholesterol level is three-seventeen. All right, anything over two-eighty for the cholesterol is supposed to be bad, and anything over one-twenty over ninety for the blood pressure bothers him. So he's got me on a fat-free, salt-free diet, and I'm *starving* to death. You know what I had for lunch? *Fruit* salad, *cottage* cheese, and a slice of protein bread without butter. I'm six feet three inches tall, and I weigh two hundred and twenty. Does that sound fat to you?"

"Well, I really don't . . ."

"My doctor says I'm overweight. He says at my *age* all of this can be a problem—the extra pounds, the high blood pressure, the cholesterol. I'm forty-six, does that sound ancient to you?"

"Well, no, it doesn't."

"He said I can either start dieting or else stop buying long-play records. That was supposed to be a joke, he's a very comical man, my doctor. So I'm eating fruit and cottage cheese for lunch, like some blue-haired old lady in Garden City. What can I do for you, Matthew?"

"Couple of things you should know," I said, and I filled him in on what both Anthony Konig and Melanie Simms had told me after Vicky's funeral yesterday.

"We got suspects coming out of the woodwork, huh?"
Bloom said.

"It would appear that way."

"So the old man is rich, huh?"

"Orange groves, motels, securities, and cash. Yes, I would
say he's moderately wealthy."

"What's an orange grove in Manakawa County worth?"

"I have a client with a hundred and four acres there, and
he's priced them at a little under a million."

"And Miller's got himself *four* hundred acres, huh?"

"That's right."

"So why was his daughter living in a crumby little development house out there on Citrus Lane?"

"Good question."

"Looks to me like he disinherited her while she was still
alive. What about this Jim Sherman? He seemed gay to me.
Is he gay?"

"That's the rumor."

"Doesn't matter to me either way," Bloom said, "except
as it might apply to the case. Said she was going to be dead,
huh?"

"That's what Melanie told me."

"Could've meant he was going to fire her if she didn't pull
the crowds in."

"Maybe."

"I'll talk to him, thanks. Few things you might like to
know. Are you interested in any of this shit?"

"Yes, I am."

"I thought you might be. First, I called this guy who used
to be lead guitarist with the group, the one up in El Dorado.
He was playing a wedding job Sunday night, give me the
couple's name, couldn't possibly have been down here putting the blocks to Vicky, so that lets him out. Next I called
this guy on the Cape, the one who used to play bass with the
group. A kid answered the phone, cutest little thing, must've
been seven or eight years old, told me her Mommy was out
shopping and her Daddy was out tuning. I gave her my name
and number, but that was a lost cause, she kept calling me
Mr. *Boom*. How do you like that? Mr. *Boom*. I'll try him
again in a little while, on the off chance he was down here in
Calusa Sunday night beating Vicky Miller to death."

"Did the airlines . . ."

"Nothing for a George Krantz. Not from Boston, where he would've most likely caught a flight, nor from anywhere else near the Cape either. But who knows, he might've *driven* down. I can't get a line on this Sadowsky character, the drummer, who was living in New York the last time Marshall heard from him. Checked all the directories, got a call in to the N.Y.P.D. right now, maybe they'll give it the old college try for a former Nassau County cop. I've been calling every hotel and motel in town, trying to locate Marshall, see if he can give me a little more information on the guy, what he looks like and so on, but he's nowhere in sight. I figure he must've headed back for Georgia already. He said he worked as a disc jockey up there someplace, didn't he?"

"Yes, he did."

"Right. He *also* said he borrowed that boat he was on from somebody named Jerry Cooper in Islamorada. That's a man, I asked him if it was a man, do you remember?"

"I remember."

"Well, there's no Jerry Cooper listed in Islamorada. That may not mean anything, lots of people have unlisted phones. But his alibi's still wide open, far as I'm concerned, so I'm eager to talk to him on *several* counts. What I did, I located an outfit in Skokie, Illinois, that puts out a publication called *Spot Radio Rates and Data*, it's mostly for people in the advertising business, tells them how much a commercial costs on any radio station in the country. Lists all the stations in all the states. I just got off the phone with them, they'll be Xeroxing the listings for Georgia and sending them to me by Express Mail. I hope there aren't *too* many damn stations there, because I plan to have my people calling each and every one of them. Provided the feds don't object, those bastards. Where's Skokie anyway? Are you familiar with Illinois?"

"I'm originally from Chicago."

"So where's Skokie?"

"Just *outside* of Chicago, actually. Very close to Evanston, where I went to law school."

"Well, I hope I get that stuff by tomorrow. I'd like to talk to Marshall again if I can locate him, ask him about this

Sadowsky guy, and find out about that boat. You think Konig might know what station he works at up there?''

"Maybe. He wants me to go see Vicky's father, by the way. Would you have any . . .''

"What for?"

"He wants to know if Vicky left a will, figures Miller might know."

"Oh? Why does he want to know about a will?''

"He's dying to know if he's been named guardian of Allison's property.''

"Tell him he has.''

"I'm sorry, what did you . . . ?''

"Tell him he's been named guardian of her property.''

"How do you know?''

"I've got the will right here," Bloom said. "We found it in a shoebox on the top shelf of her bedroom closet.''

The will was one of those stationery-store things that could be bought over the counter for fifteen cents plus tax. It was folded in three, the way most legal documents are; all it lacked was a blue binder. On the front, printed in Old English script lettering, was the word "𝔚𝔦𝔩𝔩," and beneath that "of" and then a printed line above which Vicky had hand-lettered her name, *Victoria Stephanie Miller* At the bottom of the page the same Old English script announced three blank spaces headed 𝔈𝔵𝔢𝔠𝔲𝔱𝔬𝔯𝔰, but none of those spaces were filled in. I unfolded the document.

The will itself was a combination of the printed form and the handwritten words Victoria had filled in:

In the Name of God. Amen

I, ...Victoria Stephanie Miller........., a citizen and resident of

...Calusa, Calusa.. County, State of ...Florida..., being of sound and

disposing mind and memory, do hereby make, publish and declare this to be my last

Will and Testament

hereby revoking any and all prior wills, codicils and testamentary dispositions.

FIRST: I give, bequeath and devise to my daughter Allison Mercy Konig all of my real and personal property, including but not limited to my jewelry, my furniture, my automobile, my china and my silverware.

SECOND: I designate my former husband Anthony Lewis Konig as guardian of my daughter Allison's person and property.

THIRD: As specifically regards the principal and accumulated income of a trust created by my father Dwayne Robert Miller in the year 1965, I direct the accumulated income and principal to be divided in shares three-quarters to my daughter Allison Mercy Konig and one-quarter to my former husband Anthony Lewis Konig so that he may properly and without stress or undue burden devote himself to the care of my daughter until she reaches the age of twenty-one.

That was the end of what Vicky had handwritten on the page. The rest, again, was a combination of the form's printed type and the words Vicky had filled in. A name leaped out of the page at me.

. I hereby make. constitute and appoint .... Matthew Hope ....

.... *as execut....or of this my last Will and Testament.*

I turned the page over.

. . . and direct .... him to pay all of my lawful debts. if any, and the funeral

and burial expenses.

The document was dated the fourth day of January, signed by Vicky, and witnessed by people I guessed were the baby-sitter's mother and father, an Albert Whitlaw and a Dorothy Whitlaw, who gave their addresses as 1122 Citrus Lane.

I sat alone in Bloom's office, and read the will a second time. Vicky had written it, or at least dated it, on the fourth of January, which was a week before she'd opened at the Greenery. She had written her letter to Konig on the seventh, advising him that he should contact Matthew Hope in the event of her death, a not unreasonable suggestion since she had already named me as executor of her will. It was entirely possible that Konig had possessed no prior knowledge of the will, or of the fact that Vicky had left to him a quarter of the accumulated income and principal of a trust in which, presumably, she was named beneficiary. On the other hand, it was *also* possible that Konig had known about the will all along, had perhaps even discussed it with Vicky after he'd received her letter and before her death. This would have accounted for his eagerness to have me locate the will now. I had no idea how much money was in that trust, but people have been known to commit murder for pennies.

The door to the outer office opened, and Bloom's cholesterol-laden bulk filled the doorframe. Beyond the door, two federal agents in identical blue suits were sitting at the same desk, talking on separate telephones. Bloom closed the door behind him, shutting them from view.

"Tweedledum and Tweedledee," he said, pulling a face. "They're running this place like a bookie's wire room, on the phone day and night. Wait'll the city gets the bill for all those long distance calls. Think it'll stand up?'' he asked, nodding toward the will.

"Well . . . maybe not all of it. She must've had *some* kind of advice before she wrote it, or else she looked at someone else's will as a model, had it properly witnessed, all that. But I wouldn't go spending my share of that trust money if I were Konig.''

"Why not?''

"I'm assuming the trust hasn't kicked out yet. If it had . . .''

"Kicked out?''

"Terminated. If it had, if Vicky was *already* in possession of the accumulated income and principal, she wouldn't have made reference to the trust at all. Her bequest would have been covered by the 'real and personal property' in the first clause.''

"She wasn't a lawyer, you know.''

"Granted. But I think I'm fairly safe in assuming the termination date would have been sometime *after* she wrote this will. And that's where the problem may arise. For both Konig *and* his daughter.''

"How so?''

"I don't know the terms of the trust agreement. I *do* know that unless the grantor . . .''

"Miller.''

"According to this, yes. 'A trust created by my father Dwayne Robert Miller in the year 1965.' ''

"Think it actually exists?''

"I would guess so. But unless it makes specific provision for Vicky to appoint alternate beneficiaries in the event of her death . . . well, I just don't know. I'd have to see the instrument. It's safe to say that the grantor or settlor of a trust—the man *creating* it—is the only one who can decide when and how the income and principal are to be distributed. *Unless* the power of appointment is there.''

"We're talking about millions here, you know.''

"How do you figure that?''

"The orange groves alone, from what you told me, could be worth at least *four* million.''

"That's right, but . . .''

"So even forgetting the motels and the rest of the shit,

Konig's share would come to a flat million. That's a nice piece of change.''

"Provided all that property is part of the trust."

"What do you mean?"

"We don't *know* what Miller put into that trust. The principal could have been a worthless gold mine in the Yukon, and the income on it over the years could have amounted to zero.''

"I'm betting all the other stuff is in it.''

"Not according to Konig. He says Miller put all of Vicky's earnings into his own bank account.''

"That's *Konig's* story, but what's *Miller's?*'' I sure would love to have a look at that trust instrument. Is there any way I can get my hands on it?''

"You can ask for a court order, can't you?''

"On what grounds?''

"You're investigating a homicide . . .''

"Sure, and a million bucks is motive enough for murder, isn't it?''

"Exactly.''

"But will a judge see it that way?'' Bloom shook his head. "I doubt it. He'll want to know how I can assume motive if I don't yet know what the trust *says*. I'll explain that I won't *know* what the trust says until I have access to the instrument itself. He'll say, 'You have no reasonable cause, petition denied,' and that'll be that.''

"Want *me* to take a shot at it?''

"How would you do any better?''

"My client's named in a will that refers back to a trust. It's reasonable to assume his inheritance may depend upon the provisions of that trust.''

"Mm,'' Bloom said.

"What's Miller's address?''

"He's on Manakawa Farms Road. You take the first left after you pass the City Limits sign. That's at the stop light on 41—where you'd ordinarily take a right to go to the beach, okay? He's, oh five or six miles outside of town.''

"Left at the stop light,'' I said. "Manakawa Farms Road.''

"Yeah, he's got a mailbox painted guess what color?''

"Any name on it?''

"Just numbers. Three-twenty-four. Think you'll learn anything?"

"It's worth a try," I said.

If you follow Route 41 south out of Calusa, you should arrive in Manakawa a half-hour later. Manakawa is only seventeen miles away, but during the season it might just as well be seventeen *hundred;* it took me the better part of an hour to get to the outskirts of town, and then another twenty minutes to locate Miller's orange groves out on Manakawa Farms Road, near the construction in progress for the proposed Interstate. I might have missed the mailbox painted in bright orange with the numerals 324 on it in black, and the narrow dirt access road leading into the property, had I not been alerted by miles and miles of orange trees planted in neatly spaced rows. The temperature the night before had risen to a comparatively sweltering thirty-four degrees (a little over one degree Celsius, which damn system we will *never* get used to here in America), but the smudge pots were still standing under the trees, ready to be ignited in the event of another sudden freeze.

A half-dozen cement-block buildings painted white formed a sprawling architectural complex at the farthest end of the access road. I parked the Ghia alongside a pickup truck painted orange and lettered in black with the words MILLER GROVES. Three long low steps led to a screened-in porch attached to the largest building. I opened the screen door and crossed the porch to a wooden door that opened into the building proper. A young girl in her twenties was sitting behind a desk, typing and chewing gum. She looked up as I came into the room.

"Hi," she said.

"I'm Matthew Hope," I said, "I'm looking for Mr. Miller."

"Out in the groves just now," she said. "Want to have a seat?"

"How long will he be, do you know?"

"Checking to see was there any damage last night," she said. "Shouldn't be too much longer, he's been out there quite a while now."

"I guess I'll wait outside," I said. "Get a little sun."

"You'll get the sun and the cold *both,*" she said.

"Little warmer than yesterday, though."

"Not much. Supposed to get only to the high fifties. That ain't so warm at all."

"Well," I said, "think how bad it is anyplace else."

"That's for sure," she said.

I nodded pleasantly and then went outside again, wondering as I crossed the screened-in porch just how long it had been since I'd gone native. *Think how bad it is anyplace else.* Jesus! In the distance another orange-colored pickup truck was coming up a dirt road that ran between the trees, raising a great cloud of dust behind it. I leaned on the fender of the Ghia and waited.

Dwayne Miller was wearing a ten-gallon straw hat, a blue denim jacket, blue jeans, and brown cowboy boots with white leather inserts. He seemed taller than I remembered him, but perhaps that was an illusion caused by the high crown of the hat. He saw me from the cab of the truck, but made no sign of acknowledgment as he cut the engine, opened the door, and climbed down. He was looking at the ground as he came toward the porch.

"Mr. Miller?" I said, and he glanced up. "Matthew Hope, I was at the funeral yesterday."

He studied my face. His eyes were as intensely dark as his daughter's had been, a brown almost the color of coal. His brows were as black as the sideburns showing beneath the brim of the hat. His nose qualified him at once for a member of the pig family, bulbous and somewhat tip-tilted, with overlarge nostrils.

"I don't remember you," he said.

"I was with Detective Bloom."

He kept studying me. "What is it you want?" he asked.

"I was a friend of Vicky's."

"So?"

"I'm an attorney," I said.

"*Her* attorney?"

"No, but . . ."

"Then what do you want here? Mr. Hope, is it? What do you want here, Mr. Hope? This is a place of business. We grow oranges and we sell 'em by the bushel. Did y'wish to buy some oranges, Mr. Hope?"

His tone was broadly sarcastic, his eyes burning with what

seemed unwarranted animosity. I did not know the man, this was our first meeting; I could not imagine why he was being so rude.

"Tony phoned a little while ago," he said, "told me you might be stopping by."

"Ah."

"Told him there wasn't no damn will I knew of, said his lawyer would be stopping by to ask me about it, anyway. I'm telling you the same thing, Mr. Hope. There wasn't no will."

"How do you know?"

"Vicky would've told me. I saw her Thursday night, she'da mentioned it then."

"Why *then*, Mr. Miller?"

" 'Cause it was plain to see she was worried to death about something. Knew what was coming, you ask me. Could see it plain as day on her face. Fear. Like when she was a little girl and it thundered and lightened. D'run under the bed, lay there facedown with her eyes shut, her hands clasped behind her head, sobbing and trembling. Same thing last Thursday night. Not crying or shaking, not anything like that, no, but this *fear* on her face when we were talking about the opening. I warned her against it, warned her myself, but she wouldn't listen."

"What'd you say to her, Mr. Miller?"

"Told her she was makin a mistake, openin at that little dive out there on Stone Crab. She was a *star!* A star don't go singin in a goddamn bar's part of a restaurant! I warned her. Told her I'd disown her if she went ahead with it. Wouldn't listen. Stubborn damn little bitch, same as when she was little. Coulda killed her sometimes. Just like her mother. Stubborn as a mule."

"What'd you have in mind, Mr. Miller?"

"I don't follow you," he said.

"When you told her you'd disown her?"

"I don't see as that's any of your business, is it?"

"Were you thinking of the trust?"

His eyes opened wide. He stared at me speechlessly for several moments, trying to decide whether I was bluffing. He must have figured at last that I did in fact know about the trust and there'd be no point denying its existence.

"Couldn't have had it changed, anyway," he said, "it's an

irrevocable trust. But she didn't know that. I was jess tryin to scare her is all, put a little pressure on her. How'd *you* know about it?''

"Her will," I said. "It refers back to the trust."

"Thought you didn't know if there *was* a will or not."

"I didn't say that, Mr. Miller."

"*Tony* damn well said it."

"Was Vicky in fact the beneficiary of that trust?"

"The trust is none of your business," Miller said, and took off his hat, and wiped the sweatband with his handkerchief. His hair, I noticed, was going gray on top. He looked suddenly much older. He put the hat on his head again, returned the handkerchief to the back pocket of his jeans, looked me dead in the eye, and said, "Let me make something clear, Mr. Hope. I don't own *nothin* in my own name 'cept my house. Everything else—the groves, the motels I got on the Trail, the securities— all of it's owned by the trust. Vicky was only nineteen when she got started in the music business, hit it big when she had no more sense about money than a toad. Just like her mother. I set up that trust to protect her, make sure she wouldn't end up like some of them other rock stars, you know the ones I mean, poppin pills and killin themselves or else enterin their middle years without a pot to piss in. Your average life of a rock star is maybe four or five years, Mr. Hope, six or seven if they're lucky. I didn't want my little girl endin up in the shithouse when she got to be in her thirties. Now that's all you need to know."

"Mr. Miller," I said, "Vicky's will leaves the trust principal and income three-quarters to Allison and one-quarter to Vicky's former husband, Anthony . . .''

"Don't make me laugh," Miller said.

"I didn't write the will, she did."

"How can she give away what's in a trust she didn't make? You're a lawyer, ain't you? You know damn well the man *creating* the trust is the only one can decide how and when the income and principal's to be distributed."

"She *was* beneficiary of the trust, wasn't she?"

"Of *course* she was. But . . .''

"Well, if the trust had already terminated, the principal would be hers to do with as she . . .''

"It *hasn't* terminated."

"When *does* it terminate?"

"That's none of your business."

"If it terminated before her death, it's very much my business. Your daughter has settled a quarter of the principal on Anthony Konig. That means if the money was *already* hers, a quarter of it . . ."

"Are you trying to steal all this for your client?" Miller asked, opening his arms wide to encompass the acres and acres of orange trees. "What I worked my life buildin for the time Vicky got old enough to manage it herself?" He shook his head. "Ain't no way you're goin to do that, mister."

"I'm not claiming Mr. Konig has the right to *anything* just yet . . ."

"Oh, just *yet*, huh? When *do* you plan to make such a claim, Mr. Hope?"

"After I see that trust instrument. And then only if . . ."

"Be a cold day in hell when you do that, mister."

"If the trust was in fact terminated before your daughter wrote her will."

"It *wasn't*, I told you."

"Or if provision was made in the trust for her to designate alternate beneficiaries . . ."

"There's no such provision."

"How can I know that for sure unless I see the instrument itself?"

"You take my word for it."

"Where a quarter of the principal and income is concerned? There's no way I could do that and still remain faithful to my client's interests."

"Then you can go straight to hell, Mr. Hope, because that trust is none of your damn business, and you ain't going to see it, *period*."

"A judge may disagree with you."

"What?"

"My client is named in a will that refers back to that trust. I can file suit to recover . . ."

"There's no court in the world would listen to . . ."

"Yes, there is, Mr. Miller. It's called the Calusa County Circuit Court, and that's where I'd go to ask for a declaratory judgment determining my client's rights in connection with that trust. At the same time, I'd serve you with a request for production, demanding inspection and copying of the trust instrument.''

"No court would grant you that.''

"I don't *need* a court to grant it. Upon commencement of my action, I can make my request without leave of the court.''

"Then you just go do that, Mr. Hope.''

"Your attorney may not want me to go to all that trouble, Mr. Miller. Are you sure you don't want to talk to him first?''

"You go talk to him yourself, you feel like making a long distance call. Man who drew the trust papers was David Haythorn, in N'Orleans, where we were livin at the time. You want his phone number, too?''

"I can find it, thanks. Good day, Mr. Miller.''

He did not answer. He went up onto the porch instead, and slammed the screen door behind him.

Before leaving the office, I'd asked Cynthia to call the *Herald-Tribune* for a copy of last Saturday's paper, the one carrying Jean Riverton's review on Vicky's opening the night before. It was waiting on my desk when I got back, together with a list of people who'd called while I was out. I glanced briefly at the list, and then scanned the index on the front page of the paper. The review was on page twelve of Section E. It read:

My music was swing.

I grew up in the era of the Big Bands. My feet tapped to the rhythms of Benny Goodman and Charlie Barnet. My soul responded to the sweet harmonies of Glenn Miller and Claude Thornhill. My heart soared with Harry James's trumpet or Artie Shaw's clarinet. I can still hum note for note the theme songs of Charlie Spivak, Glen Gray, Vaughn Monroe, Duke Ellington—even Alvino Rey, who

played electric guitar long before the Beatles learned to plug a "chord" into an outlet. The female vocalists I idolized were Helen O'Connell and Kitty Kallen, Martha Tilton and Connie Haines, Betty Hutton and her sister Marion, the Andrews Sisters, the King Sisters, Doris Day when she was still with the Les Brown band. I loved swing. I *still* love swing.

Victoria Miller became a recording star in 1965, when

swing was dead and the Big Band Era buried. She made her reputation with what has been called in retrospect "hard rock" as opposed to "soft rock" or "acid rock" or "bubble gum rock" or, most recently, "punk rock." She recorded three albums and a handful of 45 rpm's during her brief career. The albums were million-copy sellers, the best known of which was the first—"Frenzy." She was backed by a group called Wheat, and the style that brought them all to fame and fortune can best be described as driving, tempestuous, raging—indeed "frenzied." Last night, in her opening at the beautiful Tropicana Lounge of the Greenery Restaurant, Victoria Miller decided to sing many of the songs popularized in the Big Band Era. The results were disastrous.

It was, I must admit, difficult to resist comparing Miss Miller's rendition of "You Belong to Me" with Jo Stafford's, her version of "Why Don't You Do Right?" with Peggy Lee's, her interpretation of "He's My Guy" with Helen Forrest's. But if comparisons are odious, then they should have been avoided at all costs; a repertoire should not have

been built upon songs well known in their original versions, and remembered only too dearly by many of Calusa's residents. Miss Miller's choice of material, rather than creating a mood of familiar relaxation in the company of old friends, reeked instead of condescension. Morever, her voice—well-suited perhaps to the blaring amplification of the rock style she exploited back in the sixties—seemed tiny and tinny as she struggled with such forties favorites as "I'll Get By," "Sentimental Journey," and "Serenade in Blue." She was somewhat, but only somewhat, more believable when singing "Thanks for the Boogie Ride" (But who can forget Anita O'Day backed by the Gene Krupa orchestra?) or "Tampico" (Again, is there anyone who would not have preferred the June Christy/Stan Kenton version?), but for the most part the performance lacked the presence, the vibrance, the sheer magic those singing stars of the forties brought to each and every one of their personal appearances. John Ruggiero accompanied her admirably and bravely on piano. I suspect he may have wished he were back on the stage of the Helen Gottlieb.

I closed the newspaper.

I had never read a more devastating review from Jean

Riverton—or, come to think of it, *anyone*—in my entire life.
I could understand why she might have felt Vicky shouldn't
have invaded turf sacred to many of Calusa's pentagenarians,
but *Jesus*, did she have to rip her to shreds besides? I remembered the conversation Melanie Simms had overheard, and I
wondered now if the token insertion of a few rock-and-roll
numbers might have satisfied Jean's raging indignation. I
doubted it. One thing was certain: Jim Sherman had been
right on target when he'd objected to Vicky's choice of
material, and I suspected he would not have waited very long
before telling her she was through at the Greenery. Was that
actually what he'd meant when he'd said, "Lady, you are
dead"? I could not imagine him engaged in the sort of brute
violence that had killed her. But on the other hand, a negative
Jean Riverton review had been known to close the bravest of
endeavors. I remember the handful of people in the lounge on
the night I'd been there. A great big bundle of money was
invested in the Greenery, and if all of it went down the drain
because Vicky's appearance there had given the place a bad
name—

I didn't want to think about it; that was Bloom's job.

I picked up the phone and began doing *my* job.

Directory Assistance for New Orleans gave me a listing for
a David Haythorn at One Shell Square. It was close to five
o'clock when I dialed his number. I told the woman who
answered the phone that I was calling long distance, and she
put me right through.

"Mr. Haythorn," I said, "this is Matthew Hope, I'm an
attorney here in Calusa, I wonder if I may prevail upon your
time for a few minutes."

"Yes?" he said, cautiously.

"I'm representing a man named Anthony Konig . . ."

"Oh, yes," he said.

"Sir?"

"I didn't place your name for a moment. Dwayne Miller
said I might be expecting a call from you."

"Yes, sir, I saw him just a little while ago."

"So he told me."

"Then you know what this is about."

"More or less."

"And I needn't bother filling you in."

"It's about the trust, as I understand."

"Yes, sir."

"As it might concern your client."

"Yes, that's right."

"I told Mr. Miller we had nothing to hide here, and that I'd have no objection to discussing the provisions of the trust with you. That seemed to me the only way of satisfying you that your client would have no claim to the principal or accumulated income now that Miss Miller is dead."

"I'm making no such claim yet, sir."

"Well, from what I understand, you were waving lawsuits in my client's face, and threatening to . . ."

"Only if I couldn't gain access to the trust instrument in any other way."

"You can have access anytime you like. We have nothing to hide here."

"Mr. Miller told me that his daughter was beneficiary of the trust . . ."

"Well, I don't wish to discuss that on the phone, Mr. Hope."

"He's already *told* me this, it isn't something I'm trying to . . ."

"I still would rather not discuss it."

"Assuming she *was* beneficiary . . ."

"Mr. Hope, really, this *isn't* something easily discussed on the telephone."

"Why not?"

"A trust is a complicated thing, as I'm sure you're aware . . ."

"Yes, Mr. Haythorn, I'm familiar with trusts."

"I wouldn't want any misunderstandings concerning this *particular* trust. There's been a murder committed, there's been a kidnapping, I wouldn't want the trust misinterpreted as a possible . . ." He cut himself short.

"A possible *what?*" I said.

"I would prefer not discussing this on the phone."

"I wish you could see your way clear to do that, sir."

"No, I don't believe that would be in the best interests of my client."

"It would save me a trip to New Orleans."

"I'm sure there are flights from Calusa."

"I'm not sure they're all that frequent."

"I have no other suggestion to make."

"Other than my coming to New Orleans, is that it?"

"That's it, Mr. Hope."

"You're making this difficult for me, Mr. Haythorn, and I'm wondering why."

"As I told you earlier, we have nothing to hide here. But if you want to see the trust instrument, it'll have to be here in my office."

"I'll be there tomorrow," I said. "Let me call you back as soon as I've checked the flight schedules."

"Fine, I'll expect your call," he said. "I'll be here another hour or so."

The moment I hung up, I remembered that I had to pick up Joanna after school tomorrow. I wondered how she might react to a trip to New Orleans for the weekend. Knowing my daughter, I guessed she would be ecstatic about the idea. I checked my calendar. I had a closing at ten tomorrow, and a lunch date at noon. Joanna did not get out of school until three-fifteen, provided she didn't have Choir or Soccer or something. I buzzed Cynthia and asked her to check the airline schedules to New Orleans, reminding her of my various commitments, and she got back ten minutes later to report my best bet would be National's 127 out of Calusa at 3:10 p.m., connecting with National's 25 out of Miami, arriving in New Orleans at 6:08. I told her to book two coach seats, and then I called St. Mark's and asked to talk to Joanna's adviser there. The woman's name was Isabel Reed. She sounded harried and a trifle annoyed that I was detaining her from an imminent departure for a gallery opening. I explained that I would be taking my daughter to New Orleans with me over the weekend, but that it would entail catching a three-ten flight, which meant I would have to take her out of school at least an hour before then so that we could—

"Why don't you take a later flight?" Miss Reed asked.

"Because I have an appointment in New Orleans," I said. I did not yet have an appointment with David Haythorn, and I wasn't yet sure he'd be willing to see me after such a late arrival, but first things first.

"Why don't you take a later flight," Miss Reed said, "and make your appointment for the following day?"

"Because it's a business appointment, and the following day is Saturday," I said.

"Oh," she said.

"I'd like to pick her up at two o'clock," I said, "perhaps even a little before then, if possible."

"She has English at two o'clock," Miss Reed said.

"I'm sure she can make up the class," I said.

"English is her weakest subject," Miss Reed said.

"I'm sorry," I said, "but this is urgent."

"Well," she said.

"Thank you," I said.

I next called Haythorn again to tell him I'd be arriving in New Orleans at a little past six tomorrow night, and would appreciate it if he could see me shortly after that. He was, much to my surprise, entirely amenable to meeting with me so late in the day. He said he was staying in town for a dinner engagement, anyway, and would be happy to have me come to his office as soon as I could get there from the airport. I told him I'd be staying at the Saint Louis—which reservation I hadn't yet made—and that he could reach me there if there was any problem. He anticipated no problems.

Susan seemed to be her usual bitchy self when I called. She told me she was busy packing for her big weekend with Georgie Poole in the Bahamas, and Joanna wasn't home from school yet because she had Movie Club, and would I please make this brief. I told her I'd be taking Joanna to New Orleans with me tomorrow, and would she mind asking her to pack a bag for the weekend and to take it to school with her in the morning because we'd be going directly from St. Mark's to the airport.

"Yes, fine," Susan said, "is that it?"

"Please ask her to pack a dress because we'll be eating out, and I'd like her to . . ."

"I'll ask her to pack a dress."

"*And* a raincoat. New Orleans can . . ."

"A raincoat, yes, Matthew, if you don't mind, I *am* trying to . . ."

"And tell her I'll pick her up at two o'clock, I have Miss Reed's permission for her to cut English."

"English is her weakest subject," Susan said.

"So I've heard. Two o'clock, okay?"

"You're so fucking irresponsible," Susan said, and hung up.

Cynthia buzzed me almost the instant I put the phone back on the receiver. "It's Attorney O'Brien," she said, "on three."

I immediately pushed the lighted button in the base of the phone.

"Hello, Dale," I said.

"Hi," she said. "I want to take you to dinner tomorrow night. Are you free?"

I am, at the age of thirty-seven, too old not to be startled by today's liberated women. I had never been invited *out* to dinner by a female person before. I had been invited *in* to dinner, where I was served beef Bourguignon and red wine in a candle-lit nook off an artsy-craftsy kitchen, but never had I been invited *out*. Never.

"Matthew?" she said. "Are you there?"

"Yes, I'm . . . here. Right here," I said.

"Well, just say yes or no."

"I'm going to New Orleans tomorrow," I said.

"Oh, what *fun!*" she said. "Why don't I come with you?"

My silence now was almost palpable.

"Matthew?" she said.

"Yes, I'm still here."

"Would that be all right?"

"Well . . . my daughter'll be coming with me," I said.

"Would she mind?"

"No. I don't think so, but . . ."

"Where are you staying?"

"The Saint Louis."

"Good, I'll book a room. What flight are we on?"

"Are you serious?"

"Of *course*, I'm serious. In fact, I've been *looking* for an excuse to get out of this town for a while. What flight are we on?"

"I'll have my secretary book it for you. And the room, too, if you're really . . ."

"I am really," she said.

"Well, good. Hey, good," I said, smiling.

"Yeah, good," Dale said.

7

It was normally a twenty-minute ride from the New Orleans International Airport to the French Quarter, but the traffic on 61 was heavy, and our driver had to stop first at the Saint Louis Hotel on Bienville to drop off Joanna, Dale, and the luggage. The law offices of Foelger, Haythorn, Pelessier and Cortin were only half a dozen blocks away, but one-way streets in and out of the Quarter can pose problems of their own, and I did not get to Number One Shell Square until almost seven o'clock on Friday night.

The building was a monolithic monstrosity that occupied a full city block from Carondelet to St. Charles and Perdido to Poydras. Its entrance doors were on Carondelet, where the taxi dropped me, and access to them was gained first by climbing a short flight of steps to a landing some thirty feet across, at the outer edge of which was a standing, bronze-framed, ONE SHELL SQUARE marker, and then climbing another ten steps or so a second landing, and *yet* another ten steps to a third landing across which were the spaced doorways with their brown anti-glare glass. I felt rather as if I were climbing pyramids along the Nile. In the lobby a Burns Security guard sat inside a waist-high, oval counter fashioned of the same stone as the building itself, something that looked like a cross between marble and granite. He asked me if I was a Shell employee, and when I told him I wasn't, he pulled back the ledger he had been in the process of offering, and asked me to sign my name in a second book instead. He told me to make sure I signed out when I left, and then gratuitously pointed out the location of the elevator bank. I stopped at the wall directory first, found a room number for Foelger, Haythorn, Pelessier and Cortin, and then took the elevator up to the seventh floor.

There was no one sitting behind the desk in the ultra-modern reception area with its white Formica desk and its dark blue carpet, its Mondrian print on the wall opposite the entrance doors, its modular sofas and easy chairs. But I heard a typewriter going someplace down the hall, and I found a harried secretary who seemed relieved I was offering her a brief respite from the tyranny of her machine and all those legal-sized pages scattered on her desk. She personally escorted me to a closed walnut door at the end of the hall, and then asked if I would like a cup of coffee. I told her I would not. I knocked on the door and a voice within said, "Yes, come in, please."

David Haythorn was perhaps seventy years old, a frail-looking man with surprisingly jet-black hair and stern brown eyes set in a face that resembled browned and weathered parchment. His office, like the reception area and the other offices I'd peeked into along the hall, was decorated in a severe contemporary style that made him seem like a lost soul transported from *Great Expectations* into *Star Wars*. I introduced myself, we shook hands, and he offered me a seat beside his desk.

"So," he said, "you're here to see the trust instrument."

"Yes, sir, I am."

"Would you like some coffee?"

"No, sir, thank you."

"You're wondering why I insisted you come *here* to see it."

"Considering I could have served Mr. Miller with a request for production . . ."

"Yes, if you'd brought suit. But you weren't ready to do that, Mr. Hope, were you? Not *really*, were you? You may have scared Dwayne, but we're both attorneys, so you can be honest with me. We have nothing to hide here."

Whenever anyone says that to me—and David Haythorn had said it three times on the telephone, and a fourth time just now—the thing I run to hide is the silverware. I smiled at him. He smiled back.

"Do you know the one about the ship that sinks in the middle of the Pacific?" he asked.

"No, sir, I don't believe so."

"Well, a doctor, a minister, and a lawyer are floating around out there in shark-infested waters, and the sharks promptly eat the doctor and the minister, but they leave the lawyer alone. Do you know why?"

"Why?"

"Professional courtesy," Haythorn said, and burst out laughing. His laugh, for such a frail-looking man, was surprisingly robust, as though somehow echoing his youthful head of hair. When at last he sobered, he said, "The reason I wanted you to look over the trust here in my office . . ."

"Yes, sir?"

"Was that I didn't want it misinterpreted. I thought we could discuss it quietly and calmly here, and in that way you wouldn't come to the conclusion I'm almost certain will at first occur to you."

"And what conclusion is that, sir?"

"Why, the conclusion that Dwayne Miller killed his own daughter."

I looked at him.

"Yes," he said.

"I see."

"Which, of course, is nonsense. And yet, the trust instrument might support such a supposition. Especially in view of the fact that no one has yet heard from the little girl's kidnapper."

"Which means *what* to you, Mr. Haythorn?"

"Which means that she, *too,* may be dead by now."

"I hope that isn't the case."

"Well, naturally, naturally, but the possibility nonetheless exists. And if the *primary* beneficiary of the trust is dead—as of course Miss Miller is—and if the *alternate* beneficiary were to die before the trust terminates, why, then I think you can see why a supposition of foul play just *might* pop into someone's head."

"Why is that, Mr. Haythorn?"

"Because in such an eventuality the accumulated income and principal would revert to the grantor. And the grantor, as you know, is Dwayne Miller."

"I see."

"Yes."

"Well."

"Yes."

"May I have a look at the instrument now?"

"Certainly. I simply wanted to forewarn you against any hasty judgment."

The trust instrument ran to twenty-eight pages, and it took me close to an hour to read through them carefully, making notes as I went along. Haythorn never so much as glanced at his watch during all that time, even though he'd told me on the phone that he had a dinner engagement here in town. When I turned the last page, he looked across the desk at me and said, "Well? What do you make of it?"

"It seems simple enough," I said.

"Oh, yes, for certain, a model agreement if I must say so myself. Except for the reinvested income, of course, but that was Dwayne's idea. I told him at the time that there'd be tax disadvantages, but he said he wanted the income to accumulate rather than have it distributed at regular intervals. He always thought of his daughter as something of a financial incompetent, insisted not a penny go to her till she reached the age of thirty-five, when presumably she'd have been wise enough to take care of it."

"When would that have been, Mr. Haythorn?"

"Well, that's another thing that could easily lead to a false conclusion."

"Why?"

"Because Victoria Miller would have been thirty-five years old on the twenty-second of January—that's next Tuesday, Mr. Hope."

"Are you telling me the trust would have terminated only *nine* days after she was murdered?"

"Yes, sir, but please don't jump to the obvious conclusion."

"Who's the trustee, Mr. Haythorn?"

"Cajun National."

"Here in New Orleans?"

"Yes, sir."

"Would they know the current value of the trust?"

"I'm sure they would, but I have the most recent statements, and I can tell you it's currently worth close to twelve million dollars."

"Twelve . . ."

"Yes, sir."

"Which Victoria Miller would have received on her thirty-fifth birthday next week."

"Precisely. And which, under the provisions of the agreement, her daughter—as alternate beneficiary—will *still* receive next week."

"Unless, as you suggested . . ."

"Yes, unless she's dead by then."

"In which case all of it reverts to Dwayne Miller."

"I'm afraid so."

He looked at my face.

"Ah," he said, "I knew *exactly* what you'd think."

"Mr. Haythorn," I said, "I don't want to keep you any longer, I know you have a dinner date. Thank you for your time." I hesitated. "Could you possibly have the instrument copied and sent to me? Or would that be too difficult?"

"Now that we've talked, I'd have no objection," he said. He grinned and added, "Anyway, if I *didn't* comply, you might serve me with a request for production."

"Thank you," I said.

We shook hands. I walked up the long corridor with its doors opening onto ultra-modern offices, and past the room where the secretary was still struggling with reams of legal-sized paper, her typewriter sounding like a tap dancer on Bourbon Street, and I thought about a trust created back in 1965 and a will drawn only two weeks ago, and I thought about little Allison Konig out there someplace, and wondered if she knew that twelve million dollars was riding on her life.

I was not very good dinner company.

We had chosen a restaurant called Chez Jacques on the Rue Dauphine, highly recommended but exorbitantly expensive. I had ordered the shrimp remoulade to start, and then the turtle soup, and next the Chateaubriand for two, which I was sharing with Joanna. I kept hearing her conversation with

Dale only as a background motif; in the foreground of my mind the words, "If Allison dies," echoed and re-echoed relentlessly.

"How's the steak, Joanna?"

"Terrific!"

"Here, try some of this zucchini."

If Allison dies, I thought, either Konig or Miller will come into a sudden twelve million dollars . . .

"Do you think you'd like to hear some jazz tonight?"

"I sure would! God, I love this city!"

"Is this your first time?"

"Yep, but Dad's been here once before."

If Allison dies *before* next Tuesday, when that trust terminates, then everything in it will go back to her grandfather, Dwayne Miller . . .

"Well, then, I'll have to give you both a guided tour. A little jazz tonight, either at Preservation Hall or Mo'Jazz, then maybe O'Brien's later on for a little raucous singing and yelling . . ."

"Terrific!"

"And then breakfast at Brennan's tomorrow morning, and a walk in the French Market afterward. In the afternoon, if you like, we can rent a car and go see some of the old plantations across . . ."

If Allison dies *after* next Tuesday, when all that money in the trust becomes legally hers, then her father—Anthony Konig—will without question inherit it from her . . .

According to Section 732.103 of the Florida Statutes, the estate of a person dying intestate (and six-year-old children cannot draw wills since they do not have testamentary capacity) would pass first to any surviving spouse (Allison was certainly not married) and next to a lineal descendant (Allison had no children), or, if there were no lineal descendants, then to the descendant's father and mother—or the *survivor* of them. Anthony Konig had survived Victoria Miller. If his daughter died anytime after that trust terminated next Tuesday, he would inherit twelve million dollars from her.

Either one of them, I thought, Konig *or* Miller, has a damn good motive for bloody murder. Depending on the timing, either one of them can easily come into twelve million dollars— *if* Allison dies.

I told the waiter I did not want any dessert. The check for the three of us came to a hundred and fifty-five dollars plus tip. I refused to let Dale pay it, even though she insisted this was the night she'd planned to take me out. I told her she could treat at Brennan's tomorrow morning, and then we thanked the maître d' for a splendid meal, and went out into the streets of the Vieux Carré.

I have to explain, first, my daughter's attitude toward the various women I've spent time with since the divorce. Joanna doesn't like them. Joanna, in fact, hates them. She has come well beyond hoping that her mother and I will ever reconcile and remarry, and has even abandoned the possibility that we may one day treat each other more graciously than we now do—but this doesn't mean she feels obliged to welcome any possible contender for her father's hand or heart, or behave toward any female competition with anything even remotely approaching civility. Joanna has been known to remain utterly silent throughout the course of a three-day sailing trip in the company of a rather nice (and completely bewildered and finally routed) young divorcée from Tampa, a painter I'd met at a one-woman show in Calusa. Since the divorce I've met a lot of women at gallery openings; there is something about the creative ambiance that is conducive to fortuitous first encounters. Joanna has had the distinct displeasure of meeting many of these ladies after I'd been seeing them awhile. Her reaction has never varied. She will treat them with disdain and make it abundantly clear from the word go that the prize in dispute is none other than Matthew Hope, her *daddy*, a treasure already owned and cherished, thank you very much, by a loving daughter. So bug off, sister.

I have to explain, next, the city of New Orleans.

If a person lives on the Eastern Seaboard and anywhere south of, let's say arbitrarily, the city of Memphis, Tennessee, then he does his shopping in Atlanta and his howling in New Orleans. Move a bit farther north, into the Carolinas and Kentucky, and nine times out of ten Richmond, Virginia, will be the stamping ground for Southern tourists itching to get away from all that Bible-thumping, if only for a weekend. Head even farther northward and then westward into the states of Ohio, Indiana, Missouri, Iowa, and Wisconsin, and the mecca will be Chicago—*my* kind of town, *my* home town, and never mind what my partner Frank has to say about it remaining ever and always the *second* city. According to Frank, New York is the mecca for *every place*, wherever you live, whatever your race, religion, or political persuasion. Frank believes that the United States of America ends just west of the Hudson River. But the fact remains that there are Southerners who've been to New Orleans a hundred or more times, and who have never *once* in their lives set foot on the island of Manhattan.

New Orleans is sheer magic.

Frank has never been there because he says he can fly to New York in less than three hours, so why should he bother making a *two*-and-a-half-hour trip—what with changing planes in Tampa—to a place perhaps only twelfth on the scale of desirable American cities? (He has never told me what the cities between number twelve and number one might be; all of us in the offices of Summerville and Hope, ho-hum, already *know* what number one is.) How can anyone explain New Orleans to a partisan New Yorker like Frank? How can anyone make him believe that this city is a microcosm of all the good things about the city he worships, combined with the best of San Francisco and yes, *even* Chicago, that wonderful town? How? Where would you begin?

How do you define a city that pronounces its French street names with a distinctive Southern flair, causing Chartes to become "Charters" and Burgundy to become "Bur-GUND-ee," transmogrifying Iberville to "EYE-bur-vill" and Bienville to "Bee-EN-vill"? How do you explain that the French Quarter consists of an almost perfect grid that is only six blocks wide by fourteen blocks long if you don't count the handful of streets on the bank of the Mississippi, but that within that mote of a metropolis there is more music, more blatant sex, more souvenir shops, more fine restaurants, more hotels, more antique shops, more flower carts, more neon, more Takee Outee Chinese food joints, more shoeshine boys and street performers and beautiful women than in any comparable stretch of turf in the United States?

The music spills from the open louvered doors of the bars and clubs into Bourbon Street itself, blocked to traffic and designed for strolling, hot jazz and cool jazz, Dixieland and country-Western, you name it, we've got it. Black teenage kids sit on the curbs lacing their tap shoes, and then get up to dance to the overflow music, feet flying and clicking on the asphalt, a sly grin at the hat sitting in the middle of the street, an insistent nod toward it if the quarters and dollar bills are too slow coming. The strip joints offer topless and bottomless girls, boys performing in drag, boys *and* girls doing their timeless number in what are billed as "authentic" sex shows, the barkers out front flicking open the doors every now and then to reveal for only a second the gyrating flesh on the bartop or the stage inside—"Call the cops," they shout, "there's a naked *lady* in here!"

The souvenir shops on Bourbon are a bazaar of T-shirts printed while you wait, bumper stickers similarly emblazoned, buttons denouncing or deriding, vibrators in every size and color ("Holy cow," Joanna said, looking into a shop window at one, "what's *that?*"), French ticklers, electrified ben-wa balls, inflatable lifesize rubber dolls, aphrodisiacs, beer mugs shaped like a woman's breast with a handle and a great big nipple. There are shops selling everything from open-crotch panties to panties you can *eat* should hunger overtake you in the midst of your ardor, studded leather collars and wristlets, a machine called "Suc-U-Lator," which when plugged into your automobile's cigarette lighter will make the drive back to Biloxi more pleasurable and interesting. There are shops on Royal Street selling chocolates and pralines, escutcheons and lead soldiers, leather-bound books and Indonesian puppets, antiques dating back to the Spanish and French colonial periods, elegant luggage and lingerie, silverware and clocks.

There are galleries showing contemporary abstractions, and cheap reproductions, and fine prints, and pictures by local artists favoring "shotgun" houses, wrought-iron balconies, flower carts, and jazz musicians. Surrounding Jackson Park, just on the edge of the muddy Mississippi, there are more portrait artists than could be flushed out of the Chicago Institute of Fine Arts on any given spring day, all of them sitting behind their easels and sketching in charcoal or pastel while their subjects sit unblinkingly (and a bit foolishly) as they try to ignore the gawking passersby. In the French Market there is fresh produce brought in from the surrounding countryside, oranges and apples and bananas and carrots and white potatoes and red potatoes and onions and green beans and yellow beans, a riot of color to rival the palettes of the portrait painters in the park.

And everywhere there is music. Everywhere in this city. Round a corner, and there will be a five-piece band blowing its brains out, trumpet and tenor saxophone, piano, drums and bass. Step off a curb, and there will be three kids blowing guitar, banjo, and washboard, singing a tune of their own composition, the guitar case open before them for voluntary contributions. There are lousy musicians and fine musicians here, and you will find them anywhere—on an island in the middle of one of the waterfront thoroughfares, traffic moving past on both sides as they blow "Basin Street Blues," or playing flute in the doorway of a shop on Canal Street, or strutting to the music of yet another musician strumming a ukulele outside a shop printing phony newspaper headlines; the music is interlocking and overlapping, incessant and insidious. There is no place in the entire world like New Orleans, and my partner Frank is missing a hell of a lot.

The city's magic, combined with the loveliness and charm of Dale O'Brien, caused my poor dear daughter Joanna to become a trembling, ecstatic wreck that Friday night. She had been her usual delightful self when I introduced her to Dale at the Calusa airport ("Yeah, hullo") and had maintained her familiar silence all the way to Tampa and then to New Orleans on the connecting flight. When I dropped the pair off at the hotel, Joanna gave me a stricken look of horror—was I actually leaving her *alone* with this woman, this *person*, this *threat* to her prior rights? At Chez Jacques, while the appetizers were being devoured by a starving trio who'd had to wait till nine o'clock for dinner, Joanna thawed somewhat, but I suspected this was only because I myself had usurped her normal mute stance.

By the time the entrées were brought, however, she and Dale were engaged in a lively discussion about the inadequacies of the Calusa public school system, and about how glad she was to be at St. Mark's. Much to my astonishment, I heard Joanna telling all about a Phys Ed instructor at Bedloe

who gave passing grades to his female students if they engaged in a little *extra*-extra-curricular activity in the room
where he kept his basketballs and all his *other* sports equipment. The timely arrival of the Chateaubriand rescued me
from any further insights into my thirteen-year-old daughter's
wisdom of the ways of the world. Dale led the conversation
into an outline of the itinerary she thought we should follow
in New Orleans, and my daughter listened somewhat breath-
lessly and starry-eyed. Before we left the restaurant, I was
sure she'd already fallen in love.

Strolling between them up Bourbon Street, the pair of them
lovelier than any man in the world had any right to be flanked
by, my daughter tall and blond and brown-eyed and gorgeous, Dale even taller and russet-haired and green-eyed and
equally gorgeous, I felt strangely like the fellow who turns
two's company into three's a crowd. Assailed by the sights
and sounds and smells, the music blaring from the doorways,
the glimpses of nudity, the cooking hot dogs and hamburgers
and egg rolls, the glare of the neon, the medley of voices and
laughter and song, I walked with Joanna on one side of me
and Dale on the other, their arms looped through mine, and I
felt oddly alone. Joanna chattered across me like a magpie,
pointing out anything she saw to Dale (not *me*), and Dale
reacted as though she were experiencing all of it for the first
time instead of the fifteenth, both of them involved in a very
personal mutual discovery that excluded me almost completely.

It was to Dale, for example, that Joanna pointed out the
foot-long flesh-colored vibrator in the window of the X-Rated-
Sex Shop, not *me*. It was to Dale, not *me*, that she directed a
learned discourse (read from a napkin at Mo'Jazz) on the
invention of the cocktail right here in the city of New Orleans
a hundred and sixty-five years ago by an apothecary named
Antoine A. Pechaud, who called in a *coquetier*, since bastard-
ized into the current word. It was with Dale that she joined in
the rowdy singing at O'Brien's ("No relation," Dale shouted
over the din) while I sat by twiddling my thumbs and sipping
my cognac because I have never, but *never*, enjoyed group
singing even if it is being led by a piano player whose
mirrored image slanting overhead can be seen by everybody
in a crowded-to-bursting room. It was Dale who put her arm

around my daughter's waist as we made our way back to the hotel at three a.m., Saturday morning already, all of us exhausted, Joanna's eyelids beginning to falter and droop, her head tilting in to rest against Dale's body. I was happy for the rapport, but I felt miserably left out.

At the front desk in the lobby, I picked up a copy of the morning *Times-Picayune* and was walking toward the elevator behind Dale and Joanna when I saw the front-page story on Allison Konig. It said she had been found dead in Calusa, Florida, at eight-thirty p.m. on Friday night, January 18, in a drainage ditch on Belfast Avenue and Aspen Road. Her throat had been slit.

I tried reaching Bloom at his office at eight in the morning because it seemed to me—especially in light of Allison's death—that I now possessed information vital to the investigation. The police officer who took my long-distance call told me that Detective Bloom wasn't in yet and asked if I would care to leave a message for him. I told him this was urgent, and would he please call Detective Bloom at home and ask him to call me back in New Orleans at once. I gave him the number at the Saint Louis, but I was doubtful Bloom would ever get the message. The man on the phone sounded like one of those officious little bastards who make summary decisions based on how *they* believe an organization or a firm should be run; calling long distance was clearly against his principles, this staunch guardian of the City of Calusa purse strings. I stressed again the urgency of the situation, and he said he would make certain Detective Bloom got my message. I didn't believe him for a minute.

Directory Assistance gave me a listing for a Morris Bloom at 631 Avenida Del Sol on Calusa's mainland. I dialed the number and got no answer. I could not believe Bloom was off on a weekend jaunt the morning after Allison had been found dead. I dialed the number again and let it ring a dozen or more times before I hung up. A call to National Airlines informed me that I could catch a nonstop flight out of New Orleans at 2:35 p.m., arriving in Tampa at 4:51. The earliest connecting flight to Calusa would be on Eastern at 7:53, but I'd get home earlier if I simply took a limo from the airport in

Tampa. I asked Dale and Joanna whether they would like to stay over without me till tomorrow; Joanna seemed tempted. But the three of us boarded that mid-afternoon National flight, and indeed took the limo from Tampa, which dropped Joanna and me at the house, and then proceeded to take Dale home to Whisper Key. It was a quarter to seven when I tried Bloom's home again. A woman answered the phone.

"Hello," I said, "this is Attorney Hope, I'm trying to reach Mr. Bloom. Is he home?"

"No, he's at work," the woman said.

"Is this *Mrs.* Bloom?"

"Yes, it is."

"I'll try to reach him at the office, but if I miss him, would you please ask him to call me at home? I'll give you the number."

"Yes, just a minute," she said.

I waited while presumably she looked for a pencil and pad, and when she came back on the line I gave her my home number. As soon as she hung up, I dialed the Public Safety Building. My call was put through to Bloom at once.

"I've been trying to reach you in New Orleans," he said. "I just got your message a little while ago. Where are you now?"

"Home," I said.

"I guess you heard."

"I heard."

"Something, huh? You know the drainage ditch behind the Cushing Sports Arena? On Belfast and Aspen? Found her there last night, facedown in the water. Couple of kids necking in a parked car, the boy had to take a leak, he went over to the ditch, and there she was. Still wearing this long granny nightgown drenched with blood. The kid phoned us right away. What were you doing in New Orleans?"

"Looking at that trust instrument," I said.

"Oh?"

"I've got to talk to you, will you be there awhile?"

"Sure, come on down," he said.

He listened attentively as I reviewed for him the directives in Vicky's will, and then spelled out for him the terms of the

trust. Every now and then he nodded. When I told him the
trust would terminate in three days, he raised his shaggy
eyebrows in response. When I further explained that the
twelve million dollars in that trust would—now that Allison
was dead—revert to Dwayne Miller, he made a small cluck-
ing sound and then nodded again. I waited. He began pacing
the office. He turned to me at last and said, "From what you
just told me, if Allison had survived past Tuesday, Anthony
Konig would've got a quarter of all that money, is that
right?"

"According to Vicky's will, yes."

"Which is a legal and binding will."

"Legal and binding, yes."

"And if she'd died *after* that, Konig would've got the
whole shebang."

"Yes."

"So you're assuming that since somebody conveniently
killed her *before* Tuesday, and since Dwayne Miller now
stands to get all that money *back,* then the person who killed
her has to be Miller. Is that it?"

"I'm suggesting it as a possibility."

"Mm. Well, Matthew, let me ask you some questions.
One, are you familiar with F.S. 732.802?"

"No, I'm not."

"I know it by heart, one of the first sections I learned when
I moved down here. Here it is: *732.802. Murderer. A person
convicted of the murder of a decedent shall not be entitled to
inherit from the decedent or to take any part of his estate as a
devisee.*"

He looked at me.

"So?" I said.

"So if Miller *did* kill Vicky and his granddaughter, under
732.802 he wouldn't inherit a rat's ass."

"Wrong," I said.

"Wrong?"

"Wrong. A trust isn't a will. This has nothing to do with
inheritance, Miller's not *inheriting* anything from anybody.
The money is simply *reverting* to him."

"Mm," Bloom said. "Okay, so let's keep him up there as
a possibility for the time being. But why eliminate Konig?"

"Because unless his daughter survived past Tuesday that money in the trust . . ."

"Sure, but did *he* know that?"

"What do you mean?"

"Let's take this a step at a time, okay? Number one: let's assume Konig *knew* he'd been named in Vicky's will."

"Back up just a bit," I said. "In order to assume that, we've got to figure he talked to her *after* he received her letter."

"Why?"

"Because the letter proposes guardianship of Allison as a new idea. I think it came as fresh news to Konig."

"Okay. So he got the letter, and when he came down here to see her on Saturday, he said, 'Listen, Vicky, this is swell about wanting me to have custody of our daughter, but have you taken any legal steps to *insure* that I get her?' And she tells him all about the will she wrote, and about him getting custody of their daughter's person and property and, oh, by the way, you'll *also* inherit a quarter of the money in the trust. How does that sit with you, Matthew?"

"Fine, go ahead."

"Number two: Konig's got to know there's a trust. He was once married to her, after all, they *must've* discussed it. And he probably knew the trust would terminate once Vicky reached age thirty-five. I'm assuming he *also* had to know her birthday was the twenty-second of January. And I'm *further* assuming he knew there was a sizable amount of money in that trust. But—and this is the big *but*, Matthew—did he know that in the event of little Allison's death, all that money would go back to Miller? I'm guessing he didn't."

"On what basis?"

"You told me a little while ago that Miller thought his daughter was a nitwit where it came to money. So why would he have given her any of the intimate details of the trust? No way. I figure him for a redneck who thinks women are just supposed to smile and look pretty and not bother their empty little heads about matters best left to men. All that Southern macho bullshit, you know what I mean?"

"I still don't see where you're going."

"Here's where I'm going. If Konig *didn't* know the twelve

million bucks was going back to Miller in the event of the little girl's death, he *might* have believed *he'd* be the one to get it as her natural father. That's the law, isn't it?''

''That's the law.''

''So maybe he figured the money would *first* become part of Vicky's estate, and *then* part of Allison's, and he'd be standing next in line with his hat in his hands.''

''Maybe.''

''In which case, he *still* looks like real meat.''

''Maybe.''

''Only one way to find out about *both* these ginks,'' Bloom said, ''and that's to bring them in here and do a dog and pony act.''

He did not have to send anyone to pick up Anthony Konig at the Breakwater Inn because Konig was waiting impatiently in the outside office. He told Bloom at once (and I'm not sure Bloom believed him; I know *I* had my doubts) that he hadn't bought a newspaper this morning, and he hadn't watched television or heard a radio until just a half-hour ago, when there was a news report on his car radio while he was driving to dinner. He'd come here immediately and was advised that Bloom was in a meeting and asked if he would mind waiting. He had told me on more than one occasion exactly how he felt about Detective Morris Bloom, and it was plain now that he was smoldering with rage over the indignity of having been asked to *wait* when he was here to talk about his daughter's murder.

''Where is she now?'' he demanded. ''Why wasn't I notified?''

''We tried to reach you at the Breakwater last night,'' Bloom said. ''You weren't there. We've been trying to reach you all day today, too, still no answer in your room. Where were you, Mr. Konig?''

He hesitated.

''Let's go find a nice quiet place where we can talk, okay?'' Bloom said, scowling at the typewriter clacking away at sixty words a minute across the reception area. ''Captain's office should be empty,'' he said, and led us past an American flag in a floor stand, to where a pair of doors stood at right

angles to each other in a small alcove. He opened the door on
our left, and we went into the room. I had been in this office
before, when the son of a client named Jamie Purchase
confessed to three murders he hadn't committed. There was a
desk on the wall opposite the door, a green leatherette swivel
chair behind it. On the paneled wall above the desk there
were several framed diplomas. Bookshelves behind the desk,
a hookah pipe on the top shelf. Framed photos of women I
guessed were the captain's wife and daughters. Konig looked
around the office as though expecting a trap.

"Sit down, Mr. Konig," Bloom said. "Make yourself
comfortable." He went behind the desk and sat in the swivel
chair. Konig and I took seats opposite him. "I've got to ask
you some questions," Bloom said, "so I think we'd better
make this all legal and proper." He took a deep breath. "In
keeping with the 1966 Supreme Court decision in *Miranda* v.
Arizona, we are not permitted to ask you any questions
until . . ."

"Just a minute here," Konig said, his face beginning to
flush. "What *is* this?"

"The questions I'm going to ask you have to do with the
murders of your former wife and daughter, Mr. Konig. What
I'm about to explain to you . . ."

"Am I under arrest here?"

"No, sir."

"Then . . ."

"Mr. Konig," Bloom said flatly, "talk to your attorney."

"You needn't answer any questions if you don't want to,"
I said. "Mr. Bloom was just about to advise you of your
rights, and that's one of them."

"Well . . . *should* I answer his questions?"

"That's entirely up to you. Why don't you hear your rights
first?"

"Well, all right, go ahead," Konig said.

"Fine," Bloom said, and began his recitation once again.
Konig listened intently, telling Bloom all along the way that
he understood what was being said.

". . . right to consult with an attorney before or during
police questioning."

"I understand."

"If you decide to exercise that right, but do not have funds with which to hire counsel, you're entitled to have a lawyer appointed, without cost, to consult with you before or during questioning. Do you understand all that?"

"I do. And God bless America."

"Sir?"

"I can just imagine how this'd be handled in Russia," Konig said.

"Yeah, well," Bloom said. "Do you wish to have an attorney present while I question you?"

"My attorney's already here."

"You're willing to have Mr. Hope present as your attorney?"

"I am."

"Fine then. Mr. Konig, can you tell me where you were yesterday between four-thirty p.m. and midnight?"

"Why those particular times?" Konig asked.

"Because the Medical Examiner has estimated the time of your daughter's death as approximately six p.m., and because a police officer visited your hotel last night at midnight, after we'd tried calling you repeatedly and unsuccessfully, and he asked the security officer there to unlock your room and you weren't in it."

"That's right, I was out."

"Out where, Mr. Konig?"

"With a friend."

"Who was the friend?"

"A lady friend."

"What's her name?"

"I don't know."

"You don't know . . ."

"I know her first name. I don't know her full name."

"Okay, what's her first name?"

"Jenny."

"But you don't know Jenny *what*."

"No."

"Do you know where she lives?"

"Yes."

"Where?"

"I can take you to the house, but I don't know the address."

"Were you there last night, Mr. Konig?"

"Yes."

"From when to when?"

"We got there at a little before six."

"And when did you leave there?"

Konig hesitated.

"Mr. Konig. When did you . . . ?"

"This evening. I was heading back to the hotel when I heard the . . . the news about Allison on my car radio."

"So you were with this woman from just before six last night to . . . what time would you say tonight?"

"About six."

"Twenty-four hours."

"Yes. About twenty-four hours."

"Did you leave the house at any time during those twenty-four hours?"

"No."

"Neither of you left the house?"

"We were both there all that time."

"Neither of you left the house and drove to Belfast Avenue and Aspen Road, to the drainage ditch behind the . . ."

"Mr. Bloom," I said.

He turned to look at me.

"If I'm here as Mr. Konig's attorney, I think I'll have to object to that last question."

"Right," he said, "sorry. Mr. Konig, I'll be asking you about how we can find this mysterious lady later on, we'll probably want you to take us there so we can talk to her, if you think you can find the house again, wherever it is."

"It's near the Beachview Shopping Plaza, I'm sure I can find it again."

"Good, we'll worry about that later. Meanwhile, you keep trying to remember her last name, will you? It might save us a lot of trouble."

"I never *knew* her last name, it's not a question of trying to *remember* it."

"Where'd you meet this woman, Mr. Konig?"

"In the bar at the Breakwater. The Buoy Five Lounge."

"This was . . . when did you say it was?"

"About five-fifteen or thereabouts."

"Went down for a drink, did you?"

"Yes."

"Alone?"

"Yes."

"And met this woman whose name is Jenny."

"That's right."

"And then you drove to her house and spent the next twenty-four hours with her."

"Yes."

"In bed, Mr. Konig?"

"Much of the time, yes."

"Was she a prostitute, Mr. Konig?"

"Yes, I believe so."

"Well, did you *pay* her for her services, or were they free?"

"I paid her. But she didn't *ask* for any money."

"I see, okay. Mr. Konig, when did you get the letter your former wife sent you? I'm referring to the one where she mentioned wanting you to have custody of your daughter in case anything happened to her."

"Last week sometime."

"When last week?"

"Thursday or Friday, I don't remember exactly."

"Well, the letter was written on the seventh, which was a Monday . . ."

"I don't know when it was written."

"That was the date on the letter, Mr. Konig."

"Well, fine, if you say so."

"So let's assume it took two, three days at most to get to New Orleans . . ."

"Mr. Bloom," I said.

"Yes, yes, all right, Mr. Hope, okay. You don't remember exactly when you got the letter, is that it, Mr. Konig?"

"I told you. It was either Thursday or Friday."

"That would've been either the tenth or the eleventh."

"If those are the dates, yes."

"Those are the dates."

"Then yes."

"Did you talk to your former wife at any time between receiving the letter and the night of her murder? That would've been Sunday night, January thirteenth, Mr. Konig."

"Yes, I did."

"When did you talk to her?"

"On Saturday night. When I went to see her."

"At the Greenery?"

"Yes."

"And you had already received her letter by then."

"Yes."

"So you knew she wanted you to have custody of your daughter in case anything happened to her."

"Yes, I knew."

"Did you discuss that at any time Saturday night?"

"No."

"What *did* you talk about?"

"Her performance, and the bad review she'd got in that morning's paper. And Allison . . . she was supposed to be spending the Washington's Birthday weekend with me, we talked about that awhile. And . . . well, yes, custody, I suppose. She'd mentioned custody in her letter, so I thanked her and told her I appreciated her confidence in me."

"Did you discuss her will?"

"Her will? No, sir."

"You did not discuss a will she wrote on January fourth, three days before she sent that letter about custody?"

Konig turned to look at me.

"*Is* there a will?" he asked. "Have you found a will?"

"Yes," I said.

"Well, what does it *say?*"

"I beg your pardon, Mr. Konig," Bloom said, "but you haven't answered my question. Did you, on the night before your former wife was murdered, discuss her will with her?"

"I beg *your* pardon, Mr. Bloom," Konig said, "but I *did* answer your question. I told you we did *not* discuss a will, *her* will or anybody's else's."

"Did you know of the existence of such a will?"

"I did not."

"Weren't you curious?"

"No, I was not."

"Your former wife writes to you saying she wants you to have custody of your daughter in case anything happens, and you weren't concerned about whether she'd taken the legal steps to make this possible?"

"I figured the letter was all the piece of paper I needed. The letter clearly stated her intention, that was all I needed. I knew Mr. Hope here was her executor, I figured all I had to . . ."

"How did you know that?"

"What?" Konig asked.

"That Mr. Hope was her executor."

"Well, the . . . it said so in the letter."

"No, it didn't, Mr. Konig. I've read that letter a hundred times, it doesn't say anything about Mr. Hope being executor. It says you should *contact* him in case anything . . ."

"Well, that's what I assumed. That if I was supposed to contact a *lawyer* named Matthew Hope, then he was obviously the executor of her . . ."

Konig cut himself short. He looked first at Bloom and then at me. I said nothing.

"Executor of what?" Bloom asked.

"Her will."

"You just said you didn't know of the existence of a will."

"That's right."

"But you assumed Mr. Hope here was executor of a will you didn't know existed, is that it?"

"Well, you know what I mean."

"No, what do you mean? *Did* you know there was a will or *didn't* you?"

"I suppose, now that I think of it, I knew there was a will."

"How did you know?"

"Well . . . I suppose I asked Vicky about it. When we talked after the show that night."

"And she told you there was a will."

"Yes."

"Did she tell you what the will said?"

"Only that I was to have custody of my daughter's person and property."

"And that's all."

"Yes. Oh, wait a minute. She also mentioned that she was leaving the house and everything in it to Allison, and I should take good care of it for her."

"Uh-huh. What about the trust?"

"What trust?"

"The trust Dwayne Miller created in 1965."

"Why would I have asked her about the trust?"

"Did you know such a trust existed, Mr. Konig?"

"Well . . . yes, I did."

"Did you know that it would terminate this coming Tuesday?"

"I knew it was supposed to terminate when Vicky reached thirty-five."

"Which is this coming Tuesday, January twenty-second."

"If you say so."

"Well, you knew her *birthday,* didn't you?"

"I suppose I . . ."

"You were married to her for how many years?"

"Seven."

"So you must've known her birthday."

"Yes, I knew her birthday."

"You knew it was January twenty-second."

"Yes, I knew that."

"And you further knew that the trust terminated on that date."

"Yes."

"Did you know that you were to receive a quarter of the accumulated income and principal in that trust? Did Vicky tell you she'd left that to you in her will?"

Konig looked at me. He took a deep breath.

"Yes, I knew that," he said, "she told me that. But that doesn't mean . . ."

"Mr. Konig, please take your time before answering this next question. What did you think would happen to the money in that trust if Vicky died before the trust terminated?"

"I don't know. I never saw the trust."

"The trust instrument, do you mean?"

"Yes, I never laid eyes on it. Neither did Vicky. All we knew about it was what that crazy old . . . what her father had told her."

"And what was that?"

"That she would come into some money when she was thirty-five."

"Did he say how much money?"

"No."

"But you knew it had to be a sizable amount since her earnings as a big recording star . . ."

"I didn't know how much. It was my impression Dwayne

was socking *most* of that money into his own bank account. I told you, I never saw the trust, the trust *instrument,* and so I didn't know what he'd set aside for her. I only knew she was to get it when she reached the age of thirty-five."

"So you didn't know what would happen to the money if she happened to die before then."

"I didn't expect her to die before then."

"But she did."

"Yes, she did."

"So what did you *think* would happen to that money?"

"Vicky said it would go seventy-five percent to Allie, and twenty-five percent to me."

"That's what *Vicky* said. But what do you think the *trust* said?"

"I have no idea what the trust said."

"What did you think would happen to that money if Allison *also* died?"

"I don't know."

"Did you think it would go to Dwayne Miller?"

"I don't know."

"Or a cat hospital?"

"I don't know."

"Or do you think *you* would've got it, Mr. Konig?"

"I resent what you're implying, sir."

"What do you think I'm implying?"

"That I killed my own . . ." He stopped abruptly. "Mr. Hope, if I understood what was said to me earlier, I am not obliged to answer any questions if I choose not to. Is that right?"

"That's right."

"Can I stop the questioning now if I wish to?"

"Yes, you can."

"Then I would like to stop it."

"Fine," I said. "You heard him, Mr. Bloom."

"Okay," Bloom said. "Thank you, Mr. Konig."

"Can I go now?"

"First I'd like you to try finding that house for us. The one this woman Jenny . . ."

"Yes, I'll take you there."

"I'll call down for a car," Bloom said, and lifted the telephone receiver.

"Where's my daughter now?" Konig asked.

"At the morgue." Into the phone Bloom said, "Harry, I'll need a car, will you have it waiting downstairs for us in about ten minutes? Thanks," he said, and hung up.

"Where's the morgue?" Konig asked.

"Calusa General."

"Because I'll have to make funeral arr . . ." He cut himself short. "What are they doing to her there?" he asked. "Are they doing an autopsy?"

"Yes, they are."

"Are they allowed to do that?" Konig asked me. "Cut her up and . . ."

"Yes, sir," I said. "Under Section 406.11, an autopsy is mandatory when any person dies in a state of criminal violence."

Konig sighed and nodded his head. "Let's get this over with," he said, and rose ponderously.

Jenny lived on Avocado Way, in the black section of Calusa, across the tracks and just behind the Beachview Shopping Plaza, which apparently had been named by a visionary builder since it was fifteen miles from the nearest beach. The house Konig pointed out was a cinder-block structure with a gray shingle roof and shutters painted a bright red. A lamppost illuminated the mailbox, which was painted an identical red. There was no name on the box, just the number 479. We walked together to the front door, also painted red and flanked on either side by climbing bougainvillea. The Venetian blinds on the windows facing the street were closed. The house was dark. Bloom rang the doorbell. He rang it again. He rang it a third time. An elderly black man sitting on the porch steps of the house next door kept watching us. Bloom pressed the bell button yet another time.

"She doesn't seem to be home," he said, and looked at his watch. "What time did you say you picked her up in that bar Friday?"

"About a quarter past five," Konig said.

"Almost eight-thirty now," Bloom said, and shrugged. "Must be on the town with another John. Let's see what the guy next door has to say about her."

We crossed the lawn to where the black man was sitting under his porch light. Bloom showed his shield and his I.D. card, and introduced himself. The black man looked as if he were used to being hassled by policemen. His manner was deferential, but his brown eyes looked expectant and wary.

"Would you know who lives in the house next door?" Bloom asked.

"Yes, sir, that'd be Jenny," the man said.

"Jenny *who?* Would you know her last name?"

"Jenny Masters."

"Know where she is now?"

"Why? She done something?"

"No, nothing at all," Bloom said.

"P'lice always say somebody done nothing a'tall," the man said, "den next t'ing you know, they 'resting somebody."

"Nobody's going to be arrested," Bloom said. "Would you know where she is?"

"Wukkin," the man said.

"Where does she work?"

"Downtown. Club Alyce."

"On 301?"

"Thass d'place."

"Thank you," Bloom said.

"Don't make no fool of me now by 'resting her," the man said.

"No, no, nothing to worry about," Bloom said, and waved as we walked back to the unmarked sedan waiting at the curb.

"Where to?" the uniformed patrolman behind the wheel asked.

"Club Alyce on 301," Bloom said.

"Gonna glom you some tits, sir?" the patrolman asked.

"Sure, glom me some tits," Bloom said sourly.

Club Alyce was one of only a very few topless joints in all Calusa, which prides itself on being above such crass forms of entertainment. In addition, there are within the city limits three—count 'em, three—movie theaters showing pornographic (XXX-rated films as they are known here), and there once was a place selling marital aids and drug paraphernalia on the South Trail, but it was closed down by the police last August when they discovered the proprietor was *also* selling the stuff you *smoked* in all those pipes and roach holders. It has since been taken over by a man who sells take-out Chinese food, and maybe a little opium on the side, but the police don't know that yet. I'm not positively sure of it myself, in fact, but my daughter Joanna says that a junkie at Bedloe buys all his dope from the Hongkong House, as the place is called, and she is usually a reliable witness.

A neon sign outside Club Alyce announced TOPLESS DANCERS and a hand-lettered three-sheet on the front wall advised any potential customer that the place was open from seven p.m. to two a.m. A pickup truck was parked at the end of a row of cars outside, and a young girl with a mass of blond curls sat behind the wheel. She smiled invitingly as we pulled in beside her. The patrolman looked at the girl and then, grinning, asked, "Anybody want a quick blow job?"

"Sure, a quick blow job," Bloom said. "You wait out here."

"Sir?"

"I said you wait out here. I don't want everybody running for the exit the minute they see that uniform."

"Aw, Jeez, sir," the patrolman said.

We got out of the car, the patrolman sulking at the wheel, and walked toward the front door of the club. The door was painted an electric blue, and it opened into a dimly lighted hallway at the end of which a girl sat on a stool behind a high table. She was wearing a black leotard, black tights, black net stockings, and spike-heeled black patent-leather shoes. There was an open cash box on the table in front of her. A green light over her head washed down onto the bills in the box, making them look even greener than the United States Treasury had intended. The girl smiled as we approached.

"Hello, gentlemen," she said, "welcome to Club Alyce."

A sign on the wall behind her warned that a person had to be over eighteen years of age to enter the premises, and further advised that anyone offended by nudity ought not to venture inside.

"Are all you gentlemen over eighteen?" she asked coyly.

Bloom showed her his shield. "Police," he said curtly, and the smile dropped from her face. "We're looking for a woman named Jenny Masters. Is she here?"

"Why?" the girl asked. "What'd she do?"

"Why does everyone always want to know what someone *did*?" Bloom asked. "It's possible she witnessed an automobile accident, isn't it? It's possible she just inherited a million dollars. Is she here or isn't she?"

"*Did* she inherit a million dollars?" the girl asked.

"*Two* million," Bloom said. "Where is she?"

"You're putting me on."

"Is she inside there?"

"Yes, sir. But admission is five dollars a head."

"Don't be ridiculous," Bloom said, and pushed aside the black velour curtain that shielded the club from the corridor outside. We followed him in. The club proper, if anything, was darker than the entrance hallway. Only one part of it was brilliantly lighted, and that was a circular stage in the center of the room, occupied now by a girl wearing only a sequined G-string and a pair of red-satin spike-heeled shoes. A rock-and-roll tune was blaring from a pair of speakers hanging over the stage, on the same pipe that carried the leikos and spots. At least three dozen bar stools immediately surrounded the stage, most of them empty at the moment, the dancer wildly tossing her breasts at a clutch of four customers who sat in a row with their backs to us. Spreading out from the stage like ripples on the surface of a lake after a stone has been dropped into it, the stage itself the center of the spreading circles, were some fifty to sixty small tables. Unlike the bar stools, most of the chairs around the tables were occupied. There was a good reason for this.

The tables were in semidarkness. At each of the tables a virtually naked girl danced for the private enjoyment of the customer sitting there. Some of the girls were wearing bikini bottoms and no tops. Some were wearing tank suits cut high on their long legs, the tops pulled down to reveal their breasts. Some were wearing G-strings and baby-doll nightgowns, the hems hand-lifted to just above the breasts. All the girls were wearing four-inch spikes, and all of them were straddling the legs of their various customers as they pumped vigorously into their chests. The men all sat motionless and goggle-eyed, idiotic smiles on their faces, their hands dangling at their sides; a huge sign on the wall warned that the dancers were not to be touched. The girls were white and black and brown and yellow. Some of them were spectacularly beautiful. A blonde who looked no more than sixteen years old was sitting alone at one of the tables, clutching a giant stuffed panda in her arms. She was wearing only sequined pasties, and a G-string—the band of which bristled with folded dollar bills—and her long legs were crossed, one spike-heeled shoe tapping the air in time to the music.

"Police," Bloom said to her, and showed his shield. "Which one is Jenny Masters?"

The girl almost leaped out of her chair. She clutched the panda to her defensively and said, "I'm new here."

"So am I," Bloom said. "Jenny Masters. Which one?"

"Over there," the girl said. "Dancing for the sailor."

The sailor was sitting at a table in a corner of the room, his long legs stretched out in front of him. A tall black girl, her back to us, was straddling one of those legs and pumping away at him. She was wearing a white baby-doll nightgown, a white sequined G-string, and spike-heeled shoes. She was holding the hem of the gown up above her naked breasts. The sailor had a glazed look on his face. Because the girl's back was to us, he saw our approach before she did, and he smelled cop on Bloom from a hundred paces away. He whispered something urgently to her, and she turned immediately, letting the hem of the gown fall from her hands, the sheer fabric scarcely covering her nakedness. She may not have recognized Bloom as a cop or me as an attorney, but she certainly must have recognized Konig as the John she'd spent twenty-four hours in bed with. She put her hands on her hips, one hip jutting, and waited for us to come closer. The sailor, trapped in the corner, seemed desperately searching for a way out of the place.

"You Jenny Masters?" Bloom asked.

"That's me," she said.

"You know this man?" Bloom asked.

"I know *him*," Jenny said, "but who the hell are *you?*"

"Detective Bloom, Calusa Police."

"I thought so," she said, and nodded.

"How do you know this man?"

"He's a friend," Jenny said, and smiled. Her teeth were a

radiant white against the mocha brown of her face. Her hands were still on her hips. "Leastways I *thought* so. What's the beef?"

"When did you see this man last?" Bloom asked.

"He missing a wristwatch or something?"

"Nothing like that."

"No complaint?"

"No complaint."

"No complaint, well, well," Jenny said.

"So when did you see him last?"

"A few hours ago."

"What time?"

"What time'd you leave, honey?" she asked Konig. "Musta been about six, I reckon. Wun't it about six?"

"Where were you?" Bloom asked.

"My place."

"On Avocado?"

"Oh, you been there, huh?"

"We've been there."

"Who told you how to find me?"

"Never mind that," Bloom said. "When did you and Mr. Konig get there?"

"That your name, honey?" Jenny asked, and smiled again. "The house, you mean?" she asked Bloom.

"Yes, the house."

"Last night sometime."

"*When* last night?"

" 'Bout the same time as when you left tonight, wun't it, honey? 'Bout six, 'long about in there?"

"You were there at your house together from six p.m. yesterday to six p.m. today, is that it?"

"Just about."

"Either one of you leave the house during that time?"

"Too *busy* to leave, man."

"He was there all that time, huh? Never left the house."

"Not for a minute. Ain't no law against two people enjoying each other's company, is there?"

Bloom looked at her. His glare would have frozen the Sahara. Jenny shrugged. Konig glanced at his shoes. The sailor was busy trying to keep his face turned to the wall.

"Okay?" Jenny said.

"Yeah, okay," Bloom said sourly.

We dropped Konig at the Breakwater Inn on Tidal Street, and then the patrolman drove us back to the police station. The patrolman was silent all the way crosstown, miffed because Bloom hadn't let him into Alyce's pleasure palace. He was still sulking when he let us out at the front door of the building. In the elevator on the way up to the third floor Bloom said, "Assuming the M.E.'s right about the time of death, Konig's home free. You can't be fucking a black whore and slitting a little girl's throat at the same time."

"When do you plan bringing Miller in?" I asked.

"I've got somebody trying to reach him right this minute," Bloom said.

The somebody who'd been trying to reach Vicky's father was a detective named Pete Kenyon, a short (for a cop), stocky young man in his early thirties, I guessed, with a head of hair as bright as Dwayne Miller's mailbox, and a face blooming with freckles. He had two very white and prominent upper front teeth, and his upper lip was tented above them in a permanent wedge, so that he resembled either a chipmunk or a beaver, I wasn't sure which. I wondered at once where he would fit into my partner Frank's Fox-Face/Pig-Face view of the world. He was holding a sheaf of papers in his right hand, and the first thing he said was that he'd been trying to reach Miller by phone with no luck, and did Bloom want somebody sent out there to roust him? Bloom thought about this for a moment, and then said he wanted to keep a low profile on this, get Miller to come in voluntarily if they could get him by phone.

"Have you been calling the groves there, or his house?" he asked.

"Both," Kenyon said. "Ain't no answer neither place."

"What's all that in your hand?" Bloom asked.

"Just came Express Mail from Illinois. Whole shithouse full of radio stations in Georgia. Pages two forty-three to two fifty-nine, Xeroxed for us by that nice lady in Skokie, wherever *that* may be. Four pages of networks, and then *another* ten pages of alphabetical listings starting with Austell and ending with Wimo. Must be more'n a hundred towns listed here, Morrie, don't know *how* many radio stations. You take a town the size of Savannah, there's something like seventeen, eighteen stations there alone, AM and FM. If we started calling them all right this minute, we wouldn't be finished till next Christmas.''

"Do they list personnel?" Bloom asked.

"Yeah, but not disc jockeys. Just people like general managers and sales managers and like that."

"Shit," Bloom said.

"I had an idea, though," Kenyon said.

"Yeah, what's the idea?"

"If Marshall's working up there someplace, he's got to have filed an income tax return, am I right? So whyn't I give the IRS in Jacksonville a call, see if they can put us onto a regional office in Georgia, get ourselves a current address for this bugger?"

"They won't give it to you," Bloom said. "Not since all that funny business with Nixon."

"This is homicide, Morrie."

"They won't care if it's *gen*ocide. You can try them, but you're gonna strike out, I know it. What'd you get from the F.C.I.C.?"

"Nothing. No Georgia arrests in the past year—did I feed the right dope in? Edward Marshall, N.M.I., born circa 1941 or '42, six feet tall, one-eighty, black hair, blue eyes?"

"That's it."

"Nothing," Kenyon said. "Doesn't have a *federal* rap sheet, either. Why're you so hot on finding him, anyway?"

"Because, one, he can maybe give us some more information on this guy Sadowsky, the drummer, who the N.Y.P.D. has nothing on so far, and, two, he can maybe tell us who this fucking mysterious friend of his is who supposedly lent him a boat so he could be conveniently out on the water while Vicky Miller was getting killed. Do those seem like two good enough reasons for us to be breaking our balls?"

"I suppose," Kenyon said, and shrugged. "It's too bad there ain't some kind of union where these guys—"

"Wait a minute," Bloom said. "He's got to belong to a union, doesn't he? I mean, if he's in radio? Isn't that required? Equity or something? What the hell do they call it? For radio performers? Equity?''

"That's for actors," Kenyon said. "Actors Equity."

"Then what? It's something *like* Equity, I know it is. Find out what it's called," he said, "the union these radio guys belong to."

"Georgia's a right-to-work state," Kenyon said, "same as Florida. He wouldn't *have* to belong to a union if he didn't want to."

"Find out *anyway*," Bloom said.

8

Even God rested on Sunday.

Besides, my daughter wanted to know whether we were going to blow today the way we'd blown yesterday, what with traveling from New Orleans and then Tampa and then me rushing off to take care of business while she sat watching television all alone. My daughter has a way of directly demanding attention. She was great at this even when Susan and I were still married, but she has become expert at it since the divorce, working on the principle that parents who have split up are uncommonly receptive to their offsprings' slightest whims. She really doesn't have to try quite so hard; I would leap into a pit of molten lava for her.

What I did instead was scan the *Herald-Tribune*'s Sunday Section for a suitable amusement, proposing and having dismissed in turn: 1) the Annual Bayview Avenue Arts and Crafts Street Exhibit 2) a sculpture opening at the Wexler Gallery on Main Street 3) the annual sale of duplicate plants and orchid auction at the Agnes Lorrimer Memorial Gardens 4) the Calusa County Fair (which Joanna told me she'd outgrown, thanks) and 5) an exhibit of gem stones and Indian jewelry at Pierpont Hall. It was not until I stumbled upon the advertisements for the All-Florida Championship Rodeo in Ananburg that I captured Joanna's interest. She asked at once if we could call Dale to ask if she'd like to come with us. I dialed her home on Whisper Key and was somewhat relieved when the phone rang and rang without an answer; I really wanted to spend some time alone with my daughter. It was not my fault, as it turned out, that *some* of the time would be occupied by business—even in Ananburg, a good forty miles from the scene of the multiple murders.

To get to Ananburg, which is in adjoining De Soto County, you drive due south on 41, and then make a left turn eastward on Timucuan Point Road, driving past the Sawgrass River Bird Sanctuary and into acres and acres of cow country. In late April and early May the air out here is alive with love bugs mating in flight and smashing in conjugal bliss into your windshield. The ensuing romantic mess is bloody and gluey, and you've got to stop every three miles or so to wipe off the windshield or else drive the rest of the way on instruments. But this was January, and there were no love bugs doing their incessant thing, and the cold front seemed to have drifted mercifully out to sea, leaving behind it a day that was beautiful and bright, with a high temperature of seventy-three degrees promised by all the forecasters.

You did not have to drive very far out of Calusa to realize that the State of Florida was really an integral part of the Deep South. The regional dialects in the place I've called home for the past four years were largely midwestern, with here and there a hard smattering of northeastern edge, and—even scarcer—a dollop of Canadian English. But if you stopped for gas out here in the boonies, as we did some sixteen miles from the city limits, the Southern accent was so thick you needed a machete to slice it. The men wore bib overalls here, and boots, and straw hats, and they chewed tobacco and spit it with unerring accuracy; the women wore those patterned cotton things my mother used to call house dresses; the restaurants in the infrequent little towns along the way featured "home cooking," which invariably meant country ham and black-eyed peas, green beans and fatback, hominy, collard greens, corn bread and—particularly in this part of the country—fried catfish. As we made the drive on an arrow-straight road flanked by grazing land, I could not help but wonder how my partner Frank might have reacted to this landscape and the people who inhabited it.

My daughter had something on her mind.

I can always tell when she's about to reveal anything of monumental importance because she will sit silently for half an hour or so, nibbling at her lower lip, and fretting the problem until it finally surfaces. It pays to be patient at such times. I've discovered after thirteen years of fatherhood that probing does little to unseal Joanna's lips; she'll tell me when she's good and ready, and *only* then. And usually the revelation will come completely out of the blue, as it did that Sunday on the drive to Ananburg. I'd been rattling on about the rodeo we were about to see and about rodeos in general, and I made what I thought to be a clever remark to the effect that seeing a rodeo once every twenty-seven years was essential to my life plan, not thinking I had to explain to my daughter that since I was now *thirty*-seven, the last one I'd seen had been when I was ten, when without warning, she said, "What should you do if a boy wants to feel you up?"

I pondered this for a moment, and then answered in a manner that would have guaranteed an immediate objection from an opposing attorney. "Who's the boy?" I said.

"Well . . . *any* boy."

"You don't have a specific boy in mind?"

"Yes, I *do* have a specific boy in mind."

"Do I know him?"

"You know him, and you don't like him," Joanna said.

"Andrew the Cruel," I said.

Andrew the Cruel was a fifteen-year-old boy whose name actually was Andrew Crowell, but whom I had rebaptized when he was still fourteen and had promised my then twelve-year-old daughter that he would take her to something called the Spring Frolic at Bedloe, only to call at the last moment to advise her that he had an errand to run for his father and would have to skip the dance after all. Joanna was spending that particular weekend with me, and the way she spent it was in her room weeping from Friday afternoon at five o'clock, when the little son of a bitch called—two and a half hours before he was supposed to pick her up—till Sunday at six, when I finally coaxed her to come out and have some dinner before I took her back to her mother's. I do not easily forgive little bastards who are mean to my daughter. Joanna, on the other hand, forgave him almost at once. Two weeks later, when she was visiting me again, she spent nearly as much time on the phone with him as she had weeping in her room on the weekend of the dance. Now she wanted to know what she should do if and when, if not *already*, Andrew the Cruel felt her up.

"Andrew *Crowell*, Dad," she said, correcting me. She could call him Andrew Crowell from now to doomsday; to me he would always and ever be Andrew the Cruel, the little prick. It did not help improve my opinion of him to have learned inadvertently from one of Joanna's girl friends who'd been sleeping over for a weekend several months ago that Andrew was most likely pushing dope and that the "errand" he'd had to run that night of the dance undoubtedly involved picking up grass on a deserted beach someplace. My daughter vehemently denied this allegation. She did not, however, deny that Andrew the Cruel kept snakes. He once offered to bring to my house a pet boa constrictor. I told him that Freud might have had a lot to say about his hobby. He asked me who Freud was. This was my daughter's inamorato: a pusher, a zoo keeper, and a fucking ignoramus.

"When did this happen?" I asked.

"When did *what* happen?"

"What you said happened?"

"I didn't say it happened."

"Well, when do you *expect* it to happen?" I said.

"It's sort of come up."

"You mean he's warned you to expect it?"

"Not exactly."

"Then *what*, exactly?"

"Not exactly a *warning*, I mean. More like a *promise* is what it was."

"Oh, I see."

"Dad, don't get uptight, okay? I just want to know what I should *do* is all. In all the eventuality. If what I *think* is going to happen *happens* is all."

"He's already *promised* you it'll happen, is that it?"

"Yes. Well, more or less."

"How do you mean, more or less?"

"Well, he's indicated that he finds . . . you know . . . that all of a sudden he's, you know, sort of attracted to, you know, what there wasn't anything *there* to be attracted to a little while ago. And now there *is*. So he's sort of said he might not be able to . . . well . . . what he said was 'resist the temptation.' That's what he said.''

"He wants to taste of the fruit of the tree of knowledge, is that it?''

"What?'' Joanna said.

"Little Biblical zoo keeper that he is.''

"Dad, if *you've* got a thing about snakes, that's *your* problem, not Andrew's.''

"I definitely have a thing about snakes, yes. I *also* have a thing about Andrew.''

"*That* I know.''

"So why are you asking *me* what you should do?''

"Because I asked Mom, and *she* wanted to know if I'd like to go see Dr. Beyer to get a prescription for the pill.''

"The *pill!*''

"Yeah.''

"Jesus Christ!''

"Yeah.''

"Has your mother lost her *mind?* You're only thirteen years old!''

"I'll be fourteen in September.''

"September's almost a year away!''

"She's thinking ahead, I guess.''

"She's thinking too *far* ahead, you ask . . . I hope you told her no.''

"I told her I'd think about it. Meanwhile, what should I do about Andrew?''

"What do *other* girls your age do about Andrew?''

"Well, the only *other* girl who's ever gone steady with Andrew . . .''

"Oh, are you going *steady* with him?''

"Well, yeah, sort of.''

"What does 'sort of' mean?''

"We're seeing each other. And nobody else.''

"Joanna, you're too young to . . .''

"Come on, Dad . . .''

". . . be tying yourself exclusively to one boy.''

"Almost all the girls at St. Mark's have steadies.''

"Does Roxanne have a steady?''

Roxanne was the girl who'd told me one afternoon—while

I was squirting Charco-Lite onto the backyard briquettes in preparation for a gala hamburger and hot-dog feast—that Andrew Crowell was probably pushing dope. Joanna, at the time, was swimming in the pool, underwater like a shark. I graciously did not mention Roxanne's comment until after her father had picked her up that Sunday afternoon. Alone again with my daughter, I confronted her with the bizarre notion that Andrew might be involved in narcotics, and she told me flat-out that Roxanne was full of it. Roxanne had turned fourteen just before Christmas, which made her nine months older than Joanna. She was short and somewhat pudgy, with frizzy black hair and intelligent brown eyes. Her mother was a graduate of Vassar, and Roxanne herself planned to go there one day, as she incessantly informed anyone who would listen. In preparation, she was practicing a scholarly look by wearing black-rimmed eyeglasses. She had told me about the dope matter-of-factly, the way all the kids in Calusa—and maybe everywhere in America—talked about dope.

"Roxanne's the one who used to go steady with him," Joanna said.

"Roxanne?"

"Yeah."

"With Andrew?"

"Yeah."

This fresh knowledge seemed to lend at least some support to Roxanne's dope-pushing allegation. I wondered briefly just how "full of it" she actually was, and promised myself I'd get back to this entire subject of narcotics as soon as the more important matter of my daughter's virgin breasts had been dealt with.

"Well, when *she* was going steady with him," I asked, "did she allow him to . . . ?"

"All the way, Dad," Joanna said.

"What?"

"All the way."

"Are you saying . . . ?"

"Yep."

"That little *Roxanne* . . . ?"

"Yep."

I shook my head.

"Don't be so shocked," Joanna said.

"Shocked? I'm *appalled!* She's only fourteen!"

"Everybody does it," Joanna said.

"Ev—"

"Well, *almost* everybody. At St. Mark's, I mean."

"If that's the case, you must be considered retarded."

"Actually, I am. *Considered*, I mean. In fact, when I asked Roxanne whether I should, you know, let Andrew, you know, do what he said he was thinking of doing, she just burst out laughing."

"Thought it was funny, huh?"

"Yeah."

"Hilarious."

"Yeah. So *should* I? Let him, I mean?"

"No."

"No?"

"Not Andrew."

"Why not Andrew?"

"You'd be cheapening yourself," I said.

I could not think of any other way of putting it. I knew I was being miserably inadequate, I knew that I should have come up with some earth-shattering advice to help my daughter find the proper path to womanhood, prepare her somehow for that first tentative touch and glorious response, and all I could say was that with someone like Andrew she'd be cheapening herself, she'd be allowing a person inferior to her to . . . to *soil* her somehow.

She was silent for what seemed like a long time. Outside the open windows of the Ghia, the monotonous countryside flashed by. We were still a good twenty minutes from Ananburg, and it was close to one-thirty, and the Grand Entry was scheduled to begin at two sharp. I knew I'd said the wrong thing, and my only consolation was that Susan had given her advice even *more* stupid. Offering to put her on the *pill*, Jesus!

"Actually . . ." Joanna said.

I held my breath.

"I'm not even sure I *want* him to. I mean . . . I think you may be right about him, Dad. I'm not sure, but I think maybe you are. And I think if I let him do what he wants, then I'd be letting him take something very personal from me, something

I'm not sure I want him to have. Yeah, it'd be cheap," she said, and nodded.

I said nothing. I kept my eyes on the road ahead.

"Thanks, Dad," she said, and hugged herself.

In a little while she began humming an Elton John tune even I knew.

We missed the Grand Entry, but we took our seats on the shady side of the arena in time for the invocation and the singing of the national anthem. The first competition of the day was the bareback riding event, and a man sitting next to Joanna and me told us that the one bucking horse no cowboy wanted to draw was Dennis the Menace, whose bucking string number was eighteen. "You watch that horse when he comes out here, whoever draws eighteen," he said. "That horse'll just pitch anybody offa him in a matter of seconds." The third horse out of the chute was, in fact, Dennis the Menace, and the cowboy on his back lasted no longer than three seconds, fulfillment enough of our companion's prediction. We sat through the calf roping and saddle bronc riding events, and then I asked Joanna if she'd like a hot dog or something, and she admitted that she was starving—my daughter is *always* starving—but that she didn't want me to miss the bulldogging event, which the man sitting next to us had said was the most exciting one except for the bull riding, which was the last event on the program. I told Joanna I'd be back in a minute, and then I shuffled my way past the men and women in our row of the bleachers, noting that men and women alike were wearing ten-gallon hats, and wishing I owned the only haberdashery store in Ananburg. As I stepped through the arena gates and began walking toward the food concession some fifty yards away, the master of ceremonies was explaining over the loudspeakers that a pair of cowboys worked as a *team* in the bulldogging event, the hazer keeping the steer moving straight while the bulldogger himself leaped from his horse and "down in the pocket" to grab the steer's horns and wrestle him to the ground. A sign over a small wooden building read HOT DOGS, HAMBURGERS, SOFT DRINKS. Jim Sherman was standing in line there with a dozen or more other men and women.

I didn't recognize him at first because his back was to me

and he was dressed like most of the other men here today—jeans and boots, a western-styled shirt with pearl buttons, a ten-gallon hat. I was more used to seeing him in suit and tie as one of the Greenery's partners and official greeters, or else wearing skintight swim trunks as he strolled the beach and exhibited his gorgeous suntanned bod. He turned in profile just then to give his order to the girl working the grill, and I recognized that finely chiseled fox nose, and the clean line of his sun-bronzed jaw as he told the girl he wanted two hamburgers and a pair of Cokes. He must have seen me from the corner of his eye; he turned to where I was standing some three customers behind him, and—in a voice that sounded somewhat distant—said, "Hello, Matthew." He collected his order from the girl behind the counter, paid her for it, and then stopped just beside me where I was standing in line, and whispered, "I have to talk to you."

"What about?" I said.

"Not here," he said. "I'll meet you in about ten minutes, soon as I get this stuff back to Brad."

"Okay, where?"

"By the ticket office up there."

"Sure," I said, and watched him as he walked back to the stands.

When I explained to Joanna that I had to talk to someone, she told me it'd serve me right if she entered the calf scramble, which was the event following the bulldogging, most of which I'd already missed. The calf scramble, as the man sitting alongside us explained, was an event in which every rodeo-attending boy and girl who was so-inclined could jump down into the arena with a dozen or more calves and then try to catch one of the calves and drag it back across the finish line for a cash prize. "It's usually a boy who wins it, though," the man said, and Joanna pulled a face. I left her with two hot dogs, a side of French fries, and an orange drink, and went to find Jim Sherman.

He was leaning against the closed ticket counter, puffing on a cigarette. He ground out the cigarette under the heel of his boot when he saw me approaching, and then he took off his ten-gallon hat and wiped the sweatband the way I'd seen Miller do it that day at the orange groves. He put the hat back on his head again.

"What's on your mind?" I asked.

"I'm glad I ran into you," he said. "I was planning on coming to your office tomorrow morning. This'll save me a trip." He took another cigarette from the package in his shirt pocket, spearing just the single cigarette without removing the package, and then struck a kitchen match on the seat of his blue jeans, and lighted the cigarette, and blew out a stream of smoke, and squinted his blue eyes like Gary Cooper or whichever cowpoke he was playing here today in Ananburg, Florida. "The police've been to see me," he said.

"What about?"

"They wanted to know if I'd threatened to kill Vicky."

"What'd you tell them?"

"I told them I hadn't, of course."

"Then what's the problem?"

"The problem is I don't think they believed me."

"Who'd you talk to? Detective Bloom?"

"No, a man named Kenyon. Irish-looking guy with freckles all over his face."

"What made him think you'd threatened her?"

"I think you already know," Jim said, and looked me dead in the eye.

"Yes, I already know," I said.

"You're the one who went running to the police, aren't you?"

"I'm the one who gave them information that might have had bearing on a crime, yes."

"You didn't have to do that."

"I felt obliged to. Nixon almost got impeached for withholding similar information."

"Nixon was President of the United States. You're . . ."

"I'm an attorney. And similarly sworn to uphold the law of the land."

"So you take what's essentially hearsay . . ."

"If you told Vicky she'd be dead . . ."

"You know damn *well* what I meant! I was telling her I'd fire her if she bombed the Greenery! Plain and simple!"

"The words were spoken in anger, they *could* have constituted a real death threat. Under the circumstances, I think you'd have done just what I did, Jim."

"No, Matthew, I'm sorry. Friends don't go running to the cops when they . . ."

"Vicky was a friend, too."

"You caused me a lot of trouble."

"I don't think so. Bloom himself told me you were probably just threatening to fire her."

"Then why'd he send a flunky to see me?"

"He had to check. Nobody arrested you, did they?"

"That doesn't mean they *won't*," Jim said. "Who was the rat, Matthew? Who was so eager to tell you I'd threatened Vicky's life?"

"I'd rather not say."

"One of our dumb cunt waitresses?"

"Jim, there's no sense asking me, I won't . . ."

"Melanie Simms? The queen's handmaiden? Kissing the big rock star's ass every chance she got? Was she the one, Matthew?"

"Why? Is *she* going to be dead, too?"

"Touché," Jim said, and smiled.

I did not take Joanna back to the house I used to share with her and her mother until seven o'clock that night. Susan's car was parked in the driveway, but that didn't necessarily mean she was home yet; Georgie Poole may have picked her up in his Mercedes-Benz 450 SL before their weekend jaunt to the Bahamas. I asked Joanna to check, and then I walked over to where Reginald Soames, who used to be my next-door neighbor, was out watering his azalea bushes in the dark. Old Reggie was a bit deaf; he did not hear me approaching. He looked up, startled, when I was three feet from him and said, "You scared me to *death*, Junior. What're you doing, prowling around out here?"

"Waiting to see if Susan's home."

"You planning a reconciliation?"

"I'm just dropping my daughter off."

"So whyn't you go inside like a civilized human being?"

"Tell that to Susan."

"I will, next chance I get," Reggie said. "See you got yourself involved in another murder, huh?"

"Not really."

"Heard on the television you were the last one to see her alive."

"That's true."

"If they arrest you," he said, "I'll send you cigarettes." He burst out laughing, sobered almost immediately, and said apropos of nothing, "People claim you're not supposed to water at night. I say if you water during the day, the sun'll scorch everything out. Here's your daughter," he said, glancing past my shoulder.

"She's home," Joanna said. "Taking a bath. She says to tell you thanks."

"Tell her she's welcome," I said, and hugged Joanna close.

"And, Dad . . ."

She held me at arm's length and looked up into my face.

"*Really* thanks," she said. "I mean *really* really."

"Okay," I said.

"Do you know what I mean?"

"I know what you mean," I said.

I mixed myself a martini and then went to the desk in the living room and turned on the telephone-answering machine. There had been (and still was) a study in the house I once shared with Susan and my daughter, and that was where the machine *used* to be. I no longer had a study. The house I was renting on the mainland had two bedrooms and a kitchen, and a combination living room-dining room, and that was all. Well, it also had a swimming pool. A small one, true, but ample enough for a refreshing dip at the end of a sweltering August day, than which there was nothing worse in Calusa than a sweltering *September* day. The first call had been from Mark Goldman, who wanted to know if we were still on for tennis Thursday morning. The second call had been from a client named Arthur Kincaid, who said he was considering a coal-mine tax shelter and wanted me to look over the offering brochure. The third call had been from Dale O'Brien, who asked me to call her back as soon as I got in. I switched off the machine without trying to find out if there had been any calls after Dale's. I dialed her number on Whisper Key (I was beginning to know it by heart), and she answered on the third ring.

"Hi," she said, "where've you been all day?"

"I took Joanna to the rodeo. We tried to reach you, thought you might like to join us."

"I'd have *loved* to," Dale said. "When did you call?"

"Must've been a little before noon."

"I was out walking on the beach."

"Next time," I said. "Twenty-seven years from now."

Dale laughed, even though she couldn't have understood the reference. "What are you doing now?" she asked.

"I just got in. I've got a martini in my hand, and I plan to sip it while I listen to the rest of my messages. If there *are* any."

"Why don't you come over here instead?" she asked. "We have martinis here, too."

"Ah, but this is a *Beefeater* martini," I said.

"Will you settle for Tanqueray?" she said.

"I'll be right there," I said.

Her house was almost at the end of Whisper Key, where a narrow offshore channel ran toward Steamboat Pass and the bridge connecting Whisper to Fatback. A recent Calusa City Council vote had ordained that all bridges would be opened only every half-hour, instead of as previously, when all a skipper had to do was honk his horn to signal his approach and request an immediate raising; it was now almost eight-thirty and the boats out there in the channel were massing for an assault. A pelican, all hunched down into his own feathers, sat on a piling that marked the end of Dale's property and the beginning of the beach. The sky was riddled with stars.

She had mixed a pitcherful of martinis and had heated a batch of cheese puffs as well, and we sat on her patio and listened to the crash of the surf and the final movement of Elgar's Second Symphony, bassoons, horns, and cellos swelling from the speakers inside the house. Her cat, Sassafras, a calico almost as big as my own cat had been, lay dozing near a potted cactus, totally oblivious to the surf, the conversation, or the broken harmonies of the clarinets, harps, and second violins.

"I enjoyed being in New Orleans with you," Dale said.

"I'm afraid I wasn't very good company."

"I like your daughter a lot, too."

"Thank you."

We were silent for several moments. From the speakers, Elgar's fugal second theme moved fluidly into a reiteration of his first theme. I listened to the thunderous crash of the surf and waited for the sonorously climactic echo of the third theme.

"You took me quite by storm, you know," Dale said.

"I did?"

"Quite. I mean, asking me out so suddenly. Most men . . . well, I don't want to give the impression that I'm a vastly experienced woman of the world. When anyone says 'most men' or 'most politicians' or 'most' *anything*, they're really talking about their own experience, the people or things they know about. I haven't been very social since coming to Calusa. But *most* men"—and here she smiled—"might have been a bit more reticent."

"Does that bother you? That I . . ."

"No, no. It was very flattering. And . . . exciting, Matthew. Your obvious attraction to me. That was very exciting."

"You're a very attractive woman," I said.

"And you. A man, I mean." She hesitated. "Want to take a walk on the beach?"

I had changed into jeans, a T-shirt, and sandals before leaving the house. Dale was barefoot and wearing a flowing white cotton caftan. I took off the sandals, rolled up the cuffs of the jeans, and followed her down the path, past the pelican asleep on the piling, and onto the beach. The sand was cool underfoot. The sailboats began moving under power toward the pass; it was eight-thirty, and the bridge was open.

"About being taken by storm," I said.

"Yes?"

"*You* did, too. Take *me*, I mean. By storm, I mean. When you asked me out to dinner. And then invited yourself to New Orleans."

"You have no idea how nervous I was."

"What do you mean?"

"Making that call. To ask you to dinner. I'd never done anything like that in my life."

"You sounded very poised and self-assured."

"Pure bluster." She paused. "I was terrified on our first date—don't you hate the word 'date'?"

"Yes," I said, and smiled.

"It doesn't seem appropriate for people our age. *Teenagers* go on dates, adults . . ." She shrugged. "Anyway, I was scared stiff."

"Why?"

"Because it was happening so fast. I hate chitchat. You opened yourself to me almost immediately, Matthew. I was . . . well, honored, I suppose. And flattered." She paused. "You're the only person I ever told about my artist in San Francisco," she said. "Until then it was something very personal—and very painful—to me. I don't know why I chose to share it with you, perhaps because—all at once I trusted you." She paused again. "That's what it's all about, isn't it, Matthew? In the long run? Two people trusting each other enough to expose themselves completely? To each other?" she said, and suddenly turned to me and moved into my arms and kissed me.

We stood locked in embrace at the edge of the ocean, my mouth fastened to hers, her body tight against me; she was naked under the caftan, I realized. We kissed gently, as though we had done this many times before and would do it often again and could therefore afford the luxury of post-ponement. And then we walked hand in hand back to the house, the surf crashing against the beach on our left, the water rushing in against our naked feet, the last of the boats moving through the pass and into the bay. In her bedroom we undressed without haste and kissed again, our tongues, our hands tentatively exploring, our bodies gliding naked against each other, unhurried. The sheets and pillowcases were a pastel green, cool and a trifle damp to the touch. She took off her glasses, placed them delicately on the table beside the bed, and then lay back against the pillow, her russet hair spreading against the timid green, her nipples a fainter blush of pink. Her pubic hair was astonishingly blond, a pale distant cousin to the deeper-hued hair on her head. I hovered above her for only an instant and then lowered my mouth to hers again.

Our lips were more demanding now, our tongues boldly pillaging as she spread her legs to me and I eased myself onto her and into her. She was wet and warm and darkly entreat-ing, murmuring softly as I moved into her, lifting one hand to the back of my neck, her fingers widespread there, the other on my shoulder, my own hands reaching under her to clasp her buttocks, raising her to me, open and yielding. Our bodies móved erratically at first, thrust out of synch with counterthrust and grind, polished pelvic bones in accidental collision, until at last we discovered a furious rhythm together and exploited it ruthlessly, liberated jazz artists tumbling to an erotic beat, pillaging a chart for its hidden nuances, fashioning together a melody born of collaboration. "Yes," she said, and "Yes," I said, her lips against my ear, my face buried in masses of russet hair against the pale green pillow, "Yes, fuck," she said, and "Fuck," I said, echoing her, words and bodies echoing each other and ourselves, until we approached finally that single point in time and space where truly we became each other, no longer echoes but instead a single reverberating, melting, sliding, crumbling, exploding entity. "Oh, *God!*" she moaned, and twisted savagely beneath me, arching her hips into my own spasm. We fell back together against the tortured sheets and held each other fiercely, helpless in the grasp of the little death that savaged us.

"Wow," she said, and caught her breath.

"Dale," I murmured, "Dale."

"Oh, *God*, that was good."

"Dale, Dale . . ."

"Wow," she said again.

I explained later how the color of her pubic hair had taken me completely by surprise, and jokingly asked which she was, a genuine blonde or a genuine redhead, suggesting that perhaps she tinted herself for effect at either one place or the other. She told me she was a genuine *both* and had experienced no end of embarrassment and fear when first she reached puberty and her thatch below began coming in the color of wheat instead of rust. She learned later—at the age of seventeen, to be precise—that her oddly diverse plumage was a cause for further consternation, at least to the male of the species, or at least to the *only* male who until then had seen her in the buff and who virtually *raped* her, so bananas had he gone over her rainbow coloration. She was, at the time, a senior in high school, and a very studious one at that, having at the age of ten decided that she wanted to be either a lawyer or a doctor, and opting for the legal profession only after she fainted at the sight of a worm cut in half by an eleven-year-old playmate. A straight-A student (except for Music Appreciation, where she was the only kid in the class who got a C, due to a tin ear she still possessed to this day, no matter *how* many times she played Elgar's Second), she had no idea how she'd become involved with the school's prize jock, he who later lowered her panties on a California beach one runaway night, to discover by moonlight that the hair covering her mound below did not match that on her head, after which he'd gone totally apeshit, strewing his T-shirt and blue jeans and track shoes and sweat socks hither and yon on the sand while she trembled in virgin anticipation of allowing inside her a tool reputed (by three girls on the cheerleading squad) to be equally massive in girth and length. He impaled her on the beach ("I got sand all up me," Dale said) and then did a little sort of jigging trot afterward, similar to the one he performed on the football field whenever he made a touchdown, and then began baying at the moon like a werewolf. She was afraid he'd lost his marbles completely, and learned only later that he'd been thoroughly stoned that night on grass a friend of his had brought from Mexico, which he hadn't even had the decency to offer her.

She began to suspect that her quarterback's mouth was as big as the rest of him when the team's star tackle stopped her in the school cafeteria one day and asked if it was true about her "permanent." The moment she realized he was talking about her peculiar pigmentation, she hit him across the bridge of his nose with a convenient history book, almost giving *him* a permanent ("Disfigurement, that is," she said), and then drove herself home in the car her father had given her for her seventeenth birthday, a 1966 Mustang painted a fiery red that complemented at least the hair on her head. She then locked herself in her bedroom and began sobbing over her lost virginity and the stupidity of having chosen a moron for her first lover, but the tears magically turned to laughter when she realized he'd been bragging to all his teammates about her "permanent"—the idiot had actually believed she'd had herself touched up in a beauty parlor!

She became, after that experience, singularly gun-shy about disrobing before the act of sex, opportunities for which were not all that frequent in her home town anyway, unless she chose to take on the *rest* of the football team. It was not until she entered the University of California at Santa Cruz, eighteen years old and hotly in pursuit of a law degree still some seven years in the future, that she met a boy ("Well, actually, he was thirty-one years old and teaching chemistry") who put the matter of the disparate top and bottom hair into its proper perspective. As *usual* (her experience by then had expanded to include one other boy) she had kept herself completely clothed until the lights were out in the small apartment the chemistry professor lived in off campus, and—after they'd made love for the first time—was lying with the sheet securely pulled to her throat when suddenly he turned on the bedlamp and began rummaging in the drawer of the bedside table for a package of cigarettes. Clinging to the sheet as though it were a life raft in shark-infested waters, she waited anxiously for him to turn off the light again. But instead he alternately puffed on his cigarette and ran his free hand over her body (still protected by the sheet) and then slipped it *under* the sheet and began touching her belly and her breasts and her ribs and finally the hidden triangle of crisp golden hair between her legs, still damp with her own juices and his overflow semen, stroking her until her legs parted ever so slightly in response, continuing to stroke her, his hand under the sheet, until she was twitching with excitement, and then suddenly yanking back the sheet, pulling it free of her hands and her body and her telltale golden patch and dropping his head onto her mound, his tongue at the ready, and pulling back in surprise, and uttering only the single word, "Remarkable."

He studied her mons veneris and the luxuriant blond growth surrounding it like the mad scientist he was, poking and probing and mumbling and muttering, and finally delivered a learned discourse on the pigmentation of a person's hair as determined by his or her genes, or more exactly by the amount of "melanin" in the hair cells. If the melanin deposit was a heavy one, the person would undoubtedly have black hair, "and most likely brown eyes," her learned professor-lover said, "a usual correlation." If the deposit wasn't *quite* so heavy, the result would be dark brown hair, and then light brown hair, and so forth until the very *least* amount of melanin would produce blond hair. "But *red* hair," he said, "ah-ha, *red* hair!"

Red hair, it seemed, was caused by yet *another* gene which

could be totally overwhelmed by a stronger melanin gene to produce a person with black or brown hair. But if the red-hair gene was there to begin with, and if the melanin dose was a weak one, then the hair would be decidedly red. In Dale's case, he was willing to bet that the melanin dose wasn't too terribly weak, else the hair on her head would have been of the bright orange sort you see on so many shanty-Irish girls. A moderate dose would have accounted for the reddish-brown (''And highly attractive, I might add,'' he said) color of the hair on her head. Which brought him to the color of her pubic hair, and here he could not resist stroking it again, and even bestowing a professorial kiss upon it.

''It's relatively safe to say that if a person has red hair, then he is carrying either one or two red genes in addition to a brown gene or a blond gene,'' he said. ''In your case, I would suggest that you're carrying one red gene, one blond gene, and one brown gene, which would account for the reddish-brown hair on your head (''I prefer to think of it as auburn,'' Dale said demurely, and he answered, ''Well, russet, if you prefer'') and the blond hair on your twat. Even among Scottish Highlanders, who constitute the largest percentage of redheads on earth, one will sometimes find a man sporting either a red mustache or red pubic hair whereas the hair on his head may be a raven *black*. Which brings us once again to the color of the hair surrounding your cooze (''He had a remarkable vocabulary when it came to defining my cunt,'' Dale said now) and the possibility that the latent blond gene expressed itself only when fortified by the emergent glandular action in that particular part of your body, a perfectly normal if somewhat unusual phenomenon.''

Dale wasn't quite sure she believed a word of what he'd said, but she was nonetheless relieved that her now-acceptable ''Melanin-Mutant Snatch,'' as he'd labeled it, had not driven him to extremes of passionate lunacy, although she doubted that chemistry professors as a group were wont to perform little goalpost victory jigs. She *did* detect, however, that he achieved orgasm a bit more quickly the second time around. Attributing his alacrity to the intimate knowledge of her he now possessed, she decided that if her strange hair coloring was normal (if unusual) after all, and if it *also* served to— well, sort of *excite* men—well, then, the hell with it. She *wouldn't* shave it off, as she'd contemplated doing from the moment she turned twelve and began sprouting little blond (blond!) hairs down there, and neither would she color it to match the hair on her head. She would, in fact, *flaunt* it—the way a woman with a tattoo of Popeye the Sailorman on her backside might cunningly and fetchingly expose it to a lover while simultaneously suggesting he was now privy to her most intimate female secret.

"So I'm flaunting it," she said, and raised her hips slightly so that the light from the bedside lamp caught the thatch of blond hair between her legs, and then tossed her head forward so that the contrasting russet hair spilled down over her face. She lay that way, waiting, quite still, shrouded in autumn above, in summer below.

I parted the curtains of her Lady-or-the-Tiger hair and kissed her on the lips.

9

"It's Aftra," Bloom said on the telephone.

It was a little after nine o'clock and I was running late. I had just got out of the shower, in fact, and was standing with a towel wrapped around my waist, dripping water all over the white bedroom broadloom that must have cost the owner of the house I was renting at least twenty dollars a square yard.

"I guess maybe it's capitalized," Bloom said. "Capital A, capital F, capital T . . ."

"What is it?" I asked. "A country in Africa?"

"Aftra? No, it's a union. The American Federation of Television and Radio Artists. The union Eddie Marshall belongs to. Or—as they have him listed in their files—Edward Richard Marshall. I called the Atlanta local not five minutes ago. They checked their Rolodex and came up with a current address for him in a town called Valdosta, population around thirty-five thousand, county seat of Lowndes County, not too far from the Florida border. We've been ringing there, but no answer. Kenyon just finished going through the stuff that nice lady in Skokie sent us, came up with three FM and four AM stations for Valdosta. We're calling all of them now, trying to reach him."

"Good," I said.

"I tried you at the office first," he said. "You weren't there yet."

It sounded like a reprimand. I said nothing. I had left Dale's house at two in the morning, and I had slept—on and off—for less than six hours; felt hardly less than refreshed, even after my shower.

"We finally reached Miller. He'll be coming in here at eleven, right after the little girl's funeral. What time is it now, anyway?"

"I haven't got my watch on," I said.

"Ten after nine," he said, answering himself. "I'd like you to hear what he has to say, but if you were present he'd probably scream we were violating his rights. Maybe I can convince him to let us tape the inverview. You think he'd let us tape it?"

"Why don't you ask him?"

"I will. I'll use the old 'If You Have Nothing to Hide' routine. Where'll you be around eleven, eleven-thirty?"

"At the office. I hope."

"I'll call you there. You're not going to the funeral, huh?"

"No, I can't."

"Well, okay, I'll talk to you later."

"I ran into Jim Sherman yesterday," I said.

"Oh? Where?"

"The rodeo. Out in Ananburg. He was miffed that I'd gone to the police."

"Tell him to relax, we've got bigger fish to fry."

"That's what I told him. Who's the bigger fish?"

"Whoever killed Vicky and her little girl. I'm pretty sure it wasn't him. I'll talk to you later."

"Right," I said, and hung up and went back into the bathroom to shave. My face was full of lather when the telephone rang again. It was Arthur Kincaid, the man who'd called the night before to ask me about the coal-mine tax shelter.

"Don't you ever return your calls?" he asked.

"I got in late last night, Artie, I'm sorry."

"I just called you at the office," he said. "Do you know what time it is?"

"It's nine-twenty," I said, looking at the bedside clock.

"That's right. What time do you go to work?"

"Artie," I said, "I'm running late this morning. Send me the offering brochure, I'll look it over and get back to you."

"When?"

"When I've formed an opinion."

"When will that be?"

"I'll get to you by the end of the week," I said.

"I'll send it over by messenger."

"Fine."

"Can you get to it this afternoon?"

"I don't think so."

"Then when?"

"Artie . . ."

"All right, all right," he said. "As soon as you can, all right?"

"Yes," I said.

"Thank you, Matthew," he said, and hung up.

I had finished shaving and had rinsed my face and flossed my teeth and combed my hair when the telephone rang again. I stomped out naked into the bedroom and snatched the receiver from the cradle.

"Hello!" I said.

"Wow," Dale said.

"Oh, hi," I said. "I'm sorry, this phone's been going like sixty."

"I know, I've been trying you for the past ten minutes."

"Where are you?"

"Home," she said. "In bed."

"I just got up myself a little while ago."

"I'm exhausted," she said.

"So am I."

"I have a client coming to the office at ten-thirty, what time is is now?"

"*Nine*-thirty," I said.

"Guess I'd better get up then, huh?"

"I think so."

"I wish you were here with me," she whispered.

"Mm, me too."

"When am I going to see you again?"

"How about tonight?"

"What time?"

"I don't know what's waiting for me at the office, I'll have to call you later."

"Okay, I won't make any other plans." She hesitated. "Matthew?" she said.

"Yes?"

"No, never mind. I'll talk to you later."

"What were you about to say?"

"No, nothing."

"All right then."

We said our good-byes, and I began dressing. I was in my undershorts when the next call came. I looked at the phone incredulously. I let it ring. I kept looking at it. Finally I picked it up. "Hello?" I said wearily.

"Matthew, it's me again," Bloom said. "We located Marshall, or at least we found the station he's working for, little AM station up there in Valdosta, plays mostly rock, I spoke to the station manager, a man named Ralph Slater, he told me Marshall left for a week's vacation after his show last Friday, he's got a morning show he does from nine to twelve, took off right after it, said he was going fishing on the Keys. But he's not back yet."

"Well, maybe . . ."

"He was due back this morning," Bloom said. "So where the hell is he?"

I did not get to Bloom's office until two o'clock that afternoon because by the time I got to work there were three dozen calls piled up and two people waiting to see me, and then Abe Pollock called and asked me to have lunch with him in atonement for not having yet got those liquor figures to me, which he promised to have by tomorrow at the very latest if he could get his client off his dead ass. After lunch my daughter called from St. Mark's to say she'd left the house without any money this morning, and she had to pay for her yearbook pictures *today* at the very *latest* so could I please send someone over with a check for twelve dollars and fifty cents? I wrote out a personal check and asked Cynthia to drive it over there, and then buzzed Frank to tell him I'd have to skip the afternoon meeting with him and Karl because Bloom had called and wanted me to listen to the tape he'd

made of the Q and A with Dwayne Miller. Frank asked me
when I had begun working for the Calusa P.D.

We listened to the tape in Bloom's office.

He had told me that Miller had come in voluntarily after
they'd finally managed to reach him early this morning at his
house in Manakawa. Miller claimed to have been on a fishing
trip with some buddies, leaving Saturday morning just before
dawn and not getting back until very late last night. He had
not learned that his granddaughter was dead until Detective
Kenyon informed him of the fact on the telephone. He seemed
annoyed that Konig—instead of himself—had made all the
funeral arrangements. Surprisingly, though, considering his
normal cantankerous nature and his further annoyance over
Konig's usurpation of what he considered to be his grand-
paternal obligation, he told Bloom he would have no objection to their entire conversation being taped; all he was interested
in was finding the person who'd killed his daughter and little
Allison. The tape started with someone, presumably Bloom,
blowing into the microphone, and then his voice intoning the
words, "Testing, one, two, three, four," and then a click and
a pause and another click and then Bloom's voice saying,
"This will be a recording of the questions put to Dwayne
Miller and of his responses thereto made this twenty-first day
of January at ten-fifteen a.m. in the Public Safety Building of
the Calusa Police Department, Calusa, Florida. Questioning
Mr. Miller was Detective Morris Bloom of the Calusa Police
Department. Also present was Detective Peter Kenyon."
There was another pause, and then Bloom went through the
entire Miranda-Escobedo song-and-dance and elicited from
Miller the information that he was willing to answer police
questions without an attorney present. The interview began:

"Mr. Miller, you told me before I started the tape here that
you've been on a fishing trip from early Saturday morning till
late last night, which would've been late Sunday night. Can
you tell me what time you left your home on Saturday
morning?"

"I was picked up at a quarter to five."

"That would be four-forty-five a.m. on Saturday, January
nineteenth, is that correct?"

"Yes."

"And you returned at what time?"

"About two in the morning."

"Two *this* morning? Monday, the twenty-first?"

"Yes."

"Were you aware at any time during your trip that your granddaughter, Allison Konig—"

"No, I was not aware."

"That she'd been found dead Friday night?"

"No, I didn't know that. I wouldn't have gone on the trip if I'd known that. As it was, I only went to shake the grief I was feeling over Vicky."

"Were you on a boat all that time, Mr. Miller?"

"Yes, I was."

"Wasn't there a radio on the boat?"

"Yes, there was, but we had no need to turn it on. The weather was beautiful, we didn't have to listen for any Coast Guard reports or anything."

"Who else was on this trip with you?"

"Man named Stan Hopper, who owns the boat, and another man named Dick Oldham."

"Just the three of you."

"That's all."

"Did either of the other men know about your granddaughter's death?"

"No, sir, they did not."

"I'd like to contact them later, if you don't mind—"

"Not at all."

"To ascertain the times you've given me, if that's all right."

"Yes, that's fine."

"Mr. Miller, I'd like to talk about this trust you set up for your daughter back in 1965."

"What about it?"

"I'm sure you know the terms of the trust."

"I'm the one who set it up, of *course* I know the terms of it."

"You know, for example, that your daughter Vicky was the primary beneficiary—"

"Yes, I know that."

"And your granddaughter was the alternate beneficiary."

"Not at the time."

"What do you mean?"

"When I created the trust, there *was* no granddaughter. Vicky wasn't even married. This was 1965, she was only twenty years old."

"But from what I understand—"

"Yes, provision was made for her children, if ever she had any, to be alternate beneficiaries, yes. As it turned out, she only had the one, Allison. She miscarried with the first child."

"Mr. Miller, did you also know that if both your daughter and your granddaughter died before the trust terminated, the accumulated income and principal would revert to *you* as grantor of the trust?"

"Yes, I knew that."

"Did you know the termination date of that trust?"

"Yes. It was to terminate on my daughter's thirty-fifth birthday."

"Would you know the date?"

"January twenty-second."

"Then your daughter would have been thirty-five years old tomorrow."

"Yes."

"And you knew all this."

"I knew all of it, yes."

"Mr. Miller, did you visit your daughter on the night before she opened her singing engagement at the Greenery? That would have been a Thursday night, January the tenth."

"Yes, I went to see her."

"Where did this meeting take place?"

"At her house. On Citrus Lane, out there near the ball park."

"Why did you go there?"

"To try to convince her to back out of what she was about to do."

"What do you mean by that?"

"The job she had at the Greenery. I told her it'd be bad for her. I told her it still wasn't too late for her to call the whole thing off, get in touch with Eddie Marshall, like she should've in the *first* place, if she wanted to resume her career."

"You felt Mr. Marshall would have been of help to her, is that it?"

"Damn *right* he would've. It was Eddie who made her a

star all those years ago. You want my opinion, *he's* the one she *should've* married, and not that money-grubbing fool Tony.''

''Oh? Was there something more than a professional relationship between your daughter and Mr. Marshall?''

''You've got to be kidding.''

''No, I—''

''Where were you when all this was *happening?* On the moon someplace? Back there in the sixties, you couldn't open a magazine without there being something about Vicky in it. And about Eddie, too.''

''About their relationship, do you mean?''

''Yes, their romance, whatever you want to call it. I'll tell you, I thought *sure* they'd get married one day, it seemed so right. But I guess Tony turned her head, all his big important friends, you know. My daughter was just a country girl—a *star*, yes, but at heart just a barefoot kid from Arkansas. May've been my fault, I don't know. I put everything into that trust, you see, had all the income go right back into it, gave Vicky a modest allowance, but that was all. So she kept getting invited to that big mansion Tony had over near the university out there on St. Charles, Arabella and St. Charles, and she was meeting New Orleans society, and politicians from Washington, and singing stars from all over the country, and people who owned radio stations and record companies and whatnot, and before you knew it Eddie seemed like small-time stuff to her. Just a little Eye-talian boy from someplace in California, that's all. Never *mind* he made her a star. That didn't count anymore once Tony Konig sank his teeth into her.''

''Italian? Marshall doesn't sound like . . .''

''Well, he changed his name, you see. Years ago.''

''Would you know what his maiden name was?''

''What?''

''The name he was born with.''

''No, I don't. Don't think I ever even *heard* it, in fact. He changed it before he left California, he was Eddie Marshall time I met him.''

''What was his reaction when your daughter decided to marry Konig?''

''Well, who knows? He never said nothin about it, but I

guess it must've hurt him, wouldn't you think? Got my daughter three gold records, didn't he? Saw her day and night, they must've been sleepin together, I'd say. Kids back then were doin whatever they felt like, it wasn't like when *we* were kids. So I'm sure they were sleepin together, and I'm sure it must've hurt Eddie when she broke the news to him. Well, she made a mistake, that's for sure. I could tell right off she'd made a mistake. Tried to make up for her bad marriage by workin herself to death. That's how she lost the first baby. Drove herself and the band too hard workin on that album, the one they were gonna call 'More Vicky.'' Lost the baby, sure enough. And then quit the business.''

"Do you have any idea why she decided to try a comeback at this time?''

"No idea at all. Unless it was because she knew all that money would be coming in soon, and figured she could take a chance.''

"Did she mention anything about the money that night? Anything at all about the trust?''

"No, sir, we did not discuss money at all. What we talked about was her doing this damn fool thing out there at the Greenery. I told her it was wrong, I told her it'd be a disaster. Which is just what it turned *out* to be, didn't it. Did you read what that bitch wrote about her in the paper?''

"But Vicky wouldn't listen to you, is that right?''

"Wouldn't listen, that's right.''

"Mr. Miller, did you threaten to disinherit her?''

"I did.''

"Then you *did* discuss money.''

"Well, in that sense, yes.''

"In the sense that you meant you'd somehow change the provisions of the trust—''

"Well, yes, but I think she knew I was bluffing.''

"But you *did* mention the trust.''

"Well, yes, in passing.''

"Because you said earlier—''

"Yes, I *know* what I said, and I'll say it again. We did *not* discuss the trust, per se, we did *not* discuss the details of the trust, the money in the trust, we did *not* discuss money. Except as I told her I'd disinherit her if she went ahead with that job at the Greenery.''

"And she knew you meant the trust."

"I *suppose* she knew it. She *also* knew I was bluffing."

"In what way?"

"Well, she probably knew the trust was irrevocable, and I *couldn't* change it if I wanted to."

"Did you tell her that?"

"No, I never told her anything about the trust but what I thought she needed to know."

"Which was what?"

"That everything in it would be hers when she got to be thirty-five."

"Did you tell her how much was in it?"

"Nope."

"Did you mention that Allison was alternate beneficiary?"

"Nope."

"Did your attorney ever discuss the trust with her?"

"Nope. Why should he?"

"Then all she knew was that when she reached the age of thirty-five the trust would terminate and everything in it would be hers."

"That's all she knew."

"Mr. Miller, before we started talking here, I advised you of your rights, and I mentioned that you could stop this interview at any time just by telling me so, do you remember that?"

"Yes, I remember."

"I'd like to ask you some specific questions now about where you were, exactly, between the hours of three a.m. on Monday morning, January thirteenth, and nine a.m. that same morning. If you have any objections to answering such questions, then please tell me so, and we'll end the interview."

"That's when my daughter got killed, isn't it?"

"Yes, sir, she was killed sometime between those hours."

"I have no objection to answering any questions you might put to me. I want to help you find who *did* this, that's all."

"Can you tell me where you were that morning?"

"I was with a woman named Gretchen Heibel at her home on Westview Road out on Fatback Key."

"Do you have the address there?"

"Yes, it's 642 Westview."

"And you were with her from three a.m. that morning—"

"I was with her from *eight* p.m. Sunday night, when I picked her up for dinner, and then we went back to her house afterward, and we spent the night together, and I left for the groves first thing in the morning."

"What time would that have been?"

"What?"

"When you left for the groves?"

"About eight-thirty."

"Eight-thirty a.m. on Monday morning."

"Yes, around then."

"Did you or Miss Heibel—Gretchen Heibel, did you say?"

"Yes, Heibel."

"Would you spell that for me, please?"

"H-E-I-B-E-L. Heibel."

"Is it Miss or Mrs.?"

"Miss."

"Did you or Miss Heibel leave the house anytime between three a.m. and nine a.m. that Monday morning?"

"No, sir, we did not."

"That's *neither* of you."

"*Neither* of us, correct."

"And she'll confirm that?"

"I'm sure she will."

"How long have you known her?"

"Two or three months, it must be . . . well, wait, we met just after Thanksgiving."

"Is it a close relationship?"

"Not close enough so that she'd lie for me where murder's involved."

"Would you describe it as casual then?"

"I would describe it as an adult relationship between a man of fifty-six and a woman of forty-seven, that's how I would describe it."

"I'd appreciate it, Mr. Miller, if you refrained from telephoning her before we have a chance to speak to her."

"If you plan on visiting her—"

"I do."

"You won't find her at home, not during the business day, anyway. She works in the sales office at Timucuan Cove, that's the new condominium going up on Whisper."

"Thank you, I'll try her there."

"Quits at five."

"Thank you. Mr. Miller, I'm going to warn you again that you can end this interview anytime you—"

"Stop warning me so much, I ain't about to end it."

"Your granddaughter, as you know—"

"Do we have to talk about Allison? For God's sake, I've just come from putting her in the ground!"

"We don't have to if you don't want to."

"It's just . . . well, *damn* it, ask your questions, let's get it over with."

"Your granddaughter was found at eight-thirty p.m. this past Friday, that was January the eighteenth. The medical examiner has estimated the time of her death as six p.m., and I'd like to know now, Mr. Miller, where you were between four-thirty that afternoon and eight-thirty that night."

"I was with a woman named Gretel Heibel at her home on Westview Road out on Fatback Key."

"You mean Gretchen."

"No, Gretel."

"You said—"

"This is *Gretel*. Gretchen's sister."

"Oh."

"Yes."

"And *her* address, Mr. Miller?"

"The same as Gretchen's, 642 Westview."

"They live in the same house?"

"Yes, sir, they do."

"And you were with—"

"I went to the house Friday to have a drink with Gretel *and* Gretchen at five-thirty. Gretchen had a dinner date, so she left around seven sometime. Gretel and I had dinner alone there, and we spent the rest of the night together."

"Did either of you leave the house at any time between—"

"No, sir, we did not. I was there from five p.m. Friday till about four a.m. the next morning, at which time I got up, and let myself out, and went back to my *own* house 'cause I was expecting Stan Hopper and Dick Oldham to pick me up for the fishing trip."

"Had either of the Heibel sisters heard anything about your granddaughter's death?"

"I can't speak for Gretchen, because she didn't come home

that night. But neither Gretel nor I was watching television or listening to the radio—we had the record player going—neither of us heard a word about it. I told you before, I wouldn't have *gone* on that fishing trip if I'd known my little grand-daughter had . . . had . . . been killed.''

"Where can I find *Gretel* Heibel?"

"At the house."

"Will she be there during the day?"

"Yes, she works at home. She illustrates children's books."

"Anything you want to add to this, Mr. Miller? Or clarify? Or change?"

"Nope, nothing."

"All right then, that's it."

Bloom snapped off the cassette player and said, "What do you think?"

"Have you talked to the ladies yet?"

"Not yet, I was going to later. Figured I'd wait till Gretchen—is she the one who sells the condos?—gets home, kill two birds with one stone. Yeah, she's the one at Timucuan Cove. *Gretel*'s the one who does the children's books. Boy, I can't wait till I'm fifty, sixty years old. Konig and Miller have had more sex over the past weekend than I've had in the past two weeks out there on old Avenida del Sol. You want to know why my wife fell in love with our house? Because her father's name was Sol. I told her 'Sol' means 'sun' in Span-ish, it's Avenue of the *Sun*. She said she didn't care *what* Sol meant in Spanish, to her Sol would always mean Sol Fishbein, God rest his soul. So we live in a hacienda-style house on Avenida del Sol, and I haven't had any sex in the past two weeks because I'm on this *fecockteh* diet and I haven't got the *energy*, if you want to know."

"Have you contacted the fishermen yet?"

"Yeah, the big fishermen. Dick Oldham and Stan Hooper, or vice versa. They confirm Miller's story, he was with them from early Saturday morning to late Sunday night. Which doesn't mean he wasn't out slitting his granddaughter's throat on *Friday* night. You want to come with me later? When I go see the Dolly Sisters? It'll be after you quit work, you won't have to worry. Okay?"

"Okay."

"I'll buy you a beer afterward," Bloom said, and grinned.

*   *   *

Fatback Key is in Calusa County, but it is not within the city limits of Calusa itself. Instead, it falls within the boundaries of Manakawa to the south. Fatback is the wildest and narrowest of the county's several keys, flanked on east and west by the Gulf and the bay, two bodies of water that during the hurricane season sometimes join over Westview Road, the two-lane blacktop that skewers Fatback north to south. The bridge connecting Fatback to the mainland is a humpback that can accommodate only one car at a time. Directly over the bridge is a large wooden signpost with two dozen arrows pointing off either left or right, the names of the key's residents carved into the wooden arrows and then painted in with white. Dusk was falling as we came over the bridge, the wooden planks rumbling under the wheels of Bloom's car, his headlights on in anticipation of the dark, which sometimes comes quite suddenly in Calusa. He pulled in alongside the directional sign, and we both scanned the sheaf of bristling wooden arrows, found the name HEIBEL lettered on one of them, and turned to the left and southward.

The Heibel house was on the bay side and marked with a simple wooden plaque standing in the sand and bearing only the sisters' last name. The mailbox was just across the road, on the Gulf side, and marked with the numerals 642. The house itself must have been built back in the twenties, when land speculation was earning fortunes for those wise enough to have discovered the beauty and serenity of the county's most beautiful key. It resembled more than anything else the sort of Beverly Hills mansion a silent-screen star might have lived in, inspired by Spanish-mission architecture, with white stucco walls and orange tiled roofs, and arched windows and stone paths that meandered through cloisters of palms toward the water on the bay side, which I could see through an open patio overhung with ferns. Bloom rang the front door bell.

The woman who answered the door was wearing a paint-spattered blue smock over jeans. She was perhaps five feet eight in her bare feet, and her blond hair was pulled back into a pony tail at the back of her neck, a style that seemed too young for her age, which I guessed to be somewhere in the early forties. She had the kind of elegant Teutonic beauty typified by Hildegarde Neff, her blue eyes mildly quizzical as she peered out into the dusk and said, "Yes, can I help you?" There was only the faintest trace of a German accent in her speech.

"I'm Detective Bloom, Calusa Police Department," Bloom said, and showed her his shield and his laminated I.D. card. "This is Matthew Hope."

"Yes?" she said.

"Miss Heibel?"

"I am Gretel Heibel, yes?"

"Miss Heibel, I wonder if we might come in for a moment."

"What is it?" she asked.

"We'd like to ask you some questions."

"This is about the murders, isn't it?" she said. "I know Dwayne's daughter was killed . . ."

"Yes, that's right."

"And now his granddaughter. I heard on the television that also his granddaughter was found murdered."

"Yes, Friday night."

"*Ach,*" she said, and sighed heavily.

"That's what we want to talk about," Bloom said.

"*Ach,*" she said again, and stepped aside and said, "Well, come in, please."

The entry floor was laid with terra-cotta Mexican tiles, and the half-wall at its farthest end was lined with plants in large clay tubs. Above the low wall was a colonnade of stark white posts beyond which was a huge living room with arched doorways leading out to the illuminated swimming pool and the bay beyond. Just inside the arches a long table was set up with paint pots and jars of water and drawing paper and brushes and pencils and soap erasers and paint-smeared rags, all bathed in the glow of an angular desktop Luxo lamp.

"I was working," she said, "please forgive the mess. I like to work where I can see the bay. I used to work in a room upstairs, but it overlooks the Gulf, and the view is sometimes too wild there for my kind of illustration. I do children's books," she explained.

"Yes, Mr. Miller told us," Bloom said.

"Please sit down," she said. "Can I get you something to drink?"

"No, thank you."

"Something soft perhaps? A Coke? Some iced tea?"

"No, thank you."

"Well, then," she said, and smiled, and waited for Bloom to begin.

"We were hoping your sister would be here by now," he said.

"Yes, she should be home any time now. Did you want to speak to her as well?"

"If we may."

"Yes, surely. What is it you want to know?"

"Miss Heibel, can you tell us where you were this past Friday between the hours of four-thirty p.m. and eight-thirty p.m.?"

He had not, I noticed, mentioned anything about wanting to confirm Miller's alibi, had not given her the slightest clue that the only thing of *real* interest to him was the whereabouts of Dwayne Miller on the night his granddaughter was killed. He had told her only that he was from the police, that he was here to talk about the murders, and that he wanted to question both her and her sister. For all Gretel knew, she *herself* might have been a suspect. She sat watching him expectantly now, considering her answer, her slender hands folded in her lap, her legs crossed at the ankles, her blue eyes blinking nervously.

"I was here," she said. "Friday night I was here."

"How about Friday afternoon?"

"Yes, I was also here. Working."

"Alone?"

"My sister came home at about five. I was alone until then."

"And were you and your sister here for the rest of the night?"

"No, my sister had a dinner engagement. She left here about seven."

"Leaving you alone?"

"No, Dwayne was here, too."

"When did *he* get here, Miss Heibel?"

"At about five-thirty. We had drinks together, the three of us."

"And then your sister left."

"At about seven, yes."

"And you and Mr. Miller stayed here."

"Yes, we had dinner together."

"Did he leave after dinner?"

"No, he spent the night here. We are lovers, you see."

"What time *did* he leave?"

"Early the next morning. I was sound asleep, but I know he set the alarm for three a.m. I would say he left sometime between three and four. I know he was going on a fishing trip."

"Would you know where your sister was that night?"

"You will have to ask her."

I didn't know quite why Bloom had asked that last question. I *did* know that a medical examiner's estimate of the time of death was at best an approximate guess that took into account such variables as the temperature of the air and God knew what else. The M.E.'s report had set the time of Allison's death as six p.m., but in each of Bloom's interviews—first with Konig and then with Miller and now with Gretel—he'd asked where they'd been at four-thirty p.m., which meant he was giving the M.E. a ninety-minute leeway for error. Miller hadn't got here to Fatback Key until five-thirty on the afternoon Allison was killed. He could have made it here from the Cushing Sports Arena in less than forty minutes, depending on traffic. Similarly if Gretchen Heibel—the real-estate-selling sister—was somehow involved in this, she could easily have driven from Fatback Key to Calusa before that teenager discovered Allison in the drainage ditch. I surmised this was Bloom's reason for wanting to know where Gretchen had spent the night. Was it possible the pair of them had kept the little girl captive somewhere and that Bloom was now trying to pinpoint that place? The surmise seemed far-fetched, and I suddenly had the sinking feeling that Bloom, for all his expertise, was clutching at straws.

"Anyone pick her up here?" he asked.

"Do you mean when she left?"

"Yes."

"No. She left in her own car."

"At seven, you say."

"Yes, approximately seven."

"Well," Bloom said, and sighed. "What time does she usually get home from work?" he asked, and looked at his watch.

"She is normally here by now."

I looked at my watch. It was almost six-thirty.

"Are you sure you wouldn't care for something while you wait? Some hot coffee perhaps?"

"Matthew?"

"I wouldn't mind a cup of coffee," I said.

"I'll put some on the stove," Gretel said, and rose at once and went into the kitchen. Bloom stood up, stretched, and walked to the long work table near the arched doorways. He glanced briefly at a brightly colored drawing and then looked out over the swimming pool and the bay.

"Nice place," he said.

"Beautiful."

"Must cost what, would you guess?"

"Half a million."

"More, I'd say. Pretty woman, don't you think?"

"Attractive," I said.

"Miller didn't strike me as the last of the red-hot lovers, did he you?"

"Well, there's a certain raw power about him."

"Mm," Bloom said, and glanced again at the drawing. "Who do you suppose *this* cutie is?" he asked.

The drawing depicted, in broad strokes and a representational style, some sort of misshapen little monster leaping in the air, both feet off the ground, his tiny fists clenched over his head, his face distorted in rage.

"Rumpelstiltskin," Gretel said behind us, and came into the room, and walked to the table. She picked up the drawing and held it closer to the light. "This is just a sketch, of course, I will refine it later. Do you know the fairy tale?"

"Yes," I said, vaguely remembering something about a maiden having to guess the name of the dwarf who'd helped her do something or other sometime in the past.

"About somebody letting down her long blond hair," Bloom said.

"No, that is Rapunzel. This is Rumpelstiltskin. By my countrymen, Jakob and Wilhelm Grimm. Do you know Grimm's Law?"

"No," I said.

"No," Bloom said.

"Also by Jakob Grimm, who was famous for more than his fairy tales, you know. It is a formula describing the changes in Indo-European stop consonants. B, d, and g become p, t and k in German—and so on. But you *must* know Rumpel-stiltskin, *nein?*''

''Well, sure,'' I said, not at all sure anymore.

''It is about a German *Müller*—how do you say it in English? A man who owns a mill, and he grinds the grain there, do you know? *Ein Müller*. Anyway, he tells the king that his daughter can spin gold out of straw. The king takes her to his castle and locks her in a room and asks her to do this or else she will die. To spin the straw into gold, eh? Which of course she cannot do. But a dwarf appears to her, and tells her he can do it for her, for a price, and she gives him her necklace to spin the whole room of straw into gold. Well, the king is of course astonished, and he locks her in a *bigger* room the next night, with even *more* straw in it, and he tells her that if she values her life she will spin *this* into gold as well, which again she cannot do. Until the dwarf once again appears, and this time she gives him her ring, and he does it for her, he spins all the straw into gold. Well, the king is truly amazed, and now he takes her to the biggest room in the castle, and it too is filled with straw, and he tells her that if she can spin all this into gold by morning, he will marry her. She is crying and crying, and she doesn't know what to do until the dwarf again appears—but she has no more jewelry to give him, she has already given him the last of her jewelry. So she promises the dwarf that if she becomes queen, she will give him her firstborn child. They seal the bargain, and he turns all the straw to gold, and she becomes queen of all the land.

''Well, a year goes by, and the dwarf returns and he wants her to keep her promise, he wants the firstborn child. She offers him all the riches in the kingdom, but he refuses them, he wants the child instead, he insists on the firstborn child. She is in tears again, she is sobbing and begging, and so he takes pity on her and says if she can guess his name in three days' time, why, she can keep her child. So he comes back on the first day, and she guesses names like Caspar and Melchior and Balthazar and all the names she can think of, but it is none of those. And he comes back on the second day, and she begins guessing more exotic names, more *crazy* names like Sheepshanks and Spindleshanks and Spiderlegs and so on, but it is none of those names, either, and the dwarf goes away laughing because he knows the child will soon be his. But then a messenger comes to the queen and tells her that he saw a very strange sight in the forest, and that it was a dwarf dancing around and singing, and what he was singing was 'Today I brew, tomorrow I'll bake, next day I'll the queen's child take; for little dreams my royal dame that *Rumpelstiltskin* is my name!' Well, when he comes back the next day, the queen teases him, eh? She says, 'Is your name Thomas?' and he tells her no, and she says, 'Is your name Richard?' and he tells her no again, and then she says, 'Is it by chance Rumpelstiltskin?' So the dwarf jumps up and down in rage— that's the sketch you're looking at there—and tears himself in two, and that is the end of Rumpelstiltskin.''

"I remember it now," Bloom said, nodding.

"Yes, so do I," I said.

"It is fun to illustrate," Gretel said, and then turned toward the front door, apparently hearing a key in the latch before either Bloom or I did.

The woman who entered was wearing black tailored slacks and a pink blouse with paler pink buttons, pink shoes with French heels, a pink plastic barette sweeping her long blond hair back and away from one side of her face. She was as tall as Gretel, with the same fine features, the rather generous mouth and high cheekbones, the aquiline nose and striking blue eyes. Miller had said in his interview that Gretchen Heibel was forty-seven years old, but she looked no older than her sister, with the same slender body, the same lithe, long look. An expression of surprise crossed her face as she came into the living room and saw us standing at the work table. She glanced at her sister questioningly.

"Gretchen," her sister said, "these men are from the police."

"Ah?" Gretchen said, and strode into the room, her hand outstretched. "How do you do?" she said, shaking first Bloom's hand and then mine. "I'm Gretchen Heibel, have you offered the gentlemen something to drink, Gretel?"

"Yes, I . . ."

"Something?" she asked. "Or are you permitted?"

"I'm making coffee now," Gretel said.

"I'll have something stronger, if you don't mind," Gretchen

said and smiled, and sat in an easy chair near the work table. Slipping off first one shoe and then the other, she said, "It's been one of those days," and rolled her big blue eyes. Her English was much better than her sister's, accent free, colloquial. "I don't know your names," she said.

"Detective Bloom," Bloom said.

"Matthew Hope."

She looked directly at me. *"You're* not a detective?" she asked.

"No," I said. "I'm an attorney."

"Whose?"

"Anthony Konig's."

"Vicky's former husband?"

"Yes."

"Mm," she said. "Then this *is* about the murders. Gretel, darling, would you pour me some scotch, please, just one ice cube."

"Yes, it's about the murders," Bloom said.

"Are my sister and I suspects?"

Bloom said nothing.

"Or is it Dwayne you're after?"

"We're not *after* anyone, Miss Heibel."

"Well, surely you're after *someone.*"

"I meant . . ."

"What you meant is that you're not *specifically* trying to pin this on Dwayne—that *is* the expression, isn't it?"

"That's right," Bloom said, and smiled. "We're not trying to pin this on Mr. Miller. Specifically."

"Ah, thank you," she said to her sister, and accepted the drink handed to her. "I think I hear the kettle," she said.

Gretel went out into the kitchen again. Gretchen sipped at her scotch. "So," she said, "where do you want to begin?"

"With Monday morning, January thirteenth, between three a.m. and eight-thirty a.m."

"What about it?"

"Where were you?"

"Oh? Then *am* I a suspect?"

"No, I simply . . ."

"Ah, you want me to account for *Dwayne's* whereabouts, yes, I see. He was here with me, if that's what you want to know."

"From when to when?"

"We had dinner together, he picked me up at about eight, eight-thirty."

"Where'd you have dinner?"

"The Pepper Mill."

"On Sabal?"

"On Sabal, yes."

"Where did you go after dinner?"

"We came back here."

"What time was that?"

"After dinner. I don't *know* what time, actually. Ten? Ten-thirty? After dinner," she said, and shrugged.

"When did he leave here?"

"The next morning."

"He spent the night here?"

"Yes, he often spends the night here."

"What time did he leave in the morning?"

"Eight, eight-thirty, I'm not sure. He went directly to work from here."

"Was your sister here that night?"

"No, she was in New York, she had a meeting with her editor and the author. The *translator*, actually; this is Grimm, you know."

"When did she get back?"

"On Tuesday."

"When you say Mr. Miller often spent the night here . . ."

"Yes, for the past several months or so. With me, or with my sister . . ." She hesitated. I could not tell whether what she said next was simply designed to shock or whether it was a sort of European candor to which American men aren't much accustomed. "Or sometimes with both of us together."

"I see," Bloom said, and cleared his throat.

"Yes," Gretchen said. "Ah, here's your coffee."

Gretel had come into the room carrying a silver tray on which were two cups of coffee, two spoons, a creamer, and a sugar bowl.

"I was telling Detective Bloom that Dwayne often spent the night with both of us," Gretchen said, and this time I knew for certain that she was intending to shock.

"Yes," Gretel said quietly. "That's true."

"Is there any saccharine?" Bloom asked, and cleared his throat again.

It was dark when we left the Heibel house. Bloom was silent all the way to the sign with its bristling arrows, silent as we crossed the noisy humpback bridge, silent as he made his left onto 41 and headed the car back toward Calusa. He had promised me a beer, and we stopped for one in a joint called the Townline Rest, just this side of the Calusa city limits. A waitress wearing black tights, a black leotard, black high-heeled pumps and a short, frilly white apron took our order and seemed disappointed when it was only beer. Bloom clinked his mug against mine, said "Cheers," and then swallowed a huge mouthful of beer and foam. He wiped the back of his hand across his mouth, and said, "Looks like his alibi checks out, huh? *Both* of them."

"Looks that way," I said.

"Except for those few unaccountable hours when he could have been out there doing all *kinds* of dirty work. But still, that would've been cutting it pretty close."

"Yes."

"So," he said, and shrugged, and sighed, and drank some more beer. "I'm forty-six years old," he said, "and I've never been to bed with two women at the same time. How old are you, Matthew?"

"Thirty-seven."

"Have you ever been to bed with two women at the same time?"

"Yes," I said.

"Was it terrific?"

"There are a lot of arms and legs," I said.

It was close to eight when he dropped me off where I had left the Ghia at the Gateway Shopping Plaza, and almost eight-thirty when I put my key into my own front door. I mixed myself a very strong martini, turned on the recording machine, and listened to my telephone messages. My daughter had called to thank me for the check and to say I had saved her life. Dale had called to ask if I'd forgotten all about her and to suggest that I might like to come over if I didn't get in too late. The third call was from Bloom. I called him back at once.

"Yeah, hello, Matthew," he said. "Good news. We got

Sadowsky, the drummer. The New York cops finally reached his mother, found out he's been playing at a hotel down here in Miami ever since the season started. Kenyon moved on it while we were busy talking to the krauts. Sadowsky's coming in voluntarily, Miami's a hop, skip, and jump from here. I'm expecting him any minute. You want to sit in on it?''

"I'd like to," I said.

"Come on down," Bloom said, and hung up.

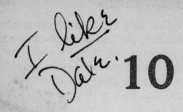

10

I called Dale just before I left the house to tell her there was something else I had to do before I'd be through for the night.

"What time do you think that'll be?"

"About ten, I'd guess. In fact, I'll make *sure* it's ten."

"Where will you be?"

"At the Public Safety Building."

"That'll mean at least forty minutes to my house."

"Will that be too late?"

"No. Come when you're finished. Whenever you're finished."

"I'll call you if there are any problems."

"Please don't let there be any problems," she said.

Neil Sadowsky was a man in his mid-thirties, about five feet seven inches tall, weighing a good hundred and sixty pounds, I guessed, with blond hair and brown eyes. A full beard covered his chin and his jowls and blended into the mustache over his upper lip, all of it as blond as the hair on his head and lending to his face a look of Victorian aristocracy that was strengthened by his straight slender nose and the deepness of his eyes. He was wearing blue slacks and a paler blue Ultrasuede jacket, a navy blue T-shirt, and black patent leather Gucci loafers. We were sitting in the captain's office; I was beginning to wonder if the captain ever came to work.

"So," Bloom said, "it was nice of you to fly over, Mr. Sadowsky, I really appreciate it. We've had a hell of a time finding you."

"Yeah, well, I've been in Miami since before Christmas," Sadowsky said.

"That's what your mother told the New York cops."

"I wish you hadn't bothered my mother."

"I'm sorry about that." Bloom paused, and then said, "I guess you know Vicky Miller and her daughter were killed."

"Yes."

"When did you find out, Mr. Sadowsky?"

"About Vicky, last Monday. About the daughter . . ."

"Well, let's talk about Vicky first. You found out about her Monday, huh? Day after the murder."

"Yes."

"Where were you the night she got killed? Were you working?"

"No, I've got Sunday off."

"So where were you?"

"I don't remember."

"Well, Mr. Sadowsky, I wish you'd *try* to . . ."

"Listen, I came here because I thought I could be of some help to you. If I knew this was going to be a third degree . . ."

"This isn't a third degree, Mr. Sadowsky."

"No? Then what is it? If you think I killed Vicky and her kid, you're out of your mind."

"So where were you?"

"I told you, I don't remember. When I get back to Miami, I'll look at my calendar, I'll tell you where I was. How the hell can you possibly believe I had anything to do with Vicky's murder?"

"A nice Jewish kid like you, right?"

"What's that supposed to mean?"

"Where were you on Sunday night, the thirteenth of January, Mr. Sadowsky?"

"I keep telling him I don't remember," Sadowsky said to me, "and he keeps *asking* me. Vicky and I were good friends, can you understand that?" he said, turning back to Bloom. "There was nothing romantic between us, like with her and Eddie, but we were *friends*, can you understand *friends?* Can you get *friends* through your thick head? So why would anybody kill his *friend?''*

"Gee, I don't know," Bloom said. "Why did Cain kill Abel?"

"Jesus," Sadowsky said, and shook his head, and let out his breath, and then said, "I can't believe this. For Christ's sake, can't you understand how *close* we all were? I mean, it happened to all of us *together*, like a dream, what was happening to us. I mean, what the hell *were* we? A bunch of kids rehearsing in *garages* until we became Wheat? Without Vicky . . . well, without *Eddie*, I guess . . . we'd *still* be playing toilets in every shitty alley in the South. Eddie's a genius. Have you ever met a genius? There isn't anything he doesn't know about music. You should've heard us back then, when we were auditioning for Regal. You'd have thrown us out of that studio in a minute. Even Georgie, who was better than any of us, maybe improved five hundred percent once Eddie started working with us. Me, I was just a half-ass dope banging on pots and pans till Eddie came along. Taught me everything I know about drumming. Hell, taught me everything I know about *music*. Before I met him, I didn't know a paradiddle from a pair of chopsticks. He was a giant in his profession, a *giant*. Had a temper could level you flat, used to explode at the slightest thing, but who says a genius has to have patience besides? I mean, he was the one *responsible* for Wheat. And for Vicky Miller, too.''

"How so?" Bloom asked.

"Well, you know, after our audition . . ." Sadowsky shook his head. "I mean, who would've thought there was *anything* there at all?"

The audition had been a total disaster.

Vicky's voice may have served in the past to mollify the scant audiences of drunks to whom she'd played in the saloons of Arkansas, but this was the big-time world of record production, and—even amplified—she had a difficult time being heard over Hamilton's driving lead guitar, the bass player's sonorous chords, and Sadowsky's own pounding. Happily for her, Regal's producer wandered by just as Vicky and the still-unbaptized group were winding up the second cut. Standing in the control booth, he listened and watched.

What he heard, by Sadowsky's own admission now, was just *awful*—but what he saw was something else again. He saw what Konig had seen earlier: nineteen-year-old Victoria Miller, tall and leggy, with midnight-black hair and eyes the color of anthracite, backed now by three not unattractive young men who, as fate might have ordained, all happened to be shorter than she was and exceedingly blond besides.

In the record business, or so Sadowsky now explained to us, a "producer" is really a combination of an arranger, a conductor, and what would be called a director if cutting a record were in any way similar to making a movie or putting on a play. The producer working for Konig was the young Eddie Marshall—originally Marciano, or Mariani, or Mastroianni, or Marielli, Sadowsky simply couldn't remember—who'd been born in Los Angeles of Italian descent, and who was working his way up in the music business doing work "far beneath his obvious talents," his constant complaint to the group. He saw in Vicky and the three young men backing her the *visual* nucleus of another of those overnight sensations that could happen only in the rock music business—if only he could get a *performance* out of them. Krantz and Sadowsky were better musicians than the lead guitarist Vicky and her father had picked up in Nashville, nineteen years old and another of those sixties kids who'd learned three basic chords and who'd then gone out to buy umpteen thousand dollars' worth of amplifiers and speakers so he could rehearse a "group." He was, however, not entirely hopeless. Blond and good-looking, with china blue eyes and an engaging smile, Geoff Hamilton would get by with a little help from his friends, and he'd fit in beautifully besides with the other two blonds Eddie planned to use as Vicky's backup. In his mind, and solely based on the color of their hair, Eddie had already decided to name the nascent group "Wheat."

The problem was Victoria Miller herself, and her pushy father. Dwayne Miller was something of a madman, a cross between a religious fanatic, a carny barker, a con man, and a shrewd entrepreneur who visualized himself as an impresario with but a single artiste in his stable: his daughter Victoria. He would settle for nothing but complete stardom for her, this despite her notable lack of a vocal instrument and an almost tone-deaf ear. But miracles had been known to happen, and Eddie Marshall was eager to try his hand at producing his first one—

"Even for Moses and Jesus," Sadowsky said, "there had to be a first one."

Eddie locked himself in with Vicky and the three musicians (whom he now officially baptized Wheat), and for three weeks they labored to produce the single that would later become part of the hit album. Eddie had written the tune himself and had titled it "Frenzy" for no other reason than that the word "frenzy" was repeated in it a total of twenty-six times, accompanied by a great many supportive lyrics like "I'm in a," and "You're in a," and "We're in a," prophetic in that the moment the album was released, *everyone* was in a.

If it took three weeks to perfect the single from which the album would derive its title, it took an equal number of months to record the other nine songs on it. Electronic wizardry aside, Eddie worked in those next three months ("This was November and December of 1964, and January of 1965," Sadowsky said) harder than he ever had in his life. His raw material consisted of a scarcely accomplished bass guitarist, a loud drummer, a lead guitarist whose repertoire had now expanded to eight chords, and a singer who—though extravagantly beautiful—could barely carry a tune. The miracle of his miracle was that he pulled it off. With more dazzling tricks and effects than anyone save Steinmetz, Edison, or Marconi had ever contrived, he produced an album that made "Victoria Miller and Wheat"—as they were billed in blood-red letters on the album sleeve—sound like the freshest thing on the rock scene since the Beatles had broken out of their Liverpool basement.

"Frenzy was released in April of '65, around Eastertime," Sadowsky said, "when Eddie and Konig figured there'd be bunches of kids home from school on vacation and roaming the record shops in search of hot new talent. The album shot to the number-one spot on the charts within three weeks, and passed the million-copy gold-record mark at the beginning of June. By then we'd pulled the single from the album, and it was in the number-two spot on the singles charts. In the long run the single sold a little less than a million copies, robbing us of a gold record in that category, but we guessed that was because so many people already owned the album.''

Vicky had told me, on the night she was killed, that her producer hadn't wanted her to perform live because he ''said it was bad for the records, he wanted everybody to go out and buy the *records,* you see.'' Given the paucity of her talent, virtually nonexistent without the help of studio gimmickry, Eddie's decision had been a wise one. The next album, appropriately titled ''More Frenzy,'' was released in 1966 and copped another gold record. The third and last album was simply titled ''Vicky.'' By then it had become apparent that she alone was the star here; it was Victoria Miller who was directly responsible for all that bread Regal Records was making, and Wheat might just as well have been chaff.

Her refusal to perform in public, her refusal even to appear on any of the television talk shows, was attributed to an innate shyness that caused severe stagefright, an ailment— according to Sadowsky—suffered even by the likes of Carly Simon. Vicky's millions of fans, the press releases explained, would have to be content with whatever glimpses of her personal life were revealed in the seemingly endless flow of newspaper and magazine interviews she granted, including a lengthy one in *TV Guide,* the voice of the medium on which she had never appeared. ''Vicky'' was released in 1967 and earned yet another gold record. It was her last album.

''How come?'' Bloom asked.

''She got married,'' Sadowsky said, and shrugged. ''To Tony Konig, in March of '68. And she got pregnant almost the minute after. Miscarried while we were working on the fourth album, as a matter of fact. Something called 'More Vicky,' which was never released. She quit halfway through, when she lost the baby. She blamed the miscarriage on the long days and hard hours she'd been putting in. Told all the newspapers her personal life was more important than all the gold records in the world. Ended *her* career and *also* Wheat's and Eddie Marshall's. He started messing around with dope, ended up working as a disc jockey at some hick radio station in . . .''

''Mr. Hope,'' Kenyon said, poking his head into the room. ''Telephone call for you, you can take it out here if you like.''

"Thank you. Excuse me," I said and pushed back my chair. I went out to the reception room and took the receiver Kenyon extended to me. "Hello?" I said.

"Guess who?" Dale said.

"Hi."

"Do you know what time it is?"

"I know precisely what time it is."

"Five minutes to ten."

"So it is."

"You said you'd be finished there at ten."

"I *will* be finished here at ten."

"Just checking," she said. "Why don't you leave right now?"

"I will."

"Matthew, I . . ."

"Yes?"

"Nothing, just hurry," she said.

There was a click on the line. I put the receiver back on the wall hook, thanked Kenyon, and went back in to the captain's office.

"Everything all right?" Bloom asked.

"Yes, but I've got to leave," I said. "I had a previous appointment, but when you called . . ."

"This may take a while here yet," Bloom said. "Go on, if you got to."

"He *still* thinks I'm involved in this fucking thing," Sadowsky said to me.

"Convince me you're not," Bloom said.

I didn't get to Dale's house on Whisper Key until twenty minutes to eleven. I was ravenously hungry, and when I told her I hadn't had any dinner yet she whipped out a leftover roast beef and a huge ripe tomato, sliced both, put up some toast for a sandwich, and then took a bottle of cold beer from the fridge. Out on the patio, I plunged into my meal while she sipped at the drink she'd mixed for herself. The night had turned a bit humid, the outdoor furniture was sticky and damp. Dale was wearing a pale blue nylon wrapper, her hair loose around her face. She kept watching me as I wolfed my sandwich and guzzled my beer, telling her with a full mouth all about the Heibel sisters out on Fatback, and then the "interview"—as the police euphemistically called it—with Neil Sadowsky. But she seemed preoccupied. When at last I finished, I opened my arms wide to her, and she came to me where I was sitting, and snuggled onto my lap, and put her head on my shoulder, and sighed.

"What is it?" I asked.

"Bad day at Black Rock," she said.

"Tell me."

"Top to bottom," she said. "First appointment to last. It would bore you."

"Tell me, anyway."

The thing that was troubling her most, *aside* from the little maddening routine annoyances that can drive any attorney clear around the bend, was a visit she'd had at the end of the day from a lawyer representing the husband in a divorce action. Dale was representing the wife, a role that displeased her to *begin* with because it seemed entirely too sexist for a *man* to be representing the husband and a *woman* to be representing the wife, all the lines neatly drawn according to gender, all the parts distributed according to sex, the boys with the boys and the girls with the girls. My hand was resting on her nylon-covered breast as she said this, and when I yanked my hand back as though burned, she pulled it immediately to her again, and said, "Don't be a jackass," and slid it into the V-neck of the wrapper and onto the naked breast itself.

She had thought, at first, that when the opposing attorney asked to see her he'd wanted to talk settlement. They'd been haggling for the past several months over alimony and support payments, and Dale naturally assumed he'd come there this afternoon to offer something more reasonable than the figures he'd adamantly clung to since before Christmas. But he didn't mention anything at all about alimony *or* support for the first twenty minutes of his visit, preferring instead to talk about the new speedboat he'd bought, and eliciting from Dale the information that she was, yes, single and, well, relatively unattached, but that she didn't much care for water sports and would really appreciate getting to the purpose of his visit, if indeed there *was* a purpose.

"He was really beginning to annoy me by then, Matthew," she said, "and *yes,* darling, I know, I *know,* the last thing in the world any lawyer should do is lose her temper with opposing counsel, I *know* that, but the man was angling for a *date,* for God's sake, instead of getting to the important matter—to *me,* anyway—of a divorce my client's been trying to get for the past eight *weeks* now, since long before Christmas when she left her husband's bed and board and took her seven-month-old son with her."

This was the second time Dale had mentioned Christmas; I suddenly thought of Vicky exchanging cards with Eddie Marshall each year. I recalled, too—and it had bothered me enough at the funeral to have questioned Marshall about it on the spot—that Vicky had made no mention in her card of her imminent opening at the Greenery, to take place less than three weeks after Christmas. This *still* seemed odd to me— but Dale was talking.

". . . in the next five minutes that what he was *really* after was two things. The first was to establish his client's lily-white purity, and the second was a fairly subtle—but not *that* fucking subtle—fishing expedition. As to his client's honesty, virtue, chastity, godliness, mercy, generosity, honesty—did I say honesty?—and ability as a second baseman for the First Presbyterian Church's baseball team, he left no stone unturned. He laid it all out as though it had been computerized—my client is *so* honest that once he; my client is *so* virtuous that he even; my client is *so* chaste that he sometimes; my client is *so* godly and *so* on and *so* on, ad nauseam. And if *that* wasn't enough, he repeated it all over again, my client is this, my client is that, like an armed robber who's been seen going into a liquor store at eight p.m. with a shotgun under his arm, and who's memorized *exactly* what time a movie goes on—at seven-thirty, as it so happens—and who can tell you just who was kissing whom at eight p.m. sharp up there on the screen in the darkness of the old Bijou on Main Street, since torn down, m'dear, to make way for yet another shopping center. Do you understand what I'm saying, Matthew? He was *alibi-*ing his client, painting him as a goddamn saint, as if his wife hadn't been wearing a pair of shiners the first time she came into my office, given to her because she'd had the audacity to find him in bed with a cheap broad who shucks oysters at Downtown Marine. She later showed me the bruises on her breasts and legs, a true paragon of Southern gentlemanliness and godliness, her husband, who plays great second base for the church team. That was the *first* thing. The alibi. The establishing of credentials."

I was still thinking about my talk with Eddie Marshall, and about how curious it was that Vicky hadn't mentioned the opening to him. And although it hadn't occurred to me at the time, it now seemed to me that Eddie had talked much too long and far too loud about where he'd been on the night Vicky was murdered. I thought now how sweet an alibi a boat on the open water could provide. Dwayne Miller hadn't heard about his granddaughter's death because he'd been out on the water with two fishing cronies. Eddie Marshall hadn't heard about *Vicky's* murder because he, too, had been conveniently out on the water—*"Didn't come back in till last night. Didn't even know Vicky was planning a comeback, learned all about it in the paper. I'd have been down here in a flash if I'd known . . ."*

". . . quite a different matter. We have *all* been subjected to fishing expeditions of one stripe or—are you listening to me?"

"Yes, go ahead."

"You have a glazed look on your face. Maybe you'd better let go of that breast."

"No, no, go on."

"Well, it occurred to me, as my learned opponent launched into his clever Snoop-and-Peep routine, that he had trotted out his client's credentials only to . . ."

"Borrowed a boat from a friend of mine in Islamorada Sunday, when I got there . . ."

". . . and was now attempting to discover, in his sly, devious way, whether I *knew* what the clod had been up to for the past eight weeks, ever since my client walked out on him, taking only the baby in her arms, the clothes on her back, a pair of black eyes, and twelve dollars and eighty-six cents in cash."

"Stopped off at Disneyworld first—have you ever been to Disneyworld in Orlando?—drove right on down afterward and went out on the water."

"Mind you, we do not drag our round little heels at Blackstone, Harris, Gerstein, Garfield and Pollock. We had put a gumshoe onto Abby's . . . her name is Abby . . . husband right after the holidays were over, and I had a report sitting in the top drawer of my desk right that minute indicating that Harlow, for such is the wife-beating bastard's name, was still seeing the cheap oyster-shucker with whom he'd been caught in bed, had in fact taken her into the shack Abby had wisely abandoned, and was now living with her in open sin—as we might have said twenty years ago. Having been through the mill yourself, you must undoubtedly know that under F.S. 61.052, no judgment of dissolution of marriage can be granted unless a) the marriage is irretrievably broken or b) one of the parties is mentally incompetent. In short, this is a marital no-fault state, so to speak, and it wouldn't have mattered if old Harlow had kept a *harem* before Abby walked out on him. Except, and this is the big except, *except* as 61.08 declares that the court may consider the *adultery* of a spouse and the circumstances thereof in determining whether alimony shall be awarded to such spouse and the *amount* of alimony, if any, to be awarded, unquote. A male chauvinist provision if ever I saw one, in that the *wife's* adultery is the determining factor, never mind if the *husband* was fucking every available woman in the state.

"But turnabout is fair play, m'dear, and I figured I could argue under 61.08—if it ever came to that—that if alimony can be reduced or even denied because of a *wife's* adultery, then by the same token it should be increased because of a *husband's* adultery. I *knew* for sure that old Harlow was still busily engaged in extramarital fornication— the detective's report detailed his round-the-clock comings and goings, no pun intended—and now his attorney was trying to find out just how *much* I knew, asking me questions to which he already knew the answers, oh, that *smart* little shyster . . ."

"At Greensleeves, is that the name of the place?"

"The Greenery."

"How'd she sound?"

"Not very good."

". . . leading me down the garden, suspecting I'd put a

P.I. on his man, and asking me all sorts of questions like did I know where his client lived, he *knew* I knew where his client lived; and did I know he'd been living *alone* there since his wife walked out, a bald-faced lie, he was living with his oyster-shucker girlfriend; and had I ever tried to call him there, which I certainly knew was unethical, but what he was trying to find out was whether *Abby* had ever called there, and whether or not the oyster-shucker had answered the phone, and whether or not Abby had reported this to me, her attorney—a fishing expedition pure and simple. I finally tipped to what he was doing, but only when he'd about run down, and then I sat there listening to him as though he'd suddenly been stripped naked and was standing there with all his circumlocutions hanging out for one and all to . . ."

"*Had someone threatened her, do you think?*"

"*I don't know.*"

"*Well, did she mention any threats?*"

"*No.*"

"*A threatening letter maybe?*"

"When he was finished, I sat very still for several minutes, and then I opened the top drawer of my desk, very dramatically I must say, and took out the detective's report, and placed it on the desk before him, and said, 'I think you'd better decide on what kind of alimony and support you're going to come up with because your client may play great second base, but that's not going to cut any ice when we lay this on the judge.' Well, his face went absolutely white. He knew he'd been caught fishing and he knew further that the fish had bit back, *he* was the one on the hook now, he was the one who . . . Matthew?"

"Yes, Dale."

"What is it? My God, what's the *matter?*"

I had suddenly remembered something *else* about that day at the funeral. I had suddenly remembered Marshall walking me to where I'd parked the Karmann Ghia.

"I have to call Bloom," I said, and eased her off my lap.

He was there at the police station, but the woman who answered the phone told me he was still busy interviewing Sadowsky. I left word that this was urgent, and asked her to have Bloom call back as soon as he could. Dale was watching me.

"Did you hear a word I said?" she asked.

"Every word."

"Do you think I was an idiot not to have realized sooner what was going on?"

"No. I think you're marvelous."

"Sure."

I kissed her. I held her close. I kissed her again. And then we went into the bedroom and Dale pulled back the cover on the bed, and excused herself and went into the bathroom. I undressed in the darkness, and then lay on the bed, listening to the sound of the waves crashing on the beach outside the window. From the bathroom, I heard the sound of water running in the sink. Dale turned off the tap, and there was silence, except for the sound of the surf. The bathroom door opened. Light spilled into the bedroom, but only for a moment. Dale flicked the switch and padded naked in the darkness to the bed. We were moving into each other's arms when the telephone rang again.

"Shit," Dale said, and turned on the bedside lamp and lifted the telephone receiver from its cradle. "Hello?" she said, and listened. "Yes, just a moment," she said, and handed the receiver to me. "It's Bloom."

"Hello?" I said.

"What's up, Matthew?"

"I just remembered something."

"What?"

"At the funeral last Wednesday, when you left Marshall and me, we talked for a while. I think he was on a fishing expedition, Morrie. I think he was trying to find out how much I knew about those phone calls. The ones . . ."

"Yes, so?"

"He walked me to my car."

"Matthew . . ."

"Morrie, he *knew* my car. He stopped at the car before *I* did. The rear plate reads HOPE-1, but he couldn't have seen that because we were approaching from the front. If he knew my *car*, which was parked in Vicky's driveway the night she was . . ."

"I've got you," Bloom said. "Come on down here, I want you to fill me in on the conversation you had. I'd better hold Sadowsky. He's clean as a whistle, but I think he's got some work to do for us."

11

Most people don't realize that police work is a twenty-four-hour business, and that police stations take the abuse of round-the-clock habitation. It's amazing that all police stations do not deteriorate down to the ground within three years after they're built; even the relatively new Calusa facility was beginning to show the strains of wear and tear. As the hour hand of the wall clock visibly lurched onto the twelve, joining the minute hand so that both hands stood straight up for only an instant, midnight might just as well have been twelve noon here at the police station. A battery of detectives and uniformed cops were sitting at desks all around the room, making telephone calls; at one of the desks, a man hunted and pecked at the typewriter before him, studying the keyboard as though it were lettered in Sanskrit. At yet another desk, an exceedingly drunken man was being questioned by a detective with his sleeves rolled up and a .38-caliber pistol in a shoulder holster. In one corner of the room a woman in a blood-smeared white blouse was talking to a uniformed cop. Sadowsky sat at one of the desks with Bloom; I had already repeated to Bloom my conversation with Marshall on the day of the funeral—and now he was getting down to work.

"Now I know it was a long time ago when you heard his name," he said to Sadowsky, "but you told me a little while ago it was something like Marciano, or Mariani, or Mastroianni, or Marielli, something like that, you couldn't remember."

"I *still* can't remember," Sadowsky said.

"Right, so what I'm going to do, I'm going to try and prod your memory, okay?"

"Sure, whatever you say," Sadowsky said, and sighed.

I suddenly realized what all those cops on the telephones were doing. They were calling every damn hotel and motel in the city of Calusa, and probably in the adjoining towns of Manakawa and Hesterville as well.

"Calusa Police," one of the detectives said, "I wonder if you can tell me, ma'am, whether you've got a guest by the name of Edward Marshall registered there?"

"That'd be Marshall," another detective said, "M-A-R-S-H-A-L-L, yes, sir."

"Well, do you have an *Eddie* Marshall?"

"Or *any* kind of Marshall at all? Any guests with the first name Edward?"

"Yes, ma'am I'll wait."

"This is a long shot, you understand," Bloom said, "and I'm sorry to be putting you to this trouble, but the possibility exists he *may* have used a name he was familiar with, the name he was *born* with, in fact, instead of cooking up a phony one. Most people registering under an alias will anyway use their own initials for the phony name, I guess you know that. There's nothing mysterious about it, it's just that lots of men and women have monogrammed items like shirts or handkerchiefs or luggage, and it'd be very strange for a guy named Eddie Marshall with his initials on his shirt to register as John Smith, do you follow me?"

"Yes," Sadowsky said, and sighed again.

"Good," Bloom said, "very good," and suddenly grinned. There was about him tonight an air of gaiety I had not previously detected, as if even the *possibility* of a good suspect had—in addition to energizing the entire staff—given Bloom a badly needed jolt.

"What I'd like to do," he said, "if you don't mind, Mr. Sadowsky, I'd like to go right down the Calusa telephone directory with you, all the M's in the directory, one by one, not because Marshall *lived* here, which he didn't, and even if he did it would be listed under his legal name and not a name he dropped however many years ago, when he was still living in California—Pete,'' he called suddenly, "did you get through to the L.A.P.D.?''

"Yeah," Kenyon said, "they'll call us back in the morning, when the courts open."

"How about Frisco and San Diego?"

"I've got Reynolds and Di Luca working on it."

"Is he back from vacation?" I said.

"Is *who* back from vacation?" Bloom asked, turning to me.

"Di Luca."

"I didn't even know he was *away*," Bloom said, and laughed.

"He's back," Kenyon said. "Got back yesterday. You know him?"

"Better try Sacramento, too," Bloom said. "Get them working on it first thing in the morning. If a guy changes his name, there's got to be a court record of it someplace."

"Right," Kenyon said, and went out of the room.

"So here's the phone book," Bloom said to Sadowsky, "and what I'm going to do, I'm going to skip over all the names that couldn't *possibly* be Italian names, like Mason or Moore or Moriarty or like that. But when I come across anything with a lot of vowels in it—well, for example, here's the first one I see, right here, Macalerro, does that sound like the name?"

"No. Well, I really don't know."

"Just think about it for a minute. Macalerro. Ring a bell?"

"No, not really."

"How about this one right after it? Macarro."

"No. It was longer than that."

"Okay, let's keep going right down the page. Macchia. That's M-A-C-C-H-I-A. How do you pronounce that, Gregorio?" he said, turning to one of the detectives.

"Spell it again," Gregorio said.

"M-A-C-C-H-I-A."

"With a hard K," Gregorio said. "*Mah*-kee-yah."

"Okay, *Mah*-kee-yah, does that sound like it, Mr. Sadowsky?"

"No," Sadowsky said.

"How about Machinista?"

"No."

"Maegli?"

"No."

"Maestro?"

"No."

"Maffeto?"

"No."

"Mafrisiano?"

"No."

"Magaletto?"

"No."

"If the guy changed his name," Gregorio said, "he probably just translated it."

"What do you mean?" Bloom asked.

"From the Italian. Friend of mine changed his name to Frank Lamb, you know what his name used to be in Italian?"

"What?"

"Francesco Agnello. That's *lamb* in Italian, *agnello.*"

Bloom was looking at him. We were *all* looking at him.

"What's *Marshall* in Italian?" Bloom asked.

"Who knows?" Gregorio said. "Get a dictionary."

It took Bloom close to an hour and a half to get an Italian-English/English-Italian dictionary because all the book stores in town were closed, and none of the owners had their home phone numbers listed in the directory. He finally found someone in the building who was able to tell him the name of the man who was in charge of Calusa's library system, and he located the name in the telephone directory and called the man at home at a quarter to one in the morning and asked him if he could get someone down to the Henley Library to open it for him because he needed an Italian dictionary right away. The man, whose name was Roger Mahler and whose job as an appointed official submitted him to all sorts of abuse, but none quite like *this* before, patiently asked Bloom if this couldn't wait till morning. Bloom informed him that this *was* morning already, and it was also a double homicide he was investigating, and he would sincerely appreciate it if someone could get down there with a set of keys right away. It was

Mahler himself who finally agreed to go down there, where he was met by Detective Kenyon, who came back to the office at a little before two a.m. and placed the dictionary on Bloom's desk.

"I already peeked," he said.

Bloom was leafing through the pages in the English-Italian section. "Margin," he said aloud, "marigold, marine . . ." and then let his finger skip down the page and said aloud again, "Marriage, married, marrow . . ." and then zeroed in on "Marsh, marshmallow, marshal, here it is, marshal," he said, and looked up at Sadowsky. "Maresciallo," he said. "Is that the way you pronounce it, Gregorio?"

"Is it C-H-I?"

"No. C-I."

"Then it's a sh sound, like you said it."

"Maresciallo," Bloom said again. "Does that sound like the name, Mr. Sadowsky?"

"That sounds like the name," Sadowsky said.

The cop who finally located the motel was sitting at the desk closest to Bloom's. "Maresciallo," he said into the phone, and spelled the name. His eyes opened wide. He nodded, and then frantically waggled the fingers of his free hand to catch Bloom's attention. "That's right, what's the first name you've got? Terrific!" he said. "When did he check in? *When?*" He was writing on a pad in front of him now, his left elbow pinning the pad to the desk, his right hand moving swiftly. Bloom had got up from his own desk and was standing behind him, looking over his shoulder as he wrote. "Hold on a second," he said, and covered the mouthpiece. "The Marjo Motel on the South Trail. He checked in on the eleventh, that's the Friday before she was killed."

"Is he still there?" Bloom asked.

"Is he still there?" the cop said into the phone, and listened, and then covered the mouthpiece again. "Checked out tonight," he said.

"Okay, ask that guy . . ."

"It's a woman."

"Ask her what time he checked out."

"What time did he check out?" the cop said into the phone, and then nodded and said, "Ten-thirty."

"Ask her . . . never mind, give me the phone," Bloom said, and took the receiver. "Ma'am," he said, "when this man registered, did you get a year and make on the car he was driving, as required by law? Good, let me have it." He began writing. "How about the license plate? Good, very good. Georgia, yes, I've got it, what was the number? Thank you, ma'am. Where are you located on the Trail, ma'am? Uh-huh. When he checked out, did he turn north or south? Well, thank you, anyway, ma'am, goodnight." He put the receiver back on the cradle and said, "A blue Oldsmobile station wagon, Georgia plate, here's the number. She didn't see which way he went, she was watching television in the office. He's got a four-hour head start. If he was headed for Georgia, where the hell would he be by now? Figure two hours to Tampa, and another two beyond that at fifty-five an hour—we've got to figure he's observing the speed limit, am I right? So where would that put him? What's Tampa plus a hundred and ten?"

"Somewhere between Ocala and Gainesville," Kenyon said.

"Marion County, right?"

"Or Alachua. Unless he headed south. *I* sure as hell wouldn't head back home if I'd killed two people."

"Think we can get a warrant?" Bloom asked.

"We've got no probable cause," Kenyon said. "Just because the man was lying about when he *got* here doesn't mean he committed two murders."

"He recognized Matthew's car," Bloom said. "I *know* the son of a bitch did it, I can feel it in my bones."

"Go tell a judge you want an arrest warrant on the basis of what you feel in your bones," Kenyon said. "Also, you don't even know where the man *is*. Even if you *got* your warrant, which you won't without probable cause . . ."

"Or even reasonable suspicion," Gregorio said.

"Yeah, yeah," Bloom said.

"Even if you *did* get your warrant, where in hell would you *find* the guy? Let's say he headed across the state and then south, toward the Keys, where he was *supposed* to've been last weekend. He could've got on a boat anyplace down there, he might be on the water *already,* in fact, heading for the Bahamas or someplace."

"All I want to do is drag him in here," Bloom said, "ask him some questions. A guy doesn't lie about when he *got* someplace if he doesn't have a damn good reason for it."

"Tell it to the judge," Kenyon said.

"We know his name, we know what he's driving, we think he maybe killed two people, but we can't arrest the bastard," one of the other detectives said.

I did not know who he was. He was bigger than Bloom, with a huge barrel chest, and wide shoulders, and massive hands. He was drinking coffee from a cardboard container.

"Maybe he'll go through a stoplight someplace," Kenyon said. "Officer'll bust him on that, we'll get him up here and . . ."

"A bullshit traffic violation," the other detective said, shrugging it aside.

"I'd settle for a misdemeanor, though," Bloom said.

"How much dope constitutes a *felony?*" I asked.

The big detective, who knew who I was but not why I had any right to be there, looked at me as if I'd just asked the stupidest question he'd heard in a long career of police work. Bloom looked at me, too, washed his hand over his face, and then fielded the question to Kenyon.

"Pete? What is it now? Twenty grams?"

"Twenty grams," Kenyon said, and nodded.

"Used to be only *six,*" the other detective said. "Fuckin law's all in favor of the *bad* guys these days."

"So how many joints would that be?" I asked. "In twenty grams?"

Bloom looked at me again and sighed. It was a little past three in the morning, and we'd all been up half the night, and he must have been thinking I was making idle chatter here while he was trying to figure out a way of arresting and detaining Marshall. "Pete?" he said wearily. "How many joints in twenty grams?"

"I don't know," Kenyon said. "Fifteen, sixteen? Who gives a shit?"

"Marshall told me he had a dozen in the car," I said.

Bloom looked at me again. This time he didn't sigh.

"He offered me a joint at the funeral, and said he had a dozen more in the wagon."

"That would do it," Bloom said, and turned to Kenyon. "Pete? Wouldn't that justify an arrest warrant?"

"When was this?" Kenyon asked.

"Last Wednesday."

"Too big a time span in there," Kenyon said, shaking his head.

"We can try it," Bloom said.

"A judge'll want to know why we're running all over the state for a lousy twelve sticks of grass some guy talked about last *Wednesday*, for Christ's sake!" the other detective said.

"I'll *tell* him why," Bloom said. "I'll tell him the dope warrant is petty bullshit, we're really after the *big* one."

"He might play," Kenyon said, and shrugged.

"Yeah, he just might," the other detective said.

The Florida Highway Patrolmen stopped the blue Oldsmobile station wagon just this side of Goulds on Florida's Turnpike, not far from the cutoff to Route 1 and the Keys. The BOLO—a Be-On-The-Lookout-For—had been fed into the computer at nine-thirty that morning, shortly after Bloom presented his sworn affidavit to a judge and requested an arrest warrant for violation of F.S. 893.13, which defined as unlawful the sale, manufacture, delivery, or possession with intent to sell, of any controlled substance defined in Chapter 893. In his affidavit Bloom had sworn there was reasonable cause to believe that close to twenty grams of cannabis were in the glove compartment of an Oldsmobile station wagon presently owned and operated by one Edward Richard Marshall, which vehicle was believed to be somewhere in the State of Florida. The judge, as anticipated, wanted to know how come all the fuss over a few joints. Bloom filled him in. The judge pondered his decision for perhaps thirty seconds and signed the warrant.

When the state troopers pulled Marshall to the side of the road and asked for his automobile registration and driver's license, he asked them what this was all about. The trooper studying the name on both the license and registration asked, "Are you Edward Richard Marshall?" and when Marshall admitted he was, the trooper told him he was wanted on a warrant from the Calusa P.D., and then promptly searched the car and found not a dozen but eight sticks of marijuana in the glove compartment.

The BOLO had carried as a wagging tail the information that Marshall was also wanted for questioning in two murders, and the judge who set bail in Dade County was aware of this. He also knew that the Dade County cops who'd booked Marshall on the dope charge had phoned the Calusa police, who'd requested that an exceptionally high bail be set for what was unquestionably a misdemeanor. The judge realized that the Calusa cops were begging for time to question this guy on the murders, and whereas five hundred dollars would have been the normal bail for a narcotics misdemeanor, and the posting of fifty dollars with a bondsman would have set Marshall temporarily free, the judge went along with the request and set a twenty-thousand-dollar bail for a crime punishable by not more than a year's imprisonment. Kenyon and the big detective whose name I *still* didn't know had flown to Miami and driven from there to the courthouse. They were waiting to put the cuffs on Marshall the moment the judge set a bail he couldn't possibly meet on the spur of the moment. Bloom was waiting for him back in Calusa when the detectives led him into the office at a little past two that afternoon.

I was not present during the brief Q and A. I was, instead, in Abe Pollock's office, going over the liquor-store inventory figures his client had finally provided. I went to the police station shortly before the end of the working day. The Q and A had been typed by then; it consisted of four double-spaced pages held together by a staple. I sat in the silence of one of the empty offices and read it through, from Bloom's opening recitation of rights to the point where Marshall abruptly called off the questioning:

Q: Are you certain, then, that you're willing to answer my questions without an attorney present?

A: Let's just get it over with, okay?

Q: Mr. Marshall, is it true that your real name is Edward Maresciallo?

A: My *real* name? What do you mean by my *real* name?

Q: The name you were born with.

A: Then why didn't you *say* the name I was born with? My *legal* name is Edward Marshall, *that's* my real name.

Q: Is it true nonetheless that you changed your name from Edward Maresciallo to—

A: Why? Is it a crime to change your name? In this country, if a man changes his name he's automatically a desperado, huh?

Q: Mr. Marshall, I'd appreciate it if you answered the question.

A: Yes, I changed my name from Edward Maresciallo, all right?

Q: Mr. Marshall, when did you arrive here in Calusa?

A: Last Wednesday. What's that got to do with what you claim you found in my car?

Q: By last Wednesday do you mean January sixteenth?

A: Whatever the date was.

Q: Wednesday was January sixteenth.

A: Then yes.

Q: And you left Valdosta when?

A: It was a week this past Friday.

Q: That would have made it Friday the eleventh.

A: If you say so.

Q: Well, I have a calendar here, and a week ago Friday would have been—

A: I'll take your word for it.

Q: Then you left Valdosta, Georgia, on Friday, January eleventh.

A: Yes.

Q: And did not get here till Wednesday, January sixteenth.

A: That's right.

Q: Where were you between those two dates?

A: I spent some time at Disneyworld in Orlando, and then I was out on a boat off the Keys.

Q: From when to when?

A: The boat, do you mean?

Q: Yes.

A: From Sunday to Tuesday, whatever those dates were.

Q: That would've been from January thirteenth to January fifteenth.

A: If you say so, you're the one with the calendar.

Q: Well, would *you* like to check the calendar for those dates?

A: I don't need to, I'll assume those are the dates.

Q: And you say you came to Calusa on Wednesday.

A: That's right.
Q: Drove up from the Keys, did you?
A: Yes.
Q: *Where* in the Keys?
A: Islamorada.
Q: This boat you were on. Where'd you get it?
A: I borrowed it.
Q: Who from?
A: A friend.
Q: In Islamorada?
A: Yes.
Q: What's this friend's name?
A: Jerry Cooper.
Q: We haven't been able to locate anyone named Jerry Cooper in Islamorada.
A: That's your job, not mine.
Q: Uh-huh. Mr. Marshall, does the name Marjo mean anything to you?
A: No.
Q: Where were you staying here in Calusa, Mr. Marshall?
A: I don't remember the name of the place.
Q: Well, do you remember whether it was a hotel or a motel?
A: A motel.
Q: Would you remember its location?
A: On the Trail someplace.
Q: Would it have been the *Marjo* Motel?
A: I don't want to answer any more questions.

That was it. I slipped the stapled pages back into the manila folder, picked up my briefcase, and went out into the reception area again. The woman typing behind the desk near the letter-elevator told me that Bloom had someone with him just then and she didn't know how long he'd be. I asked her to please buzz him and tell him I was waiting. She gave me a look that told me it was already five-thirty, and she was still here typing, and she really didn't have time for interruptions—but she buzzed him anyway. "He'll be right out," she said, and put up the phone, and went back to her typing. Bloom came out of his office not a moment later.

"I got problems," he said. "There's this lady in my

office, she runs the Marjo Motel, her name is Mary Gibson. Her husband's name was Joseph Gibson, that's how they named the place, but he's dead now. I want to ask her some questions about Marshall, but the cop who drove her down here mentioned this is a homicide we're investigating, and she's clammed up on me. You want to talk to her? Tell her what the law is, tell her there's nothing to worry about?''

"Sure," I said.

Mary Gibson was a short, squat woman with iron-gray hair, deep blue eyes, and a determined look of resistance on her square face. She sat in a leather chair opposite Bloom's desk, her hands gripping the top of the pocketbook in her lap. She turned toward the door as we came into the room, and then studied me as though I were the Grand Inquisitor flown in especially to put her in thumbscrews.

"This is Mr. Hope," Bloom said, "he's an attorney. Matthew, this is Mrs. Gibson, she owns and operates the Marjo Motel."

"How do you do?" I said.

"What *kind* of attorney?" she asked at once. "From the *State* Attorney's office?"

"No, ma'am, I'm in private practice," I said.

"I don't need an attorney," she said, "I didn't have nothing to do with any murder."

"No one's suggesting you did, Mrs. Gibson."

"Then why do I need an attorney?"

"Mr. Bloom thought I might explain the law to you."

"I don't *need* the law explained to me. When the police asked me to come down here, I didn't know there was a murder investigation going on. I don't want to get involved, plain and simple."

"Mrs. Gibson, you're not a suspect, you don't have to . . ."

"No, then what am I?"

"You're a witness who may have information vital to the investigation. As such, you're obliged to answer any questions the police might put to you."

"No, I'm not obliged to do anything I don't *want* to do."

"Mrs. Gibson, if you refuse to answer Mr. Bloom's questions, it would be within his power to subpoena for deposition."

"What does that mean?"

"You'd be *ordered* to answer. By the court. And if you *still* refused to answer . . ."

"Yes, then what?"

"You could be cited for contempt. I'm sure you don't want that to happen."

"I won't answer any questions unless my lawyer's here."

"Mrs. Gibson, a witness doesn't *have* the right to counsel. You're not being accused of anything, Mr. Bloom simply . . ."

"Let her call her lawyer," Bloom said, "that's okay with me."

"I don't *have* a lawyer," she said.

"Well, Mr. Hope here is a lawyer, will you settle for him?"

"What school did you go to?" she asked.

"What?" I said.

"Tell her what school you went to, Matthew."

"Northwestern."

"Where's that?"

"In Evanston, Illinois."

"You didn't go to Harvard?"

"No."

"Or Columbia?"

"No."

"Well," she said dubiously, "I guess you'll be all right anyway. But if he asks me anything I shouldn't answer . . ."

"I'll object, ma'am."

"Just see that you do," she said, and turned to Bloom. "What is it you want to know?"

He talked to her for only five minutes.

That was all the time he needed.

12

The jailer on the second floor of the building led the three of us to a steel door at the end of the corridor, lifted a ring of keys from his belt, and fitted a key that was color-coded red into the keyway. He twisted it and swung open the heavy door.

"This way, please," Bloom said.

We walked parallel to a long row of iron bars, down a narrow corridor, made an abrupt right turn, and came into a cul-de-sac at the end of which was a pair of cells. Eddie Marshall was in the cell at the end of the hallway. The jailer used the same color-coded key to open the cell door. Mrs. Gibson hesitated.

"It's all right," I said, and the three of us entered the cell. The jailer locked the door behind us.

"Mr. Marshall," Bloom said, "this is Mrs. Mary Gibson, she runs the Marjo Motel on the South Trail. I'd like you to . . ."

"What are *you* doing here?" Marshall asked me.

"He's her attorney," Bloom said. "I'd like you to hear what Mrs. Gibson has to say, but first I want to be sure you still understand what your rights are. Earlier today, before I talked to you, I told you that you had the right to remain silent, that you didn't have to answer any questions, and that whatever you said could be used against you at a later time. Do you remember that?''

"I remember it," Marshall said.

"Well, you've still got those same rights. Do you want an attorney now?''

"We've got one attorney too many right this *minute*," Marshall said.

"Does that mean you *don't* want an attorney?''

"If I can sign off whenever I want to, why would I need an attorney?''

"Yes or no, Mr. Marshall?''

"No."

"Okay. I'm going to ask Mrs. Gibson some questions, and she's going to give me some answers. I want you to listen carefully to what she says, because I'll be asking you about it later on. Okay?''

"Sure," Marshall said.

"Mrs. Gibson, do you recognize this man?''

"I do," Mrs. Gibson said.

Her earlier qualms seemed to have vanished entirely. She stood directly in front of Marshall where he sat on the cell's single, wall-fastened cot, looking him directly in the eye, as though challenging him to deny the truth of what she was saying.

"Is he someone who registered at the Marjo Motel?''

"He is."

"Did he register under the name Edward Maresciallo?''

"That's the name in my records."

"And this is the man who registered under that name?''

"Yes, he's the man."

"Have you looked at your records recently, Mrs. Gibson?''

"I looked at them last night when you called me."

"By *me* . . .''

"The police."

"Can you tell me when Mr. Maresciallo . . . ?''

"Listen, that's enough of this," Marshall said.

"No one's questioning *you*," Bloom snapped. "You just sit tight and listen to this, okay?'' He turned back to Mrs. Gibson. "Can you tell me when this man registered at your motel?''

"Yes, it was Friday night, January the eleventh.''

"Did he check in alone?"

"I don't have to listen to . . ."

"Just keep your mouth *shut,* Marshall!" Bloom said. "No one's violating your goddamn rights. Did he check in alone Mrs. Gibson?"

"Yes, he did."

"When did he check out?"

"Late last night."

"What time would that have been?"

"Ten-thirty or thereabouts."

"Now, Mrs. Gibson, during all that time Mr. Marshall was staying at your motel, did he *remain* alone?"

"I don't want to hear any more of this," Marshall said, and suddenly got to his feet.

"Sit down," Bloom said.

"No, I don't *want* to sit down! You're a lawyer," he said, turning to me, "tell him I want him to quit."

"He's not asking you for incriminating testimony," I said. "He doesn't have to . . ."

"No, then what the hell *is* it when he drags somebody in here and . . ."

"You're not covered by law," I said, "so forget it. If he wants to, he can ask you to submit to a blood or breathalyzer test, take your fingerprints or photograph you, put you in a lineup, ask you to put on a hat or a coat, put your finger to your nose, pick up coins, repeat in your own voice words he's written on a piece of paper—*and* listen to what a witness has to say. The difference is between nontestimonial and testimonial responses. When he gets to you, you can refuse to answer any questions. But so far, he hasn't gotten to you. I suggest you listen quietly, Mr. Marshall."

He sat on the cot again, and in that instant I knew he was finished. There was something in his look of resignation, his entire body stance, that told me all the spirit had suddenly drained out of him, it was all over. He knew *exactly* what Mrs. Gibson was going to say next, knew that Bloom had him dead to rights, knew further that there was nothing more he could do about it, nothing more he could say in denial or rebuttal; this was the end of the long road that had begun in Valdosta, Georgia, eleven days ago—or perhaps even longer ago than that.

"Mrs. Gibson," Bloom said, "did he *remain* alone all the time he was registered at the Marjo Motel?"

"No, he did not remain alone."

"Can you . . . ?"

"All right," Marshall said softly.

"Can you tell me who was there with him?"

"A little girl."

"When did she join him, Mrs. Gibson?"

"On Sunday night, the thirteenth of January."

"Can you describe . . . ?"

"All right," he said again.

"Can you describe the girl to me?"

"She was about six or seven years old, with long black hair. She was wearing a granny nightgown, I saw him carrying her from the station wagon to the . . ."

"All *right*, goddamnit!" he shouted.

The cell went utterly still.

"Want to tell me about it?" Bloom asked.

"You know it all, the hell with it."

"Tell me anyway," he said, more gently this time.

"I killed them," he said, and looked down at his hands. "I killed them both."

"Let's start from the beginning," Bloom said.

The beginning had been a long time ago, back in New Orleans, when he'd taken the basic straw of Victoria Miller's meager talent and turned it into the pure gold of three million-copy albums. In return she had graced him with her favors. As Victoria's father had told me earlier, Eddie and she became lovers, a relationship that lasted until fame and the heady lure of Konig and his sophisticated friends convinced Vicky that he was the man she should marry. Marshall made love to her for what he thought would be the last time (and here Mrs. Gibson turned away from him and stared in embarrassment through the bars at the wall in the corridor outside) in a farewell assignation a month before her wedding to Konig. When she returned from her honeymoon, she called Marshall to say she was pregnant with his child.

"Your child?" Bloom said.

"Mine."

"Mr. Marshall . . ."

"My baby. She was married to Tony, but this was a week

after the wedding, the baby was *mine*—from the last time we'd been together. And she killed it. She pushed so hard on that album, the last album, *knew* she was pregnant but worked herself like a dog, anyway. That was what caused the miscarriage, her working so hard, driving everyone so hard. She killed my baby."

He left New Orleans shortly after Vicky's retirement and the dissolution of Wheat, taking a job with a small record company in Nashville ("I was an industry giant, working for a firm with a list of midgets"), and when the company collapsed finally managed to get himself a job as a disc jockey in Georgia. In 1973, five years after he'd last seen her, he went back to New Orleans for a visit. She was still married to Konig, but the marriage was in serious trouble and when she came to see Marshall at the Royal Sonesta, where he was staying, she told him she hadn't had sex with her husband in months. Inevitably, she and Marshall made love again. And inevitably, or so it seemed to him now, she got pregnant again. Two months after they were together for the last time, she called to tell him the news and to announce that the child was without question his.

"She promised me she wouldn't lose this one, she'd take good care of it forever and make sure nothing happened to it. I got a birth announcement when Allison was born. Allison Mercy Konig, the card read. Konig. *My* daughter—with Konig's name."

After that there was silence—except for the Christmas cards each and every year with the little handwritten notes telling Marshall how the daughter he'd never seen was coming along. And then, this past Christmas, a card with a note saying she was going back into the business again, and would be opening a singing engagement at the Greenery on the eleventh of January. He called her on New Year's Eve. He was drunk. Little Allie answered the phone. There must have been a party going on, he could hear a lot of noise in the background, could hear his daughter yelling to her mother that there was a "Mr. Marshall" on the phone. Mr. Marshall. *His* daughter, and she was calling him Mr. Marshall. Vicky sounded drunk, too. He told her she'd promised him she'd take care of their little girl forever, make sure nothing ever happened to her the way it happened to the first one and she just laughed and said she'd have plenty of money soon, she'd be able to hire a dozen governesses to take care of Allie, he had nothing to worry about. He didn't know what she meant. How did she plan on making any money singing in public when she had a voice like a flat tire? He told her she'd better not do it. He warned her. She told him to go to hell, and hung up. He was sitting in a chair near the dresser in the room he was renting. He yanked the phone out of the wall and threw it at the mirror over the dresser, smashing it.

On the eleventh of January, the day of Vicky's opening, he drove down to Calusa from Valdosta, Georgia. He hadn't planned to kill her. He planned only to talk to her, reason with her. When he got down here that Friday night, he went to see her. This was just before the opening, he begged her not to go through with it, begged her to take care of their baby the way she'd promised. She told him Allie wasn't a baby anymore, Allie was already six years old, and besides she'd be coming into a lot of money very soon, and he didn't need to worry. He asked her *what* money, and she said the trust. He didn't know anything about a trust, he thought she was lying, thought she was still planning on making millions singing again, the way she had back in the sixties. He warned her again. He told her not to go ahead with it, or he'd come take the baby from her as sure as he was standing there. She said he'd better get out of the house before she called the police. He left without even seeing his own daughter. She was staying at a friend's house that night, sleeping over, so Vicky could get ready for her goddamn opening!

"It was happening already," Marshall said. "She was already neglecting Allie for her dumb *career!*" He shook his head, and suddenly he began weeping. Mrs. Gibson, startled by the sound, turned from the bars to look at him. An expression of pity crossed her face. She stood watching him as though wanting to take him in her arms and comfort him. Bloom waited. Marshall took a handkerchief from the back pocket of the dark blue prison trousers. He blew his nose. He dried his eyes. He sighed heavily, and blew his nose again, and then shook his head and said, "I . . . I still . . . still didn't plan to kill her. All I wanted was my daughter. I only planned to take my daughter. That's why I registered under my old name, I guess. Because I planned to take my daughter from her. And then only if I couldn't talk her into giving up this . . . this dumb *move* she'd made. I mean, she'd got that bad review in the paper on Saturday, she *had* to know it was a lost cause. On Sunday I . . . I called her at about ten to eight, I figured she'd still be at the house, I'd catch her before she left for the lounge. But she'd already gone, I talked to a baby-sitter instead. It was beginning, you see, she was leaving my daughter with a sitter while . . . while she . . .'' He shook his head again. He had begun wringing his hands. Mrs. Gibson was watching him, unable to take her eyes from his face.

"I called again at about ten-thirty, figuring she'd come straight home after the show ended. It ended at ten, you know, I figured she'd go straight home to Allie, but no, the god-damn *sitter* again! And then I called at about a quarter past eleven it must've been, and this time I asked the sitter to tell Vicky I'd be stopping by to collect. I was parked up the street when she got home at about eleven-thirty, I guess it was. I watched her go inside the house, and then come out again to where Mr. Hope here was waiting in his car. I saw both of them go in the house together. I . . . I waited till he was gone, he left about three-thirty in the morning. There was only one light on in the house, I guessed she'd fallen asleep with the bedroom light on. I found a sliding door unlocked at the back of the house, and I went in. She was naked in bed. A light was burning on the table alongside the bed. I woke her up and told her I was taking Allie home with me. She . . . she went for the phone right away, and I shoved her away from it, and she . . . she started screaming . . . and . . . and hitting at me with her fists and I . . . I just . . . just lost my temper, I guess. I started pushing back at her, just trying to keep her away from me, you know, and then . . . punching her, I guess, and then I . . . I don't remember, I guess I . . . I banged her head against the tile floor until she was . . . I guessed she was . . . dead.''

He looked down at his hands. A shiver shook his body. He kept looking at his hands. I was surprised to see tears running down Mrs. Gibson's cheeks. Bloom waited for a moment, and then very gently said, "What about your daughter, Mr. Marshall?''

"God,'' he said.

"Will you tell me about her now?"

"God," he said, "God," and began wringing his hands again, and then abruptly brought them to his face, and buried his face in them, and spoke through his hands, hiding his face, his voice muffled. "I took her to that motel, I knew they were looking for her, they thought I'd *kidnapped* her, my own daughter! I couldn't move, I couldn't chance having her seen, she was still wearing the nightgown she'd had on Sunday night, when I took her from the house, I didn't know whether to go out and buy her some clothes, I didn't know *what* to do. When I went to the funeral last Wednesday, I had to leave her tied up in the room, tied and gagged, my own *daughter!* I just didn't know what to do."

"Why'd you go to the funeral?" Bloom asked.

"I figured if I was there, I mean if I was there expressing my grief, then nobody'd know I did it, nobody'd suspect me, you know what I mean? And then, when I talked to Mr. Hope, I found out he knew about those phone calls I'd made, and if *he* knew, then the police had to know, too, am I right? So I had to get out of Calusa, I had to take Allie someplace far away from Calusa. But I didn't know where. I couldn't go back to Georgia with her, I just didn't know. I mean, the job in Georgia is nothing, I wouldn't have cared about leaving it, but I didn't know where to *go.* I mean, how could I get a job *anyplace,* take my daughter *anyplace* when the whole damn world was looking for her?"

He kept his face buried in his hands. It was difficult hearing him. Bloom had moved closer to him. I was standing alongside Mrs. Gibson, who took a surprisingly delicate lace-edged handkerchief from her pocketbook, and dabbed at her eyes with it, and then put the handkerchief back in the bag, and closed the bag. The brittle snap of the catch sounded like a gunshot in the small cell.

"It was . . . it was Fri . . . it was Friday night when I decided I'd have to make a run for it. Go down to the Keys with her, rent a boat there, take her out on the water till I figured out my next move. I told her we were leaving. I'd brought some fruit back from the market, and some cheese, and a bottle of wine, and we were having supper in the room when I told her we'd be leaving in the morning. We'd be going out on a boat, I told her, did she like boats? She said she didn't *want* to go out on a boat with me, she wanted to go home to her mother. I told her . . . I said your mother is dead, darlin. And then, for the first time since I'd taken her from the house, I . . . I told her who I was. I said, 'I'm your daddy, I'll take good care of you, don't worry.' And she looked at me, I was peeling an orange, I had this knife I kept in the wagon for whenever I went fishing, I . . . I was peeling an orange with it, for *her,* the orange was for *her,* and she looked at me and said, '*You're* not my daddy, Tony *Konig* is my daddy,' and got up and ran for the door. I caught her before she could unlock the door, I yanked her back by her hair, and I . . . she was struggling to get away, I had the knife in my hand, I . . . I just . . . I guess I . . . lost my temper again, her saying *Tony* was her daddy, damnit, *I* was her daddy! So I . . . I guess I . . . I used the knife. I guess I . . . slit her throat.''

''All right, Mr. Marshall,'' Bloom said.

''I guess I killed her.''

''All right,'' Bloom said.

''I'm sorry,'' Marshall said.

In the reception area upstairs Mrs. Gibson apologized for not having been more alert during Marshall's stay at the motel. She'd seen him bringing the girl in, she'd seen pictures of the missing girl in the papers and on television, but she'd never once made any connection. Bloom assured her she wasn't at fault, thanked her for her cooperation, and then arranged for a police officer to drive her back home. It was almost six-thirty. The office seemed surprisingly still. Bloom was worried that Marshall's confession might be inadmissible because he'd made it in the presence of Mrs. Gibson and me. I told him I saw no reason for any objections on those grounds, but he still seemed worried about it, and said he wanted to check with the State's Attorney right away.

''They always have their reasons, don't they?'' he said, and shook his head sadly. ''Remember what I told you that time? They always have their reasons, Matthew. It's only in the movies that guys commit murder for the money in a goddamn trust. In real life it's things like husbands and wives and daughters.'' He shook his head again. ''Killed two people and wrecked his own life. How does that happen to somebody, Matthew? Man who used to be a giant in his profession.''

"He was a dwarf inside," I said.

I phoned Joanna the moment I got home. I wanted to hear her voice. I wanted to hear her call me "Daddy." She told me she had talked to Andrew the Cruel just a little while ago and had told him she didn't want to go steady with him, and in fact wasn't even sure she wanted to *see* him again. She had called him Andrew the Cruel, I noticed with some satisfaction.

"So that's that, I guess," she said.

"Are you sure it's what you want to do?" I asked.

"Yeah, I'm pretty sure," she said. "Dad," she said, "thanks, I mean it."

"I love you," I said.

"I love you, too, Daddy," she said.

I put the receiver gently onto the cradle and sat looking at the phone for several moments. I felt like crying. I sat very still for what seemed a long time, and then I picked up the receiver again and dialed Dale's number.

ABOUT THE AUTHOR

Ed McBain has won fame as the author of the long-lived 87th Precinct police procedural novels, which have been popular reading since 1956, and as Evan Hunter, author of a number of strong novels beginning with *The Asphalt Jungle* to the most recently published, *Love, Dad*. Ed McBain continues to write 87th Precinct novels as well as this new series featuring Matthew Hope, who made his debut in *Goldilocks*, published in 1978. Mr. McBain lives in Connecticut.

Ed McBain's Classic

87th PRECINCT

Mysteries...

"The best of today's police stories...lively, inventive, and wholly satisfactory." *The New York Times*